Ashes and Bone

David Andrew McGlone

PROLOGUE

'GO, GO, GO!' The tense silence was broken by the Detective's urgent demand, sending the grim faced men in uniform rushing towards the faded white door. As the metal battering ram smashed through the entrance, PC Marlin looked on; poised for action should he be required, his heart pounding with fear and excitement. Young but with good experience, Marlin was nevertheless new to the world of serial killers and apprehensive as to how this arrest might pan-out. To calm himself, he drew in a long deep breath of cold air, fogging his view as he blew out.

The anxious face of the Chief Inspector looked on as his officers forced themselves into the small property, a maelstrom of indistinct shouting and crashing as adrenaline overwhelmed careful consideration. The atmosphere was electric and all of the men were as one as the wave of anticipation washed over them. All but one.

To the left of the Inspector stood a slim, casual, but well-dressed man. His longish blonde hair obviously civilian, he stood smoking with a look of almost nonchalance on his handsome face, though his sharp blue eyes were fixed on the house. As he sensed Marlin looking, the man turned his head and smiled as he nodded slightly; then turning once more he focused intently as he sat back against the bonnet of the police car. The brilliant Dr Andrews had brought them to this point with his profiles and plans of action and it had been Marlin who had been there to see that he had everything he needed. A quiet, almost unseen presence, but happy to be there. Happy to see the man in action and privileged to be somehow a part of the process.

Amidst the chaos unfolding before him, Marlin heard the sound of breaking glass as the front window to his left exploded and a balled figure hit the ground and rolled before standing into a run. All eyes were drawn to the movement, a slight figure in jeans and a blue hooded fleece top, as it sped away from the building. Chief Inspector Jones screamed a demand to halt with more anger than belief which duly went unheeded, but Marlin moved instinctively and quickly after the fleeing man.

As he gritted his teeth and focused on the speeding suspect, Marlin heard a crack to his right hand side as a firearms officer reacted with a wild shot. The figure hunched as he ran and Marlin heard him let out an excited yelp as he accelerated - was the bastard laughing? Over the green hedge he leaped with Marlin close behind and now he could hear it, the almost hysterical high-pitched giggling as the man ran. Anger swept over Marlin and his muscles tensed.

'Stop, Rennie! Police.'

The words were almost screamed in desperation as the shrieking figure continued to vault garden fences and sprint across lawns, but Marlin did not slow down or end his pursuit, if anything he pushed harder.

Temple Mills was a built-up block of houses and flats used as a local university campus and, whilst there were plenty of gardens and hedges, there was little in the way of real cover, especially with a pursuer so close. The noise had brought students spilling from their rooms, some cheering as they saw the uniformed officer being evaded, some just caught-up in the spectacle. The sounds seemed to spur the man on and Marlin began to wonder where all of his support had gone as his legs tired. Then, as they reached the second last garden, Rennie slipped, not enough to fall, but enough to ensure his leap was too low; the would-be escapee caught the hedge squarely and fell out of sight as Marlin took two large strides and leaped over, balling his fists as he did so.

Mark Rennie was 22 years old and a student at the University of East London, a psychology major with a quick and evil mind. He had plotted the deaths of four female students, as a Leopold and Loeb style experiment that had proved only too successful and caused terror throughout the campus and the city beyond. He chose his victims carefully and approached them in specific places; he was not a brawler and in no condition to fight with a policeman such as Marlin. He was built on ideas not brute strength, so his surrender was quick and inevitable.

'AGH, be careful. There's really no need for such roughness officer! Agh, too tight. Don't you see I'm not resisting?'

'Shut up, you sick bastard, tight cuffs are the least you deserve.' Marlin was scowling now and trying to catch his breath. Around him were now a good number of officers, some with weapons aimed and all sharing the exhilaration of capture. Through the uniformed crowd walked Andrews, the studied calmness of his features only betrayed by the keen fascination in his eyes. Walking slowly forwards, he raised an eyebrow and almost smiled as he spoke.

'So this is him? This is the cause of so much terror?'

'Not anymore Dr Andrews, thanks to you…and of course this officer.' The Chief Inspector patted Andrews' shoulder as he spoke effusively. Rennie was trying to find some relief from his cuffed discomfort, but the name caught his attention.

'You're Dr Andrews?' His voice was almost mocking. 'I'm genuinely disappointed.'

Andrews looked momentarily surprised and then irritated by the comment, yet he still felt able to smile as he leaned in close to the man.

'I wasn't aware that I was supposed to impress you, Rennie. Just catch you. Although it's now quite hard to take any pride in the capture of such a small man. Such a small mind.'

Now Rennie was visibly angered and his half-smile became a vicious baring of teeth. Then from his tight lips came the cackle once again, a cruel impersonation of a child's amusement.

'A small man? Oh I'm far, far bigger than you can ever imagine. Far bigger than you'll ever be, Doctor. I let you catch me to end the tedium of waiting. I don't have a small mind; I have a low boredom threshold.' Again he cackled and Andrews seemed about to speak, but only smiled and shook his head slowly. Turning, Andrews nodded at Marlin and moved away from the crowd once more as the prisoner was forced towards the car. 'Was it worth it, officer? All of that work only to have the credit taken by him?' Again the giggle, but Marlin kept silent, only fixing Rennie with a stare. The eyes of his prisoner were wild and excited, unlike any he had seen before or wished to see again, but he knew he couldn't argue with that or try to understand. He'd done his job and that was all that mattered.

SUNDAY GIRL

She woke, stretching for a sheet that was no longer there. The material now pushed away, embarrassed by its stained memories, awash on a thin mattress that would not absorb the dampened guilt. A weave beyond her grasp.

Rolling over she cursed a night of easy passion and, having reached across, brought her hand down with a 'Smack' to the cold hollow 'he' had left. 'Fucking typical'.

Standing up carefully, trusting in momentum rather than balance, she stumbled towards the bathroom. She noticed her stomach grumbling ominously as her bladder was gratefully emptied and suddenly it felt good to be alone. Jesus, wine kills me she thought; not for the first time.

As she walked through her compact living-room, her eyes fell on a half-finished vodka and coke; half drunk and available, just like me, she mused. Smiling at the pun she shook her head and padded away from the alcohol. Move away please, nothing to see here folks.

She laughed loudly and, looking up, caught a brief cameo in the window. Her dark hair, longer than she liked, danced untidily around her head and shoulders as she smiled at her reflection. She turned to admire her image, shaking her hips as her sudden good humour played a futile game of hide and seek with her hangover. *Not bad for 35 – but bed*, she thought as she almost skipped forward before coming to a halt. 'Juice' she announced as she turned.

It was only visible for an instant. Less a sound as a breath aloud, an echo when the first sound was nought. She was aware of the ground rushing up to meet her, but the first contact would remain a mystery. The muffled 'oh' of her involuntary sigh merged with the piercing flashes of colour that fringed her view. The pain, both heavily dull and sharply intense, dispensed with all other considerations.

Then the silence, the terrifying, numbing silence. A warm sweet sensation invaded her mouth, over her tongue, on her lips. That strange metallic taste of blood, of death.

In that moment her future, her plans, became her present and her past. Her body panic, her grooming, her pedicured perfumed self would ensure only a beautiful corpse. Designer clothes and dream weddings would remain unseen. She would be cloaked in the earth and wedded to the grave.

The man now allowed himself to move. He went to sit, but then thinking better, bent his knees to a crouch; his outstretched hands hovering as if he was viewing this scene through a glass case. He breathed deeply and stared at his victim, basking in the warm glow of exhilaration that he knew would be only too fleeting. From his chest pocket he carefully withdrew his phone camera and lined up the photo. An android 'click' captured his victim.

'My Sunday girl' he whispered. And then he was gone.

THE GHOSTS OF PAST MISDEEDS

The loud grunt that finally awoke him was his own, a self-alarm for no fixed time that brought him round to a dimly recognisable present. This was a world authored by alcohol and presented via the medium of hangover. So dimly recognised and not at all unfamiliar. Just lie back and wait for the mental replay, he thought as his eyes slowly closed but nothing came. The only thing worse than the drunken memories was no memory at all. He could accept the blackouts, if only he was not racked with a fearful guilt of acts imagined; or was it imaginations enacted?

With no great ease he slid from the settee and got to his feet, finally focusing on the whiskey bottles on the table. The empty whiskey bottles. This quantity of empties was always a bad sign. Guilt and his head throbbed in unison as he involuntarily reached for the back of a chair, stretching the kinks from his neck as he scanned the room.

Where the fuck is my phone?

Seeing that his hand was resting on his jacket, he carefully checked the pockets. As each one came up empty he found religion, please God don't say I lost my phone. Then success as he patted the right hand front. The night can't have been that bad then, he thought.

Heading through the expensive mess that his house had become, Al found the bathroom and showered. Washed and brushed he dressed to face the world. All that remained was a strong coffee and a lot of water, a task he easily achieved on auto-pilot before taking his cup into the living room. Breathing deeply he picked up his phone with no little trepidation. 'So to the day.' He exclaimed to no-one so much as the ghosts of past misdeeds. He had messages. Long, repeated, anxious, angry messages. He had missed calls and he had seemingly missed Wednesday.

Al was Dr Aldous Andrews, a psychologist almost famed for his (long since written) book on the psychology of the serial killer. In recent times he was Dr Al, almost famed for the sound bites for which he was always available. One consistent feature, even in these days as Dr Al, was the public's fascination in his name - that hated name - Aldous. A dubious gift from his father.

Francis Andrews, Frank to his friends, was the editor of the South Shields Bugle, a paper so small it was now gone and all but forgotten. A well-read and serious man, Frank was a picture of the disappointment he seemed to carry on his slumped shoulders. His wife and children he viewed as an inevitable consequence of age; an expectation of a life realised but entirely unexceptional. His career was his everything and it was supposed to be spectacular.

His journalistic skills would propel him quickly through the ranks, earning the respect and envy of his peers. Offers to edit the nationals would be nonchalantly waved aside to concentrate on the first of his great novels. He would have his experiences as a war correspondent to draw upon and his association with world leaders would lend a definite gravitas. In his forties he would worry only about literary short-lists and the blossoming brilliance of his children; the beauty of his wife.

The reality of life came quicker and more harshly than a dreamer such as he could ever have imagined. Employed by a local paper, he was hard working and tenacious but his copy was dry, his insight anything but. Joe Green, his editor, said that he had never seen someone as driven as the 21 year old Frank. He would need that drive however, as his natural talent was lacking and there would always be more gifted individuals. In short, local news was as far as he was going and he would have to fight to stay there.

Crushing to his spirit, this was compounded by his literary creations, still-born every one; artistic impotence. He was aware that his dreams were dead by the time of his 29th birthday; a humourless, grey and almost silent figure by the age of 35. In this year his son was born, his only son and Francis Jr. became Aldous; named after a real writer and unmistakeably so.

Beneath the shadow of his father's disappointment, Aldous grew up in an atmosphere of quiet tension as a reticent and rather sullen child. At school he was initially teased about his 'posh' name and, as he retreated into himself, his aloofness. At home his mother Kate bore the resentment of her husband with a defeated resignation, but was determined that her son would have a better life. Although physical contact was rationed, there was no lack of focus on the boy and his academic progression; his ticket out of there. Granted, laughter was only an occasional visitor and the rod not spared, but Al emerged as a thoughtful and polite young man;

top of his classes and ready for the next challenge. Kate, for her part, was ready to set him free, confident that he had a chance in the world and hopeful he would amount to more than simply his father's son.

Reasonably handsome with a winning smile, he had his mother's piercing blue eyes and a quiet vulnerability that made him something of a hit with the girls, if only he had noticed. As it was, a certain social awkwardness meant he was largely oblivious, as his eyes remained fixed to his books and the road sign pointing south. Al would become, or appear to become, the person he wanted to be; but he could never quite leave the childhood Aldous behind. He saw the name as an embodiment of those days and he was embarrassed that it still generated laughter and curiosity in equal measure. As with many things in life, the small things can seem too important and for a time it prompted an unnecessarily sharp response from Al.

His abridged and infinitely more polite response to all questions, was now a weary:

'His Father. Yes, Huxley. Yes, the writer. No, not a man with a grasp of the cruelty of children or adults for that matter. Yes, his sense of humour regarding the matter was mostly exhausted. Al or Dr Al will do.'

Dr Al was wanted by Radio London Live to contribute to the Linda Dear show. It must be a slow week he thought. Nothing gets those phones ringing quite like a ripper or two, maybe Myra?

He was more than available for the right price. Anyway, he had never done her show and debut appearances were rare these days.

IDENTIFY THE SYMPTOMS

Radio shows were no big deal for Al now, despite the odd butterfly in the stomach. A combination of experience and psychological relaxation techniques meant he was able to believe that no-one was listening. To ensure this he always made it plain that any 'phone-in' segment should be after he had left the studio. He now no longer did TV appearances due to the 'dumbing-down factor'. That was his official reason, he didn't wish to admit that he was embarrassed by the paunch and the now thinning hair that he felt ruined his once attractive appearance. Drink and the lifestyle had aged Al more than he liked to admit in recent years and, whilst vanity was not a conscious consideration, he was more than happy to avoid the camera's attentions.

The red light glowed waking Al to the present, his eyes suddenly alive. Calm with an edge was the PR, so treat him nice. Linda Dear edged forward and smiled. Her bleached hair, pulled back into a pony-tail, stretched her skin tightly; dark make-up hid her eyes. A woman in her late twenties Al guessed, although her voice suggested the confident assurance of one much older.

'Hello Dr Al and welcome to the show. Is it ok to call you Dr Al or would you prefer Aldous? I did notice that it was Dr Aldous Andrews on the book cover. A very literary name for a very literary subject.'

'A literary name yes, from Huxley, but that was my father's idea and I can't say that I'm crazy about it. Dr Al is fine.'

'That's ok, so Dr Al, I'm rather curious about your background. The man behind the science so to speak,' she smiled 'You've mentioned your father but, for instance, is there a significant other?'

'Father, Mother or significant other is personal. And personal, as I've always said, remains personal. I don't believe that it's important to know anything about my life in this context. I haven't written an autobiography, not yet anyway, so that area's not relevant to me.'

'Nothing at all to tell?'

'Nothing, that's the idea.'

'Dr Al, please don't think I'm trying to pry. It's simply unusual these days to have someone in the public eye with such a degree of privacy. There'll be those who'll wonder if you have something to hide?'

'Look Linda, please don't think that I'm being rude, but I'm not trying to hide anything. I'm simply not making my business public. Also, I can assure you that it's not at all interesting.'

He tried to smile but false displays of emotion were particularly difficult with the level of hangover he was experiencing. He succeeded only in looking slightly pained; perhaps he was.

Linda Dear returned his faked expression of warmth, but was clearly more comfortable with this than Al.

'So Dr Al, Serial Killers; who are they and why?'

Al relaxed and became Dr Al.

'I'm not sure that I, or anyone for that matter, can really rationalise the why. It's perhaps a case of being able to identify the symptoms, without really understanding the disease.'

'Please go on, Dr Al.'

'From the list of people caught we can establish types and generally there are three. There are some who will argue that there are four major types and also those who break characteristics down into a large number of categories. All are valid, but I tend towards the three type explanation.

'Firstly there's the thrill seeker, a man who enjoys the publicity, the chase. In general, this type of killer will actively enjoy the killing and won't spare a thought for the victims or see them as being anything less than expendable.

'Second would be those who believe they are on a mission, possibly to improve society. In past cases this has manifested itself in the killings of homosexuals, prostitutes, people of a different ethnic background or those of a different religion. Whilst these people can be said to be very clearly and obviously disturbed, they are probably not psychotic.

'The third type is often the cruellest, as they kill and torture to establish power and control over their victims. It's usually true to say that they feel powerless or inadequate in everyday life. In many cases, it can emerge that they were abused themselves as children. These are the types we know.'

Linda Dear screwed up her face in what Al took to be a quizzical expression.

'The types we know? You say that as if there are types we don't know?'

'Linda, what you have to realise is that there are many serial killers that have never been caught. We can hypothesise as to whether these people fall into the categories we know, but as long as they evade capture it can only ever be a hypothesis.'

'Very interesting. Now you wrote the book 'Inside the Mind of the Serial Killer'. What was it that drew you to this subject?'

'The focus of my doctorate was personality and, in particular, personality disorders. An element of this concentrated on criminal behaviour as a possible personality trait. Since the days of Galton, with his somewhat misguided facial measurements and the like, we've looked for factors to identify people and explain their behaviour. I was just as curious and it led me, after many years, to be quite adept at profiling people in general and criminals in particular.'

'Is that when the police contacted you?'

'Yes, it must have been about 1998 I think. The Metropolitan Police asked me for help with a series of murders around Stratford in East London. It looked like the same person was responsible, but they wanted to know what sort of person he might be.'

'This would be the murders of the female students along the Romford Road. I'm sure many of our listeners will remember that.'

'That's right. I put together a profile which helped to locate the killer Mark Rennie, a fellow student of the murdered girls and a very disturbed young man.'

'That's one of the cases in your book isn't it?'

'Yes, that was in my third book.'

As Al spoke he could see a hive of activity behind the glass in the production room. Sign language and serious expressions, urgent whispers into microphones. Linda Dear was enlivened again.

'That's fascinating Dr Al, but I'm afraid we have breaking news on the venue for the Royal Wedding. We're going across now to our royal correspondent Trudy Little, live from Buckingham Palace. Hello, Trudy.'

Al removed his headphones and stood up stretching. Linda Dear's eyes followed him with a puzzled half-interest, yet she maintained her dialogue with the royal rambler unfailingly. Stepping from the room he was met by a pretty young production assistant.

'We're so sorry Dr Al. We're expecting a press conference any moment, but it shouldn't be longer than ten minutes or so. If you could wait for that long we can continue the interview.'

'Thank you, but I think I've well and truly had my time. I've got to go.' Stepping past the young assistant Al paused, ' Please make my apologies to your listener. If there was one, that is?' he smiled weakly.

In a parked car in North London there was at least one listener and DCI Marlin was a particularly receptive audience. Dr Al, I'd almost forgotten you.

A LETHAL UNDERTOW

The man didn't really care. He had felt most emotions as keenly as everyone else once, but he didn't really let it get to him anymore. He was five foot nine and although quite slim he had a strong and wiry torso; his arms were scratched and marked but with prominent muscles like wire cable. His dark eyes gave nothing away at first and to strangers he looked a bit slow or disinterested; closer inspection showed a glint that was anything but. His dark brown hair was mostly obscured by the hood pulled tight about his face, a face no longer shrouded in a beard but dark all the same, shadowed with thick stubble. Where he had been and what he had done was a matter of some dispute as he had changed his story many times. So many times in fact that he had forgotten many details himself.

He did however have a hunger for knowledge and he voraciously devoured books of all kinds. The information he read stuck and from trivia to philosophy he had it all filed away. The quiet demeanour was all the better for the silent approach, his strength all the better to exploit the moment of surprise. He lived for these moments.

From conspiracy theories to revenge or crimes of passion, from proclamations of 'true evil' to unfortunate chemical imbalances, nothing really came close to an explanation. They say that 'Still waters run deep', but in this case there was a lethal undertow for all who broke the surface. To become tangled up with the man was to surely drown, but to avoid him was not a simple matter either. He was as indiscriminate as the elements when it came to striking the innocent down.

Torrential rain turned to snow as it fell heavily on Oxford Street; the leaden sky hung dark and low. The man felt that the atmosphere was reaching out to him from the shadows and whispering of foul deeds as yet unseen. He tapped into the dark mood of the day and realised that he must emerge again and act with grave intent. As people huddled in doorways for cover, he pulled up his collar and stooped into the wind and snow, feeling elated by the cold numbing of his face. He strode purposefully forward, glancing to his left down each of the streets that led away from the main road, not knowing exactly what he was looking for, but feeling sure that he would recognise it when he did. As he pushed through the gauntlet of leaflet pushers and con merchants, he was brought to a halt. He had found it.

Among the bright lights of mega-stores and the noise and bustle of the gullible tourists was a small arcing road; no, more an alleyway which was dark and surprisingly quiet. A silent recess amongst the pandemonium of commercial excess. The man slowly walked down the alleyway and saw that it split into two paths, one a dead end and the other curving round to meet the street at a much advanced point. It was like a place forgotten, hidden away in the darkness. The streets were cobbled and even the street lamps suggested a much earlier age. Scattered throughout were failed bistros and cafes, elitist record shops with shuttered windows, seedy doorways barely illuminated with red lights and closed shop doorways now the resting place for the homeless. The man noted all of this and revelled in it. He chose the path back out onto the street and slowed his pace.

Back on the main street his head was swimming with thoughts of what could or would be. His body tingled and twitched and he had to admit that he felt extremely aroused by it all. He felt alive, so alive and yet driven. He could not enjoy any of this until the deed was done however, but he didn't want to rush things and find that it was over too soon; he wanted this to last forever. He had to have some time to think and he had to get out of the snow, but looking around he didn't want to go into a shop as it would break his concentration. His mouth was dry, but he didn't want a drink; it would change the sensation, the excitement, the desire. Seeing a phone box free he made his way along the street and stepped into the booth.

Holding the phone to his ear he looked out of the glass box and tried to contain his excitement, he must be calm. He watched the traffic and gradually the childish excitement drained away, replaced by a cool self-assurance. A Japanese tourist tapped at the window, hoping to make known his desire to use the phone, smiling, apologising, but making his feelings known. The man turned and glowered, his teeth exposed in a cruel caricature of a smile, his eyes suddenly blazing. The Japanese tourist was visibly shaken by this and quickly turned away, walking rapidly, afraid to look back, praying he was not being followed. The man was glad of this interruption as it had crystallised his mood. Turning to replace the handset he was suddenly aware of the overbearing presence of cards in the booth. A shop window for sex in the modern world. 'Young schoolgirl type needs discipline', 'strict mistress', 'naughty boys', 'massage, caning, whipping, bondage', on and on with the same. The man smiled to himself. If these rich old men wanted humiliation, discipline or punishment, he could oblige. No fees included, just the donation of a life.

Pushing open the door he bowed his head and slipped back into the alleyway. It was still surprising to note how dark it was in there. Looking back he saw that he was not being followed and so he continued along, towards the sign with a large white moon that once signalled 'New Moon Records'. Past the shuttered record shop he heard a voice, pleading with a bitterness borne of too many cold nights on the street, 'Spare some change please?' He stopped and slowly reached into his pocket. Huddled on the ground the tramp looked as many others with his grey or brown faded clothes, ripped and shabby, cloaked in a long heavy coat with its stains worn as badges of abuse. His hair was long and grey, his beard white except for the browning stain of nicotine. The filth of the street was a tattoo on his skin and his eyes showed no life, no hope. Looking up at the man he felt his bitter defiance turn to utter terror; he could not meet his gaze any longer.

The man picked a pound coin from his pocket and as the tramp looked away he threw the money to the floor. The tramp looked down as the money hit the pavement but didn't know if it was safe to pick it up; there was something about this man that spelled danger. The money should not go to waste however, nothing should go to waste. He watched the feet of the stranger as they slowly moved away and he reached out for the coin, pulling it quickly into his chest, holding tight. The sound of footsteps had ceased and the tramp began to raise his head.

In the blink of an eye the tramp felt every breath forced out of his body as he was propelled back into the wall. His head cracked off the corner of the doorway and a sharp band of pain shot through his body, burning white-hot into his senses as he realised his arm was broken. No breath for screams and no time for thought, the tramp struggled to focus on his attacker's eyes. The man held the old man's throat with a vice like grip, feeling the cartilage cracking beneath his pressure. He thought of breaking the man's neck, but throttling had come first to mind and he liked to act on first instincts. Seeing the man begin to struggle, he stamped hard onto his ankle, hearing it crack like a whip. The tramp writhed but was pathetically weak and no match for the man. He approached death.

The elation was at its peak, but he was aware of his open surroundings and in the back of his mind he knew that this was no real sport. Forcing the man's head back into the wall he squeezed with all of his might, ignoring the slight wheezing sound and the cracking of the neck. Unable to fight, the tramp simply slipped away, dying in the pain and squalor that had typified his life. Even in death life had dealt him the poorest of hands.

Laying the sad corpse to the ground he stepped back and looked at his work. For a brief second he felt an emotion wash over him that made him feel uncomfortable. It may have been shame, but if it was it was certainly short lived. Next to the body was the pound coin, a small price to pay for a life but too much for the man. Picking up the coin and putting it in his pocket, he turned up his hood once more and headed out onto the main street. Looking into the crowd it was not long before the figure of this executioner melted into the throng, neither standing out or attracting attention. In the alleyway it would be some time before the body of the tramp attracted any attention. People saw only another down and out, unconscious and drunk no doubt. It was only the man who had seen the human being there, the life. It was he who had taken it.

MARLIN

It was almost five o'clock when Marlin pulled up in the street opposite Aldous'

window and lit a cigarette, slowly releasing the blue smoke as if to hide in a nicotine cloud. He was in no rush to go across to the door; after all, he was not even that sure why he had come. With one last long draw, he threw the cigarette end out of the window and adjusted his coat and tie. Glancing at his tired eyes in the rear view mirror, he registered the anxiety staring back at him and reached for another cigarette. 'One more and then inside.'

Savouring the nicotine that allowed his delay, he tried to view the only slightly faded grandeur of the Victorian property. The fine oak door that led to a world within his aspirations, but well beyond his present reality. If he didn't make some progress with the current spate of killings, even the Audi he was sheltering in would be beyond both. This was a gamble but what the hell else could he do?

He checked the mirror again, smoothing his cheeks and chin - he needed a shave but it would do. Moving his fingers across the dark shadow above his lip, he wondered how many times he'd considered growing back his moustache but, at the age of 38, he'd finally grown into his face and he liked seeing how the years were treating him. The greying of his temples also made him reconsider, after all, what was the point of going from 'baby-faced' to distinguished old man without some middle ground? No, he had some character now and he liked it.

Looking across again, he saw the oak door open and in the half-light he could see Andrews and a girl. Blonde and somewhat younger than Andrews, she was not dressed for the cold. Well, well Dr Al, you surprise me.

Al gave Lara a quick hug.

'I'll call you about Friday'

'I've only got late afternoon or the evening free at the moment, so the sooner you decide the better.' She pecked his cheek and turned, hurrying away in the cold.

'Dr Al?'

The door ajar, Al squinted at the figure approaching.

'Yes, detective is it?'

Marlin stopped and raised an eyebrow.

'Detective Chief Inspector actually.'

'The polished shoes are a dead give-away. What can I do for you Detective Chief Inspector?'

'Marlin, DCI Marlin.'

Having opened the door and signalled to come in, Al lead the way to the living room and picked up a whiskey from the table.

'Can I offer you one?'

'No thanks, on duty and all that'

'Ok. Well then.' Al stopped and looked intently at Marlin. 'Don't I know you?'

'I was one of the officers working on the Romford Road Murders. I arrested Rennie.'

'Ah, of course, Marlin.' Al pointed to his lip. 'Didn't you...?'

'Yes, the moustache has gone.'

'Well, well, Marlin,' Al looked closer and shook his head. 'It's good to see you again, and a DCI now, you've done well. I shouldn't be surprised though, you were always the bright one. When I could get a word out of you that is.'

'Thanks. I see you still like your whiskey.'

Al smiled and raised his glass. 'It helps the thought process.'

'So you still think a lot?' Marlin smiled.

'Ha, yes, you could say that. Now it's good to see you again, but I get the impression this isn't a social visit.'

'No it's not. Dr Al, I need your advice and your help. I don't know how closely you follow the local media, or national for that matter, but there've been a number of murders over the past week or so.'

'I can't say that it had caught my attention. How many murders are we talking about?'

'Of particular interest, seven or so.'

'Seven, really?' Al drained his glass and swallowed heavily.

'What's the link between the 'particulars'? I'm assuming there must be something if you're bringing this information to me.'

'That's the thing; there's no link that we can see. Men and women, rich and poor; even homeless one of them.'

'And so....,'

'Wait.' Marlin interrupted. 'Seven days and at least seven bodies, all in London and not a clue among them. No sexual assaults, no robbery, no pattern we can see; nothing but corpses. Random it might be, but I find it odd that the murder MO should suddenly be so bloody tidy. I suppose what I'm trying to say is that it's clinical. Too clinical to just dismiss anyway, and I'm not really sure what to make of it.'

Al leaned forward and poured himself another drink, unable to disguise the interest in his eyes. 'Tell me more.'

SEVEN BODIES

Having seen that Al had lost none of his love for whiskey, it was no surprise that he had suggested they continue the conversation in the pub. 'More relaxed' he'd said, but Marlin had noticed that the bottle was empty. Still, he was able to call in to confirm his off-duty status and could now have a drink himself.

The Red Lion afforded one a warm welcome, good beer and prices that were of only slight concern to the average wallet. Al was not concerned; at home and well known to the staff a pint of lager and a shot of whiskey arrived unbidden.

'And for your friend?'

'A pint of lager's fine, thanks.'

'And a shot.'

'On the slate, Al?'

Al smiled at the barman and, collecting his drinks, moved to a table in the corner. Marlin followed, walking stiffly and straight-backed, his body yet to relax from duty. He sat down, wiping the foam moustache from his upper lip.

'That's some house you have Dr Al, life has been treating you well?'

'Just Doc or Al, remember?'

'Ok, that's some house you have Doc. Is it just you and your girlfriend?'

Al looked slightly puzzled for a moment and then his face relaxed into a wry grin as he shook his head.

'No, no girlfriend. The young lady is a different kind of girl altogether, although very friendly. I'd better leave it at that, Detective Chief Inspector.'

'Marlin. It's still just Marlin, even with the promotions, and there are two things you should know. First, I'm off-duty now and secondly, I really don't care who's in your bed or why they're there. I've seven bodies and literally not a clue. Help me out here and I'll get my friends in Vice to give you a list of recommendations and a get out of jail free card.' He downed his shot but was still half a pint behind Al as he watched him signal for the same again.

'For God's sake you drink quickly Doc.'

The drinks arrived and Al composed himself.

'Tell me about the first body. Where and when?'

*

Tuesday

Stepping from the bus into the rain of a dismal Tuesday evening, Janet Pearson was stopped by a strong hand on her shoulder. Flinching slightly, she turned her ample frame to see a smiling young man holding an umbrella

'I think this is yours'

'Oh thank you. Thank you so much. I'd lose my head if it wasn't screwed on.'

The last words were lost as the doors slid shut and the bus slipped away.

'There's hope for this world yet,' she whispered.

Turning into the wind with a grimace, she struggled to balance her bag inside her elbow whilst opening, or trying to open, her umbrella. The rain numbed her face as she looked down the lane that ran along the field and cut 10 minutes off her journey. It was quiet but, as it was not yet dark, it was worth a gamble, surely? An icy gust proved convincing.

'Damn it,' The umbrella finally open, jerked, inverted and then pulled her forward like some ghost dog, her eyes blinded by the rain. Stopping, she regained the shape out of the wind and carefully pulled the umbrella shut.

SMACK, CRACK, CRACK.

Fists unseen landed sure and heavy. Three notes so quick as to be a chord of concussive simplicity. Janet was without senses long before she landed on the hard concrete that connected fatally with her head.

The man did not pause or glance back. Hooded and grey he was swallowed by the rain, the whispered 'Mardi Gras' unheard and lost to the wind.

*

'Tuesday, Leytonstone, a 58 year old woman was punched to death in a quiet lane in broad daylight. There were no clues and apparently no witnesses. Nothing.' Marlin shook his head, exasperated by his own brevity and the reason for it. He was reminded of the phone call from a reporter that morning asking, 'Any news about who killed the old fat woman?' Crude and thoughtless, yet he had accounted for her life and death in one sentence. Excusing himself he stepped outside and lit a cigarette.

Al had checked Marlin's full pint and ordered himself another round, then taken a small notepad from his pocket to make some notes. Resting the nib of the pen on the virgin sheet he glanced out at Marlin drawing heavily on his cigarette.

'Notes on what? There's no fucking information here!'

Marlin returned to his seat.

'Doc, you might want to slow down a bit, I need you to be able to think.'

'I'm ok; one of the few gifts I inherited from my father is an absurdly high tolerance for alcohol.'

'He was a drinker?'

'No, he was a failure. Now, if you really want me to help you, it would be useful if you could give me something to work on or with.'

'What I'm giving you is all that I have.'

'Ok, what about the others?'

Marlin downed his whiskey and reached for his cigarettes again, halting as the realisation of the ban occurred to him.

'Well, we're not too sure how it all fits, but each day there has been a killing with no evidence whatsoever; no witnesses, no fingerprints, no bloody murder weapon, nothing. We just don't know what to dismiss as coincidence.'

'Just tell me your thoughts and whatever it is that you do have.' Al signalled for two more drams.

'Alright, Wednesday we had a shooting in Balham, but it was a kid and we know that gangs are involved. A stabbing fatality during a robbery, but there are prints everywhere. And a strangled prostitute, although without going into details, the MO is somewhat different. Then there's an as yet unidentified body in Fulham.'

'Unidentified?'

'Burned to a crisp about a mile from Fulham Broadway, under a railway bridge. We know it's a male. It was on the news all of Thursday.'

'Thursday wasn't a good day for me. Not a lot of TV. Tell me about the prostitute.'

'As I say, she was strangled in premises near Oxford Circus but there was a message,' Marlin paused.

'What message? Don't drag it out.'

''Now are you satisfied?' scrawled in lipstick on the mirror.'

'Classy and clichéd.' Al half-smiled and returned to his whiskey.

'Well anyway, on Thursday we have a hit and run in Ilford but the CCTV seems to have caught a few images. Then there's an American tourist in the toilets of the *Travellers Rest Pub* in Victoria. He was beaten to a pulp and left in a cubicle; it was only his case left by the table that alerted anyone. The CCTV cameras were focused on the till and the daytime crowd in there all saw someone different. To be honest I wouldn't trust those guys to recognise their own faces in a mirror.'

'I've had a drink or two there myself so don't knock the patrons,' Al was grinning.

'Are you...,'

'No Marlin, I'm not drunk, go on.'

'Friday, we have a fatal stabbing in Wembley - assailant caught. And a teenage charity worker; neck broken and found behind a line of recycling bins in Stepney.'

Al was now writing, a keen concentration sharpening his expression. Marlin signalled to the bar.

'Another two whiskeys please. Shall I...,'

'If there's more, go on.' He looked up and for the first time Al showed a genuine concern.

'Are there more?'

'Maybe, you tell me. All of this might be nothing.' The drinks arrived and Marlin was glad to pause and sip, appreciating the warm burn in his throat.

'Saturday was a busy day but only one fatality, a heavy metal fan hit by a train near Shoreditch. Seemed like a suicide, but the pathologist thinks he was dead before he was hit by the train. From the bruising to his wrists and elsewhere, we think his neck was broken and then he was thrown from the bridge.'

'Why do you mention that he was a heavy metal fan, is it relevant?'

'With the state of his face; his hair and what was left of a Black Sabbath t-shirt were all that was recognisable.'

'Black Sabbath, ok?' An interested Al scribbled furiously for a few minutes and, having absentmindedly gestured towards the bar, fixed Marlin with a piercing stare.

'I make that five, go on.'

'Sunday we found the body of Gillian Watson, a 35 year old woman, in her Mile End flat. Half-dressed, she had been killed with one blow from a blunt instrument we have yet to find.'

'Could it have been a hammer?'

'No, not a hammer. We think something with a heavy base but no weapon has been found. There was no sexual assault or robbery, no fingerprints we can match.'

'Had she been undressed?'

'Unlikely. Panties and a dressing gown - it looks like she had just gotten out of bed.'

'And you say no sexual assault?'

'No, she'd had sex - we found a used condom - but no signs of assault. She brought someone home but we don't know who. Enquiries are on-going.'

'Mm. Ok then, what about Monday, yesterday?'

'Monday, we found a homeless guy off Oxford Street with his neck broken. No CCTV there. Now this one could be nothing, it might be completely random; they all could.'

Al finished scribbling, then downed his short and stood.

'Time to go Marlin, I need to think about this.'

Coats fastened, they stepped outside and Marlin lit a cigarette.

'Do you think it's anything? I mean, is there something here worth taking a closer look at?'

'Honestly I don't know, but I hope so for your sake. I don't think you really want to have to deal with a whole new breed of 'elite' killers.'

'Thanks Doc, for the drinks and the cold comfort.'

Al arrived back at his house having stopped at a 24/7 to restock with whiskey. He poured a generous glass and then brought a large oblong of hardboard from the small cupboard under the stairs. Balancing this against the wall, he took a box of pins from the top drawer of the desk that sat inside his front door. He had plotted famous cases and even book structures this way, but he could not help but be amused, as he pinned notes to the board, just how much he was copying film detectives.

Swallowing deeply and refilling, he brought himself back to the serious reality of the moment as his eyes settled on the name of Janet Pearson. This was no film. Days, names and details were pinned carefully and studied as Al made more notes.

He knew this was a chance to get his career moving again, in much the same way as the Romford Road Murders had brought him into the limelight a decade or so earlier. Play his cards right and there was surely a book in there somewhere. It was an exciting and slightly frightening prospect as he looked at the clues pinned to the board. Where the hell should he start? Could he do this anymore? He looked for associations, for a type, a thread of sense to get hold of. He scanned and drank, drank and scanned, until the words swam before him and he floated away from memory or consciousness.

A PRIEST

In the hinterland between night and day, disturbing dreams and living nightmares, Al found himself struggling to make sense of the not unpleasant buzzing on his thigh. The odd noise troubled him, until his hand found the vibration and his scrambled senses once again searched for their rightful places. He allowed the phone to go to voicemail and dared to open his swollen eyes. The half-light was almost physically painful and his bladder was now screaming for mercy. Fully clothed, he was sprawled across his bed, stale whiskey oozing from every pore. Standing gingerly, he made his way to the bathroom then to the kitchen and the solace of coffee. Now he could face the phone; and as he looked at the board of scrawled notes, some sense of context invaded his damaged consciousness.

The phone was a horribly familiar sight, the previously clear screen now tattooed and disfigured by insistent envelopes and calls unheeded. He started with the calls as normal so as to find his role in the dialogue. As always he ignored the content on first listen, preferring to gauge the tone and most importantly the introductory time and date. He was always somewhat excited and anxious to get to this and once sated he would return for specific information. People wanted decisions; Lara about Friday and Marlin repeatedly about everything, then anything and eventually just recognition of his calls - all six.

Having finished his two cups of coffee, Al moved back to the bathroom and undressed before stepping into the shower. A powerful blast of hot water brought Al into a refreshing present as his mind disengaged auto-pilot and took control. Palms flat against the wall; he extended his arms and leaned his head forward to let the cascade wash powerfully over his neck. What answers did he have for Marlin? Did he know what to say to Lara? The three empty bottles on the living room table - where had the third one come from? Since his phone had announced that it was Thursday, what had happened to Wednesday? Al tried to hide his own anxiety but it was clear that he was becoming elusive even to himself.

Dressed and trusting in the healing powers of caffeine once again, Al took note of Marlin's instructions to check his e-mail. Sitting with his lap-top on his knees, he scanned the message.

Al

There have been no notifications of any fatalities on Tuesday as far as I know.

Maybe I got it wrong. Did you come up with anything?

Oh and could you try answering your phone?

Get in touch when you can.

Marlin

Al did not know whether to be relieved or not. Surely it was a good thing if it was over? Or that it had never been anything at all? No, his gut feeling was that it had been something and that feeling had not gone away. He looked towards the board and studied hard, a reminder to himself that this mattered; it mattered to him as a serious piece of work. It mattered that he had been picked to help and not just provide a trite one-liner. It mattered that his mind was away from the black blanks in his head.

His phone jerked on the table, an electric fish out of water and he grabbed blindly, nerves shredded.

'Hello, Al Andrews?'

'Doc, where the hell have you been?' Marlin exclaimed, his annoyance poorly disguised.

'Hello, Marlin. Look I'm sorry but I wasn't too well.'

'You were too ill to answer a phone?'

'I took to my bed and was sleeping most of the time.'

'Dead drunk and sleeping it off more like.'

'Hey, I was ill ok!'

'Christ Doc, you're hard work. Did you at least check your messages? Your many messages?'

'Marlin, calm down, I checked all of the messages and the e-mail. You think it may have stopped at seven. Or it's a random several? But it's stopped.'

'No, it hasn't. There's a possible eight and nine now.'

'What? When?'

'Found yesterday but time of death Tuesday night. A priest.'

*

Father John

St Michael's RC church in Paddington was never a hive of activity;
those busy masses were memories of Sundays long gone and a Tuesday
night at 8pm was never going to be anything to stick in the mind. Father
John shivered slightly as he moved through the church and, as he
became aware of the echo of his footsteps, he decided to lock up for the
night. He was cold enough to lose hope in any potential visitors and
hungry enough to be pleased with an early finish. Feeling oddly self-
conscious, he checked the empty pews for the imagined eyes he could feel
and sighed at the vacancy.

'Father, full of grace?' a voice whispered close and intense. Father
John turned in horror but only found blackness as the man brought the
candlestick onto - and through - the back of his skull. He watched as the
priest slumped, heavy with death, on to the floor. The black blood
glistened in the light of the candles and the man paused to breathe in the
silence, savouring the taste of finality. One being where only moments
before there had been two; he spread his arms and felt his body pulse
with a perverse elation. A savage unforgiving ecstasy.

Al felt sick and not a little panicked. It occurred to him that the saying,
'Be careful what you wish for' was eerily applicable.

'You there Al?'

'Yeah I'm here. Jesus Marlin, where's all this leading?'

'I came to you for that answer, Doc.'

'I'm working on it. Now, Marlin?' Al felt his whole body become
taught. 'What about yesterday?'

'What about yesterday? I'm glad you ask because yesterday raises
some interesting questions.'

'Another killing?'

'Two killings, Doc. Another prostitute has been strangled, in Old Street
this time, and a guy about 30 killed near Vauxhall.'

'OK, let's start with the prostitute. Was there a message?'

'Yes. Lipstick again - 'Now you are fucked.''

'Are we looking at some sort of comedian here?'

'I'm not finding it funny.'

'Prints?'

'Plenty of prints, but then she was not unpopular. Nothing to go on
yet.'

'And the guy?'

'Well I can't really tell you too much at the moment. About 30 years old, worked as an administrator for MI6, less than a quarter of a mile from where his body was found. Neck broken but little sign of any struggle. As you can imagine though, from his place of occupation, there are others involved in this investigation. I'm somewhat out of the loop and kept at arm's length. With that in mind, this would be a good time to tell you that you know nothing about this and I certainly didn't say anything.'

'Ok.'

'Just get me something, Doc. I don't know if we have a madman branching out to killing prostitutes or whether all the other murders are random and this is the guy we should be concentrating on? Scarily, I'm beginning to think we have another psycho out there and we have two to find.'

'I'm sorry to say it, but I think I agree with you. But let me concentrate on psycho number 1 for now.'

'Ok, will do. Now try and answer your phone and lay off the whiskey, Doc.'

Al pushed the button ending the call and then reached forward and poured what remained of the bottle into his glass and drank greedily. Staring at the board again he sighed wearily and stood. I'm going to need another bottle of inspiration.

The bottle was procured more easily than any inspiration, but it served only to keep his hangover at bay and his tired eyes open. The fresh air on the brief trip outdoors was a welcome relief, but he ached and it was all he could do to get a bottle and a pizza before struggling home. Afternoon eased into evening and the pizza was washed down with a bottle as Al stared blankly at his television, little more than white noise with pictures. His phone was thankfully quiet and e-mails merely solicitations for Viagra or illicit pastimes. The heaviness of the world in his bones, Al knew that although today was ruined, tomorrow was another day to try. Putting down his drink he clicked off the television and headed for bed. 9pm and he was as old as he had ever felt and ready for sleep; sleep was ready for Al and greeted him warmly.

Friday arrived earlier than Al was used to and he showered for a long while, trying to wash the fatigue away, succeeding more than he hoped due to his hours in bed. The start of the day was devoted to ease and comfort as he reclined on the sofa. Drinking strong coffee and sipping on the remains of his whiskey, he was unsurprised that the 24 hour news channel did not bear glad tidings. He did know that today was for work however. Just past midday Al moved to his board and began to insert notes. He didn't have too much information, but he needed to be clearer about what he did know. The days, the people, the geography. If nothing else he had to establish the questions he hadn't asked:

DAY: Tuesday
NAME: Janet Pearson
PLACE: Leytonstone
FEATURES: Punched, alleyway, overweight woman in her 50s.

*

DAY: Wednesday
NAME: u/ kn
PLACE: Fulham
FEATURES: Male, burned completely

*

DAY: Wednesday
NAME: u/ kn
PLACE: Oxford Circus
FEATURES: Prostitute, strangled - message so seems a different killer 'Are you satisfied now?'

*

DAY: Thursday
NAME: u/ kn
PLACE: Victoria
FEATURES: Beaten to death in pub toilets, US tourist

*

DAY: Friday
NAME: u/ kn
PLACE: Stepney
FEATURES: Charity worker, broken neck

*

DAY: Saturday
NAME: u/ kn
PLACE: Shoreditch

FEATURES: *Neck broken and thrown off bridge onto train track, rock fan?*

*

DAY: *Sunday*
NAME: *Gillian Watson*
PLACE: *Mile End*
FEATURES: *Bludgeoned with blunt instrument, 35 yr. old female*

*

DAY: *Monday*
NAME: *u/ kn*
PLACE: *Oxford Street*
FEATURES: *Neck broken, homeless man*

*

DAY: *Tuesday*
NAME: *Father John*
PLACE: *Paddington*
FEATURES: *Bludgeoned*

*

DAY: *Wednesday*
NAME: *u/ kn*
PLACE: *Vauxhall*
FEATURES: *Male 30, worked for MI6, strangled*

*

DAY: *Wednesday*
NAME: *u/ kn*
PLACE: *Old Street*
FEATURES: *Prostitute, strangled - message 'Now you are fucked.'*

Sitting back, Al shook his head and sipped the last remnants of his whiskey slowly. He was so lax it was an embarrassment and he knew that he had allowed alcohol to cause, and then disguise, his lack of focus. He remembered his studies; he could vividly recall all of the books, reading about Bundy, Son of Sam, and Neilson. Scanning the pictures, page after page of victims, he had returned the dead-eyed gazes and felt the pain, the loss. These were people with hopes and dreams who were torn from this life literally kicking and screaming. These were people who mattered for their lives and not just their deaths.

He examined his list, looking through the missing names, and he saw a catalogue of bodies and victims. He hadn't even started to look at this properly. He had become an expert at suppression, hiding his own dark secrets in a bottle, but now was a time to emerge into the light. It was time to open his eyes.

Opening his laptop he e-mailed Marlin.

Marlin

Sorry for going AWOL. Back in action now. I need to have all of the names, places and any other details you may have picked up since we spoke. I am looking for a connection and I am ruling out the prostitute murders for now.

Thanks

Al

SABBATH BLOODY SABBATH

Determined but weak, Al had scouted for whiskey and the cold wind was both numbing and invigorating. He stopped at Mario's café and devoured a full English eagerly. Mario's, the Italian named English café, run by an unnaturally cheerful Turk and a Polish chef. United Nations it might be, but all Al cared about was his stomach and the breakfast was hot, greasy and good. The day could begin and he knew it was going to be a long one.

Inside his house once more, Al prepared a cafetierre and placed it on his living room table along with a cup, some milk, a glass and his new bottle. He opened his laptop and checked his mail, smiling as he saw that Marlin had been as quick with his reply as he'd been with his 'Benetton' breakfast.

Al

Here are the details as I have them but the MI6 kid is only listed as Jackson. He was an accountant of some sort but they seem keen to make sure he was not part of some spy ring. If they allow me more details I'll let you know.

Call me later and let me know what you think. Friday is rapidly progressing.

Marlin

Al was only too aware of the timing of events. He looked at the attachment sent by Marlin and opened a new page on the laptop, quickly copying the details from the board and updating them both electronically and physically. He felt like a nervous schoolboy sent off to revise, yet spending his time ordering pens and pencils to postpone the need to concentrate. He placed his iPod into the overly ornate speaker system and pushed the shuffle button - an unconscious nod to younger days when music was a source of much inspiration. As My Morning Jacket soared from the speakers he sat and focused, eyes darting from laptop to board. What did the new details say about a pattern? There had to be a pattern.

DAY: *Tuesday*
NAME: *Janet Pearson*

PLACE: *Leytonstone*
FEATURES: *Punched, alleyway, overweight woman in her 50s.*

*

DAY: *Wednesday*
NAME: *Ken Cohen*
PLACE: *Fulham*
FEATURES: *Male, burned completely*

*

DAY: *Thursday*
NAME: *Don Simpson*
PLACE: *Victoria*
FEATURES: *Beaten to death in pub toilets, US tourist*

*

DAY: *Friday*
NAME: *Chris Bailey*
PLACE: *Stepney*
FEATURES: *Charity worker, broken neck*

*

DAY: *Saturday*
NAME: *Charles Glover*
PLACE: *Shoreditch*
FEATURES: *Neck broken and thrown off bridge onto train track, rock fan?*

*

DAY: *Sunday*
NAME: *Gillian Watson*
PLACE: *Mile End*
FEATURES: *Bludgeoned with blunt instrument, 35 yr. old female*

*

DAY: *Monday*
NAME: *Daniel Riley*
PLACE: *Oxford Street*
FEATURES: *Neck broken, homeless man*

*

DAY: *Tuesday*
NAME: *Father John Tracey*
PLACE: *Paddington*

FEATURES: Bludgeoned

*

DAY: Wednesday
NAME: Jackson
PLACE: Vauxhall
FEATURES: Male 30, worked for MI6, accountant, strangle

Alternating sips of whiskey and coffee, Al settled into a quiet intensity. The music, at once strident and forceful, became aural wallpaper; the plaintive pleading for a Child in Time nothing but an old conversation that required no more attention. He stared at days and days and days. He thought of days stained by death and written in blood, he thought of days unremembered and lost. He looked at Tracey, Jackson, Riley and all of the names. He pictured gravestones. He searched the internet for connections as he thought of dead presidents, rock stars, film stars, sportsmen and women. He considered broken necks and cracked skulls, shattered noses and burned remains. Sticking virtual pins in electric maps he could not grasp any geographical shape, in much the same way that he could not grasp any philosophical reason.

The minutes tiptoed by unheeded and were joined by hours slipping silently out of sight. Al sat back and sighed heavily, a hand on the glass jug spoke of coffee, cold and almost exhausted. He poured a large glass and stared ahead, trying not to admit defeat, although the size of the drink alone was a signal that seemed a prelude to surrender. Rolling his neck he felt the tightness across his shoulders and he drank deeply, closing his eyes. The music came into the forefront once more. He smiled gently at the crunching chords of his youth as he looked across at the illuminated album cover; the demonic image seemed fitting.

Immersed in the music, Al drank and tried his best to dwell only on simpler, happier times. Days when loud guitar was a panacea. Relaxing into nostalgic reverie he drank again and sang along enthusiastically, stopping himself suddenly as the chorus played out. The words sung seemed to hang in front of him and he was frozen in time; a full-back under the ball hoping to catch his idea cleanly. There was no fumble or drop.

'Sabbath Bloody Sabbath,' he spoke slowly as his eyes scanned the board.

'Mr Glover, you wore a Black Sabbath t-shirt on Saturday - the Sabbath?' Is this something? Anything? He felt that it was, that it had to be, but he had to convince Marlin.

Thursday

'See you later Davie,'

'See ya big man,' Davie shouted, surprising himself with the volume.

'Pished' he thought 'But happy.'

A laugh escaped from his lips and he leaned into his meandered journey smiling. Tom's a good bloke he thought, could do with talking less and working more, but a cracking guy to have a few pints with. What was he like with the wee barmaid in there? Ha! He grinned again and slalomed onwards, slowing slightly as he realised his bladder was once again ready to be emptied. He looked for a pub and realised there were none in sight; worse still he could not work out where he was. He knew the general area was Angel but he had taken a wrong turn. His bladder throbbed insistently and he cursed life, no longer such a happy man.

Continuing forward his eyes searched desperately for cover, more so as the discomfort increased. Passing a now inviting bus shelter he saw a small road passing between two houses as the main road curved. His step quickened. Looking around him he did his best to slip into the quiet darkness unseen and, once alone, he gratefully emptied his bladder, groaning with relief in a fetid cloud of steam.

Davie would have recognised the orange 'dead- blow' hammer and known of the internal cavity filled with steel or lead shot. He may have known how this was to even out the time-impulse curve of the impact, enabling a more powerful blow to be delivered without risk of marring the target. He had never felt the impact however, the incredibly dense thudding agony, sound and pain as one. By the third blow there was no pain, by the fifth barely a head. The man stepped back and regarded the viscous mess that was once a man and he breathed in heavily. Urine and the soiling of death combined in an acrid scent that was sickly sweet and strong enough to taste. The man breathed deeply once more and bared his teeth in a grotesque perversion of a smile as he turned and left, hooded and unseen in the evening's darkness.

Al called immediately. 'Marlin'

'Al? It's nearly 9pm, what is it?'

'Look just tell me, the boy on the Saturday, the heavy rock kid. Where he was found, was it anywhere near a rock club or somewhere that rock bands play; a pub or something?'

'Al, have you been anywhere near Shoreditch recently? There are probably more music venues than bands.'

'Yes, but rock music?'

'Christ Al are you researching or going gigging? Yes, rock music. Any music you like will have something or someone playing it.'

'Right. Thanks Marlin, sorry for ringing out of hours.'

'Out of hours? I'm not a GP for Christ's sake, you're the Doc,' he laughed. 'Now are you going to tell me what this is about, because if you're not, I'm going to get really pissed off.'

'Ok. I've gone over the days of the week scenario, and apart from the obvious fact of there having been a killing or more every day, I saw nothing. For some reason it suddenly struck me that the young rock boy was killed on a Saturday. He was wearing a Black Sabbath t-shirt. The Sabbath is often Saturday.'

'Are you not getting too coincidental here, Al? I mean that's some leap of faith. I think we may need a bit more than that, don't you?'

'Maybe, but it's at least a possibility. Just think for a moment, what if there is no discernible connection among the victims? Just a connection to the days? What if the kid was selected because he was wearing a Sabbath t-shirt on the Saturday? What if this guy was looking around rock clubs?'

'Find me a second link and I'll think about it. Oh, and don't have any more whiskey. Night Al.'

Al sat back and sighed. Of course there would have to be more than just one link. He was also embarrassed that even over the phone there was obviously whisky on his breath. To his surprise the doorbell rang. Peering through the peephole on his door, Al was somewhat astonished to see a 'J&B' whisky label in close up.

'Come on Al, hurry up, I'm freezing out here.'

'Lara?' He jerked the door open quickly and there before him stood Lara. Her pretty blonde head tilted, she viewed Al with a smile and fluttered her long eyelashes exaggeratedly. Then, shaking her hips in a mock dance, she moved the bottle in front of his eyes.

'If it isn't your favourite, whiskey and coked up Lara, ha.'

'Lara. Come in.' He stepped back and Lara skipped past into the hallway.

'You owe me extra for the bottle, Doc.' She effortlessly slipped off her short jacket and placed it over the staircase banister before glancing into the living room. 'It looks like you started without me. Can I have a glass too?'

'Oh, er, yes of course.' Al was unusually flustered and not a little confused. He picked a glass from the cabinet and filled a generous measure before passing it to his guest.

'So Lara, what brings you here?'

Lara was circling the living room inquisitively until she leaned forward to read the board he had set up. His storyboard of murder and misery. As she did so her skirt, the thin band that was her skirt, rode up to reveal her stocking-tops and Al was left staring. She turned and, seeing his look, pulled down the material with mock indignation.

'Doctor Al, really.' He could not help but smile at the pantomime and innuendo that was his sex life now.

'I'm here because you asked me to come Doc, and we both know you're pleased to see me don't we?'

'I asked you?'

Lara stopped and tutted, 'You rang on Wednesday night. You said to be here at nine and to bring a bottle. How many have you had?'

Al was embarrassed that the darkness that was Wednesday had brought a physical reminder, but he couldn't pretend that he wasn't pleased to see her.

'Oh yes of course, sorry, I'd lost track of the time.'

'That's ok Doc, but time is money, is it not?' She extended her hand and, back on familiar ground, Al reached for his wallet. Not needing to count the money, Lara turned and sashayed suggestively as she moved to her handbag, carefully placing the notes inside. The economics of the situation resolved, Lara turned again and slowly approached Al, her eyes wide in an intense gaze, her mouth closed and serious.

'SLAP!' she brought her right palm hard across his cheek. 'Now get upstairs and get undressed.'

MARCH MOURNING

Marlin sat at his kitchen table looking out of the window into the yellowed night of streetlamps and domestic illumination. He lit a cigarette and drawing deeply, he considered Al and his thoughts on the Sabbath and Saturday. He looked down at the files spread out before him on the table and wondered if he was wasting his time. The opinion of a half-drunk, has-been mentalist who is talking about days of the week? What does that even mean for Christ's sake? What if the big connection is days of the week? A connection to what and how does that help with the investigation? A slight touch on his finger brought him back to the present as a thin tube of ash lost its fight against gravity. He automatically reached for a replacement to reignite his thought process.

Peter Marlin was a good policeman in his own opinion and, in truth, there was pretty much a consensus in this respect. A good policeman and a good man from a good family, married to a good wife with a beautiful child. A good father to his son, a non-smoker and a moderate drinker. Only some of this was now true and all in all Marlin did not feel good. The man admired by many was now a lone, somewhat isolated figure, who had all but lost his self-respect. He knew that he was becoming a cliché but he was now defined by the job and how he did it. Any inherent self-esteem and achievement could be measured against his ability to get results at work. It was not what he had wanted, but he had taken some comfort in moving from a man of the police to a policeman.

Trying to ignore the link between his increasingly regular coughing fits and the constant chain of cigarettes to accompany the sour black coffee, he pictured Diana; she was smiling wryly and gently shaking her head. Even in his imagination she could make him feel like a small boy again. Her disapproval was always a needle-sharp reminder, a rein on his behaviour and a guide to his future conduct. She had been his conscience and his inspiration; his strong woman. She did not stand behind her 'great' man; she supported and enveloped him, steadied his feet and inflamed his ardour. That she had become his life was of no surprise to anyone except Marlin himself. He knew now, though. Christ, he knew now.

Marlin was ready for fatherhood in the same way that he had been ready for his marriage, in that all of the planning had not diluted the utter shock of the actual day arriving. Marlin had a tendency to live in the present, whilst plotting for the tomorrow that would never be today. Diana had a plan and little Thomas was all too a part of it. There can have been no more attentive mother to the little boy, 'the most beautiful little boy with the bluest eyes'. Thomas was Diana's angel, her little man, her life; much as Diana was Marlin's.

He had too few sleepless nights as she took control of changing, feeding and all that seemed necessary. He tried not to resent his young son, but it was an effort that led to a withdrawn silence, a sullen sulk of unspoken jealousy. That he felt unable to bond with the boy - or even get close - left him frustrated. To Diana he was merely a man/child, unable to step-up to his responsibilities and selfishly coveting the kisses and caresses that were Thomas'. No wonder she felt the need to do everything herself. She knew best and until he grew up there was no alternative. She immersed herself in motherhood and he worked incessantly as he slowly sank into a deep well of guilt.

The day in March three years ago was still a blur to Marlin. The absolute horror of the day was acutely raw and real, but the detail had gone. He had drunk to forget and he wanted none of those minutes, those agonising seconds back. That morning 'the most beautiful little boy' had lain still and peaceful and cold. That he was unprepared to deal with the cot-death of his son was natural, but his obvious shock and grief was as nothing compared to Diana. She plumbed depths of despair that he could never have imagined and he could not help her. She spoke of his jealousy of the boy and how he must be glad now. She wept and she screamed, she pleaded with God and asked why? Again and again she cried out why until, with no answer forthcoming, she fell silent - deflated and desolate.

It had been a birthday for a friend of a friend in the *Argyll Arms* pub, just off Oxford Street. Marlin had had a little too much to drink, but buoyed by Dutch courage he was able to speak to the red haired girl with the smile and 'those eyes'. He remembered how he had remarked on the incredible beauty of her brown eyes and how she had berated him for his 'line'. He was however speaking the truth; her brown eyes were quite stunning; she was stunning. The light in those eyes dimmed after

Thomas, replaced by a slight flicker of anger or distaste when she looked at him. Occasionally he saw a violent malice directed towards him when he mentioned the boy's name. For the most part he just felt her palpable irritation at his presence. To avoid seeing him she began to stay with friends, stays that became longer as her phone stayed silent. One day the 'bag' she packed was three cases and he knew she wasn't coming back. They neither hugged nor kissed - as they had not done since Thomas - when she left; the atmosphere cold and lifeless. He had since felt a grief that he had lost both his son and wife that March morning. It was a hole in his life he needed to fill and whilst he had no idea how he would do so, he had resolved to become a man; to take control of his life once more.

Stubbing out the cigarette butt, Marlin rubbed his hands down over his face. Surprised to feel the warm wetness of his tears he reached for a towel. Shaking the packet to make sure he had enough cigarettes left he stood and put on his jacket, feeling instinctively for the unopened pack in the inside pocket and patting down to his trousers for the car keys.

'Let's see what the fuck the Doc is talking about.'

ASHES AND BONE

The drive was not a particularly long one, nor the roads particularly busy, but Marlin idled absent-mindedly on his way across town. When he did arrive at the old Victorian building he sat as before and rolled down the window, lighting a cigarette as he did so. The smoke blew into his eyes, stinging one shut, and he coughed into the cold night air. Checking his watch he saw that it was gone half-past eleven. He figured the Doc would be up at this time but sober? What the hell, he was here now.

Ringing the bell Marlin looked at the light peeping out from the bottom of the thick red curtains and stepped back from the door. No sound came from inside and he wondered if a malt induced sleep was in progress. As he was turning to leave he saw a twitch of light from the upstairs window. Standing his ground he leant forward and pressed the bell two, three times more. A light in the hall flickered into life before a fumbling of locks brought the Doc into view.

'Jesus Doc, are you ok?' Marlin said to the dishevelled figure in front of him. Untidily tied into a white dressing gown, the Doc had a vivid red left cheek and was sweating profusely.

'What is it Marlin? It's late.'

'Yes, sorry Doc, I was just going over what you said earlier and I wanted to discuss it with you. Are you sure you're ok?'

'I'm fine; look come in and take a seat through there while I get some clothes on. You could have phoned ahead you know. Some warning would be nice.'

'I'm sorry I wasn't thinking.' He heard a 'humph' and steps on the staircase as the Doc disappeared and then what he thought were voices above. Or was it just the TV? He paced the room until he came upon the board and stood staring intently.

'Maybe not so much of a has-been?' he murmured quietly to himself.

Walking through to the kitchen he picked an ashtray from the windowsill and a tumbler from the draining rack. Returning to the living room he felt sure he heard voices above, giggling even. Maybe this wasn't such a good idea? Pouring himself a generous shot of whiskey he sat by the board and stared. A gentle click of the door upstairs allowed for a whispered conversation to float into the silence of the living room.

'You call me this time you naughty boy or you know what you'll get,' Lara giggled as she whispered in an overly exaggerated and over loud manner.

'Shhh. I'll call. Now be quiet, the door's open.' A stolen kiss was followed by slow padding footsteps and Marlin eyed the door with no little curiosity. The blonde girl he had seen before, small and pretty, paused at the bottom of the stairs and put on her shoes. He saw that her skirt was holding few secrets and her long legs did not suffer from their disclosure. She glanced into the living room as she pulled on her leather coat and, eyes sparkling, she brought her index finger to her lips.

'SHHHHHHH.' Then she smiled broadly and stepped forward and out of the door.

Marlin saw a small black bag on the settee next to him and, picking it up quickly, moved to the door and then outside where she had stopped, aware that something was missing.

'Excuse me, is this yours?' he held up the bag self-consciously.

'Ah, there it is. Such a gentleman.' She smiled again softly as she took the bag. 'Now don't let on to the Doc that you saw me, ok?'

'I won't, goodnight.' She was already moving towards the street as he spoke and it was now that he noticed the cab waiting. Lara stepped inside and, as it pulled off, the small blonde stared out across the road with no discernible focus.

'Come on, you'll get cold out there,' the Doc stood at the door barefooted but dressed and washed; a drink in his hand as he looked past Marlin and into the road where the cab had stood. Lost in thought, his face was at once serious and sad.

Once inside the Doc regained his composure and gestured animatedly as he recapped the details from his notes. From his bag Marlin produced the official files and his own notations. He studied Al.

'My boss, Chief Superintendent Thomas, wants you off this case, Doc. He thinks that you're not bringing anything to the table.'

'And he wanted my involvement in the first place?'

'Well no, I kind of went with that decision on my own.'

'It's ok, I'm not sure I'd want me on this if I was him. But for your sake let's try and come up with something here.'

'Fine with me Doc, but I have to ask you a question.'

'Fire away.'

'This Sabbath/Saturday link of sorts.'

'Yeah?'

'Well, even if it does point to a link between the death and the day of the death, what does that really tell us?'

'Us, probably very little, but me? I'd take something from it. I need to know what I'm looking for here and then that will point the way to who. Look Marlin, even serial killers don't go out and kill every day. This points to a very dangerous, very disturbed person. I've no doubt that this psycho gets off on the killing itself, but even a freak like this must know that a daily fix is odd. If the victim is being linked with the day in some way, it would be an unconscious distraction from the lack of control over these urges.'

'Right then, we better look at these again.' Marlin spread the files along the table and Al picked up two at random as he sat down. Marlin looked to the board and forced himself to scan slowly, deliberating on each word.

'Doc, I don't really know what I'm looking for here.'

Al stopped reading and looked across at Marlin. Slightly puzzled he poured them both a measure and then sat back down. Pulling his laptop towards him, he turned it on, shaking his head.

'Me, neither, if I am being honest Marlin. I've been so eager to get a theory that I've forgotten to back it up with solid evidence. You were right before when you said that this was just a coincidence without more. However, for now let's forget about the details of the investigation, they're few enough anyway. Look at the killings from the point of view that I'm right about a link to days and see if we can identify a pattern.'

'So what do you have on the laptop?'

'I have the modern world, Marlin. I have Google and Yahoo.' Al smiled and raised his eyebrows, but he was tired and generated no genuine amusement.

'Al, I've had forensic officers going over each crime scene with a fine toothcomb and you think we can Google the answer?'

'This is for the profile, Marlin. A way to see what the freak is thinking; how he's thinking. Once I get something we'll need your good police skills, so let's get every link to every day and then search through the killings. What's the first?'

'Er, Tuesday, Janet Pearson, Leytonstone. Punched and beaten to death.'

'Black Tuesday, Patch Tuesday, Shrove Tuesday (Mardi Gras), Super Tuesday and Tuesday's child is full of grace. Associated with Mars, the God of War.' Al sat back and stared at the ceiling as Marlin's eyes stayed fixed on the notes for Tuesday. The silence was tangible and it was some minutes before they allowed themselves to emerge from its cold embrace.

'Nothing here, Al. The more I look the less I see.'

'There has to be something here. The murder scenes are spotless in terms of clues but the killings are vicious and random; and yet there is one each day. That's too much blood for our psychopath to remain completely anonymous. And don't forget, he'll not see himself as a psychopath, so there must be some design. There is something, trust me.'

'Maybe the guy is a fucking music critic.'

'Maybe.' Al looked deflated and frustrated. He looked across to his board, but it was nothing but over familiar words now. Words with no particular meaning anymore. Tuesday to Monday and then on to Wednesday again.

'What day is it, Marlin?'

'Friday, well actually it's Saturday morning, just.'

'Was nothing reported on Thursday or today?'

'Nothing that I was told of. Let me check with the duty sergeant.' Reaching for his cigarettes Marlin stepped outside and Al filled his glass anew.

'Wednesday.' He peered at the pages on offer. Ash Wednesday, Holy Wednesday, Sheffield Wednesday, Spy Wednesday. Associated with Wodin/Odin the Norse God.

Marlin appeared again, still smoking, his face grim.

'A man killed in the Angel area. Looks like he was bludgeoned with a hammer.'

'Yesterday? I mean Friday?'

'Found early yesterday, but killed on Thursday night. No witnesses.'

'Christ's sake Marlin, Norse Gods. Fucking Norse gods.'

'What?'

'Thor, hammer of the gods. Thursday.'

'So it's Norse gods now?'

'Yes, well no, not all Norse gods, but yes to Thursday. Well, maybe to Thursday.' The Doc's eyes were slightly wild as he spoke, all the more so as he drank in the air of scepticism around Marlin.

Marlin spun the laptop round and looked at the page Al had been studying.

'So Wodin? How does that fit in?'

'It doesn't, well I don't see anything. Look Marlin, it's not one link if it is a link.'

'Yes Doc. If, if, if.'

Al scanned the table and picked up the file of Ken Cohen - Wednesday. No link between Wodin and Fulham that he knew of. He almost smiled but he knew this was not the time, Marlin was clearly irritated and his anxious smoking was a clear indication of the tension in the room. He recoiled slightly as he returned to the file and saw the pictures of Cohen, or what had been Cohen. The report confirmed that he had basically been cremated following death, leaving nothing but ashes and bone.

'Ashes,' Al murmured, almost surprising himself.

'What?'

'Cohen, ashes and bone, Wednesday. Ash Wednesday.'

Marlin looked to the board and in his mind the horror of the burning was brought back to mind. Mental images not easily forgotten.

'Doc, I think you're right, we may be on to something here.'

Al was already typing in Friday and staring, desperate for the connections to emerge. Saturday, Sunday, Monday. He stood and leaned in to his notes, a finger tracing the details, as if his touch would cause the words to reveal themselves. He knew he had to calm himself and he sat again and picked up his glass. Marlin was engrossed in a file, only his eyes and a thin swirl of blue smoke visible. It was unspoken but they were both aware of the reality of the charged, excited atmosphere. Was there really a psychopath with a sick line in themed killings? If so, who and where was he? Where was he? How did this information move them forward?

'Marlin.'

'What now, Doc?'

'You didn't say anything about yesterday, Friday?'

'Nothing to report.'

'Sounds a bit too good to be true?'

'I'm not complaining.' Marlin returned his gaze to the file, a slightly puzzled look on his face, and then he turned the laptop around and began to type.

'What is it?'

'Wait. It's just something that a reporter said to me. Something that stuck out and stayed with me; disturbed me to be honest. 'Any news about who killed the old fat woman' he asked me. He reduced that woman to a statement of age and weight.'

'The press surprise you?'

'No, no, not surprise as such. It was just so stark and cold it depressed me if anything. But it stuck in my mind.'

Marlin turned the laptop side-on to share the view and slowly pointed - *Shrove Tuesday also called Mardi Gras- fat Tuesday.*

'Old fat woman? Janet Pearson? It was on Tuesday.'

'Christ's sake Marlin, this is the world according to fucking Google.'

'So Doc. What do we do with this information?'

'You keep getting the connections, just in case I have this wrong. I don't have it wrong, and I think you see that now, but we have the likes of Thomas to convince. But I now have a basis for a profile. Let me sleep on it?'

'You want me to get the fuck out of here don't you Doc?'

'It's half-two in the morning and it's been a long day.'

'I could see that Doc. What's the story with the young blonde girl? The mark on your face? And your wrists?'

Al looked down at the now light pink indentation along his wrist and blushed deeply as he rubbed, unable to erase this evidence. His private moments were for the quiet darkness, they appeared ugly in the light and this was a source of great discomfiture.

'Another time, Marlin.'

Marlin picked up his jacket and drained the last of his whiskey.

'Ok then, see you later Doc, I'll call tomorrow.'

He left without waiting for confirmation and lit a cigarette as he climbed behind the wheel of his car. He knew he was over the limit but he, too, was tired and he could not face the thought of calling a cab. He wanted to be home in his bed. Alone. His mind drifted to the blonde girl again and he half smiled to himself. Not at that stage yet Peter, but she was nice. He swung the car out into the road as he allowed his mind to drift, navigated by his libido; it made a welcome change. I can see why the Doc likes his Scotch so much he thought. Al had reprimanded himself for his carelessness and taken himself to bed. He pictured the raw splashes of livid colour across his body and drifted off to sleep, vowing not to open the door to unbidden guests again. With the exception of Lara of course. Behind his locked doors he drifted deeper into the dark, yet warm, solitude of slumber.

*

In the dark but untouched by the peace of rest, the man sat, still and intense; watching patterns of his own making in the dusk. He felt restless and disturbed. He felt the itch that pulsed under every inch of his skin and the emptiness of the moment echoed. Standing, he moved towards the window and paused at the dark wooden table against the wall, the unremarkable furniture on which stood candlestick and hammers. Bloodied and stained they bore silent witness and judged him not. He bent slowly and breathed in deeply, then bent further until his lips caressed the polished gold, his tongue gently searching for the taste of the dry blood. For a moment he glowed and throbbed with a delicious electricity, then shuddering slightly he returned to his bed and lay still and unblinking.

GOOD JUDGEMENT AND DISCRETION

Seeing Saturday before midday came as a pleasant surprise to Al, although it didn't mean that he would change his rehydration regime. Sipping on a strong coffee, he enjoyed the bright sunlight that brought a warm glow to the living room. He enjoyed that his phone sat still and quiet; no electronic notes speaking of death or memoranda of murder. Refilling his cup he picked up his notebook from the table and considered the days gone by. What was necessary for an explanation, what or who was accountable?

Beginning on a seemingly random Tuesday, brutality and murder had been brought to bear on ten innocent victims. Ten so far? Did this really start less than two weeks ago? Was it over? From his knowledge it seemed certain that the killer was getting a thrill; to emerge day after day and slaughter there must be a gratification and a strong one. However there was no contact so far. No cat and mouse. No taunting. Nothing really. Al looked down at the paper on his lap. Who? Why? Who?Why?Who?Why?Who?Why? Again and again and again he wrote.

He paused, looking ahead and slowing his breathing. Picking up the pen he wrote:

Male. Loner. Strong, so possible background of manual labour. A true sociopath so certainly intelligent from the details of his design so far. A keeper of trophies, if the taking of items at crime scenes is anything to go by. Angry but at what, who?'

Standing, he flung the notebook down beside him and picked up his phone. 'More detail,' he thought.

'Marlin.' Al spoke sharply into his phone.

'Hello to you too, Doc.'

'Any more news? I'm trying to paint some sort of picture here, it's taking shape but not fully formed. I need to have some definites to work with.'

'Definites and certainties? You don't think they might help me as well?'

'Ok, point taken. I'm e-mailing a preliminary profile if you want to use it. Any news yesterday or today?'

'Nothing. I would have called to let you know if there was something to report. However, I'm glad you called. Thomas, our DCS called for an update, so I told him about the theme of days and all of that.'

'Pleased?'

'No, not really. Distinctly unimpressed actually. He did say that he wanted to make mention of this at his weekly news briefing; or at least mention the run of deaths and the fact that there may be a nutter out there.'

'It might be worth saying something to see if we get a reaction but, based on what I've profiled so far, I'd suggest that anything said is carefully worded and prepared. It needs calm consideration and a very wise choice of words. Would it be possible to have an input or see what he's going to say?'

'I don't think so; he gave the briefing half an hour ago. I'll e-mail you the briefing note.'

'Jesus Marlin, couldn't you stop him? We needed to think about this. I could've used this opportunity to get a reaction and maybe bring him out of hiding.'

'He's my boss. I don't get to tell him what to do and neither do you. Check your e-mail and we can speak later, although I don't think your mood's going to be improved somehow.'

'What do you mean?'

'Just read it Doc, see you later.'

As the phone fell silent the sun disappeared from the room, taking his earlier good humour with it. He opened the laptop and clicked on mail. There was a message. He opened the attachment.

Ladies and Gentlemen of the press

We trust in your good judgement and discretion to avoid creating any panic among the public, but there is an issue that requires care and vigilance.

Over the past week or so there have been several murders across London - many of which you will have reported already. We now suspect that there may be one person responsible for these killings. This person is obviously very disturbed and very dangerous and we request that the public are vigilant when going about their daily business.

We have a top team working on this and have consulted with Dr Aldous Andrews in the interests of creating a profile of the suspect.

We are not at liberty to give out any further details at this time.
DCS A Thomas

Al filled his glass and sat back heavily.

'Fucking idiot. Good judgement and discretion? You must be fucking kidding. Consult Dr Aldous Andrews? You throw me open to the fucking press and you use that fucking name!'

Al realised that he was shouting and stopped himself by drinking deeply. He now noticed his phone was buzzing. Of course it's buzzing he thought bitterly. I'm a story now. He drank again and emptied the last of the bottle into his glass. After a while he slowed his breathing deliberately and checked his phone. The missed calls were racking up and the vibration almost took the thing out of his hand. Glancing at his computer screen his mail inbox flashed urgently as the numbers rose. The press!

Requests for interviews, his agent Shirley asking to speak to him urgently and even one from Lara, 'Hey, Doc seems you're big news again.' His heart sank and he pulled on his jacket and an ugly old black woollen hat. Checking outside for activity he thanked God they hadn't thought enough to approach his house for a quote yet. He slipped quickly away down the street and was soon at the 24/7 where his half hidden appearance was of some concern to Mr Khan on the counter.

'Oh, it's you Dr Al? I thought I was being robbed.'

'Please Mr Khan, just a couple of bottles of J&B and don't say that you've seen me.'

'I find it fairly unlikely that someone will ask Dr Al. But if they do I won't let on, ok? Anyway, with that outfit on I'm not sure I have seen you,' he laughed, and Al also smiled as he paid and made his way furtively from the shop. Moving quickly, the irregular clink of bottle against bottle made a lie of his attempts at clandestine movement, but he escaped attention for long enough to once again arrive at his home. Having refreshed his glass and himself he glanced through the e-mails. The curse of a public persona was a public e-mail, not that too many had been bothered to use it before. Now there was an interest and it would seem that morbid curiosity was big business.

Where to start? He picked up his phone.

'Marlin.'

'Hi again Doc, I said you wouldn't be pleased.'

'An assumption of pure genius; I can see now how you got so far in the police.'

'Doc, this isn't my fault.'

'No? Well how do you explain your DCS being unhappy with my involvement and then throwing my name to the press?'

'I don't think you are his favourite person but I didn't know he was going to do that.'

'And Aldous, he had to use Aldous? What a fucking bastard.'

'Look I'm sorry, but it's really not my fault.'

'You know I've got the press all over me now.'

'It'll die down; just refer them to our press department. Anyway, I thought the media was your chosen field?'

'Don't be fucking smart, Marlin.' There was a genuine anger in Al's voice and although Marlin felt that there may be some hypocrisy and over-reaction to the situation, he fell silent. A silence that then hung uncomfortably as neither man continued. As the tension became palpable Al spoke.

'Still no new killings?'

'No, we are at 10.'

'What about your research into the other days? Anything?'

'I have a few possibles or probables maybe. I've no doubt that we are looking at themes relating to days though. I came across the poem 'Mondays Child' and found myself looking for links. Take Tuesday, 'Tuesday's child is full of grace,' couldn't that apply to the priest, Father John, on Tuesday?'

'Ok, that seems feasible.'

'I also checked the files again, unlike you I find that sobriety actually helps me to concentrate better and I did see something.'

'Yeah?'

'The homeless guy always seemed the ultimate in random killings. So, once you started looking for themes, I wanted to see how it fitted more than any of the others. I suppose as a final proof for myself.'

'And did it?'

'With a bit of a stretch, yes, well, maybe.'

'Tell me then.'

'In the file it happens to mention that he was killed in an alleyway, by an old record shop called 'New Moon Records'. I checked with the PC who was first on the scene and he happened to mention that there was a large white 'moon' sign outside the shop - visible from the street. Monday is derived from Moon Day.'

'You know how much I hate coincidences. It has to be.'

'I think so, but does it help?'

'It does. It says that my profile is right. Use it.'

The doorbell rang loudly and Al was slightly startled.

'I've got to go Marlin, someone at the door.'

'Ok Doc, keep in touch.'

Tapping to end the call, Al moved to the front door and surprised himself by opening it without checking, his mind racing somewhere else. Leaning casually against the door jamb, a bearded figure tried to mask surprise behind a fake disinterest.

'Dr Al?'

'Maybe. Who are you?'

'Jeff Stanley, *The Herald.*' At this the man flashed some sort of id that might as well have been a bus pass for all the sense it made to Al. 'I just want to ask you a few questions about the killing spree.'

'Killing spree?'

'Is this a serial killer we're looking for? Is that why you were called in? Does he have a nickname?'

'What?' Al did not know whether to be disgusted or angry, so he stuck with his initial disbelief with a hint of exasperation, until he could find his focus. Then it hit him.

'Mr er...,'

'Stanley, Jeff Stanley.'

'Well Mr Stanley, I'd love to be able to give you some information, but you'll have to contact the Metropolitan Police Press Office. Or maybe you could try DCS Thomas?'

'Yes, yes but can you tell me if it's a serial killer?'

'I can't say anything Mr Stanley, goodbye.'

He began to close his door when he was caught by a bright flash and then another. It was then he saw the photographer leaning against the far wall, now studying his camera intently.

'Thanks for nothing, Dr Al.' He closed the door firmly.

BROUGHT TO BOOK

Standing in DCS Thomas' office, Marlin felt as though he was back in his old headmaster's office. That too had been a room that was rarely seen except in times of trouble. Feeling uncomfortable as his senior officer studied the file in front of him, he tried to cultivate an intense interest in his shoes with no success. His own studied disinterest having made the point he sought, DCS Thomas looked up and removed his black-rimmed spectacles, his hand unconsciously smoothing back hair that no longer graced his balding pate.

'DCI Marlin, I don't wish to learn about the origin of the word Monday. Nor about Thor or a child's rhyme. I want the killer, or killers, responsible for the madness of the last couple of weeks. This file, this report, is frankly a joke Marlin and I'm seriously thinking that you may not be the man for this job anymore.'

'Sir, I realise that we do not have any suspects as yet, but given the random nature of these events and the lack of evidence or witnesses, it has required a slightly different approach. And it was never an expectation as far as I was aware, that immediate results were anticipated.'

'As far as you were aware? Expectation, anticipation, a slightly different approach? You and your 'Doctor' friend really do make a pair. It's all flowery language and talk, talk, talk with you college boys. Why don't you just keep it simple? We have a killer, we have crime scenes and we have victims; so go and catch the man. Do you even know the word arrest? Police work has not changed a hell of a lot since my days on the beat Marlin, and neither has the aim of the job. Get a result for fuck's sake and get one quickly!'

'Yes sir.'

'Well you have a week to get out there and make one or I am reassigning this case. Now get out.' DCS Thomas returned to his case files dismissively, indicating loud and clear that the meeting was over.

Once out of the office Marlin relaxed and couldn't help smiling to himself as he thought about the absurdity of his situation. I'm literally clueless, working with an alcoholic psychologist, who may or may not be paying a woman to knock him about, yet my boss hates me for being able to string together a coherent sentence. Well at least he didn't give me '24 hours or you're off the case.'

Sitting at his desk he picked up the file of Gillian Watson. Flicking through it he looked for the name of the officer who was first on the scene and asked dispatch to connect him.

'PC Wilkes? This is DCI Marlin.'

'Yes sir.'

'The killing of Gillian Watson, the girl in the flat in Mile End; did you ever find out who spent the night with her?'

'Not yet sir, we've asked for anyone with information to come forward, but nothing yet. We're also trying to find any CCTV footage from the night out, but we're not having too much luck. We talked to her friends, but the bars were full and everyone was hammered. To be honest, it's a bit of a meat market there on a Saturday night. Sorry, sir.'

'That's ok Wilkes; the last thing I am expecting right now is a lucky break. But Wilkes, this is a case of a murdered girl so don't go talking about meat markets, ok? Now can you talk to her friends again and check with the bar staff? Now the story has hit the papers there may be more chance of someone remembering something.'

'Yes sir.'

Marlin stared at his desk and wondered where to start. It was well known that he worked best alone and, for the most part, that was how things were left, but sometimes he felt abandoned and adrift. Never more so than now. His finger was tapping a gentle but insistent Morse code on hollow cardboard, an act which brought his mind back to reality. He needed more details so, picking up his cigarettes and jacket, he strode out to his car. Sucking deeply on the first flame he pushed the car out into the road and drove aggressively through the London traffic. Unconscious movement, for no other reason than to go forward in some sense.

After some time spent on the staccato stop/start roads of a Saturday afternoon, Marlin pulled across sharply to his left. Oblivious to the gesticulations and curses of his fellow road travellers, he finally came to a stop within a small walled car park. He looked at the shared entry door to a small three storey block of flats and then up to the window on the third floor. He lit a cigarette as he slowly realised that he had driven to the home of Gillian Watson in Mile End. Subconsciously hoping that proximity might provide some 'eureka' moment.

Stepping from the car he looked about the small car park and shivered against the wind. Moving across to the entry door he went to buzz one of the flats to see if they would let him in when he saw that the door was open. The catch was damaged and he made a note to find out how long it had been that way. Going inside he made his way along to Gillian Watson's flat, the entrance to which was still covered by police tape, and reached for the keys. Covering his hand with his handkerchief he reached to the door knob and turned it open then pulled away some tape and ducked through the gap into the room. There was a strange quiet to murder scenes, or so Marlin thought. An eerie silence, and a coldness the like of which he had experienced only in one other situation. The feeling of loss was palpable and he felt it keenly every time he crossed the line, but he was here to work so once again he went on.

Stepping softly and carefully, he ran through the report in his head as he tried to look with fresh eyes. At the taped outline of the body, he paused and looked around, finally coming back to the blood stain on the carpet. Breathing deeply he moved on through the flat sensing that, fresh eyes or not, there was nothing to be found. At the door he bent to step through the gap once more when his eye was drawn to the table inside the door. Beside the fast food menus and junk mail he could see a light film of dust with a distinct circular gap in the middle. Stretching his forefinger and thumb he saw that it was about a 5 inch diameter. So, ornament or lamp, he'd taken it with him. Not only that, it was now clear that he had not planned the method of killing, he'd picked up what was close to hand. Like the Doc had said about the Sabbath kid, he was seizing whatever chance he had that would fulfil his theme; the profile rang true. Stepping back to the landing he quietly closed the door and headed for the car, glad to get out of the bleak atmosphere.

Door locked, curtains closed and glass full, Al felt safe and secure again. He picked up his phone and steeled himself as he dialled his agent.

'Hello Shirley.'

'Oh Al, how nice of you to deign to call me. I'm so honoured.'

'Now, now Shirley, please don't get pissed off. I've been busy.'

'Of course you have Al, I heard about it today on the radio. Were you going to tell me you're working for the police now? Given that I'm your agent, details like that are quite useful.'

'Look, it is only an unofficial type of thing.'

'I have to say that the radio made it sound pretty official.'

'That wasn't my fault.'

'Jesus, it's never your fault. Whose fault is it then? Mr J & Mr B once again? Christ Almighty Al, at least tell me you are being paid?'

'Well, to be honest I didn't really get into details like that. As I said, it's all kind of unofficial.'

'Why do I bother? Really, can you tell me? Oh and by the way, that radio gig I got you was a total disaster. They don't pay to have you there sulking for 10 minutes and then bugger off for a drink when they pop to a breaking story. And while I have you on the phone, a real rarity in itself these days, may I point out something to you? I'm going to anyway. Aldous is your bloody name. It's no-one else's fault if they use it or try to. So in future turn up sober, smile, talk about your death theories or whatever and then take the money graciously. Even if the cheque is made out to Aldous.'

'Finished?'

'For the time being. Now, have you spoken to any of the newspapers?'

'Some guy from *the Herald* was round, but I gave him a no comment.'

'Ok, now secondly, is this really some sort of serial killer? And if so, have you thought about maybe getting a book out of it?'

'What?'

'Have you come up with a name for the suspect? There's usually one and it would be useful to know in case they try and contact me. If we are in the news we might as well make the most of it, no?'

'For god's sake Shirley, this is actually a sensitive matter and I don't know what we have here, although I feel pretty sure it shouldn't be public. At least not in this way. If someone contacts you put them onto the police press office. Play it down for now.'

'You think they want to hear that answer?'

'Help me out here Shirley, just for now ok? And I didn't say there wouldn't be a book. Just let me get to the end of the story first or the middle even? There's a lot of strange shit going on here Shirley, stuff I can't even start to get into, but I can get past all that if I'm left alone. I don't want to talk to reporters or TV crews and I don't want my picture in the paper. I don't want to be sharing my views at all, do you see? Not at the moment anyway, later will be different.'

'Now then that's better, Al. It's nice to see that at least you have some sort of a strategy. So, I keep the press out of your hair and let you get some good stuff for the book? Very good, Al. But remember to keep in touch ok?'

'I will Shirley, but also remember that I've got some work to do here. Now bye.'

Sitting back and drinking, Al found that he couldn't get the book out of his head. After all, the idea had been there all along, it just felt nobler for Shirley to be the one to come up with it. Maybe he should look for a nickname? Putting on some music he took a large refill and smiled to himself as 'Cross Eyed Mary' boomed from the speakers. Whiskey and Tull is so good.

PHANTOMS IN THE NIGHT

Marlin sat at his desk and considered the files in front of him. Alone in a darkened office he was searching for a new way to work, a way without witnesses, a way without clues. The trip to the flat in Mile End had provided a spur, but no new ideas as to who was responsible. How was she chosen and how did the killer get in? Did she pick up her killer the night before? Entry was not insurmountable from what he'd seen, but the internal door hadn't been forced, so was it someone she knew? He was pretty sure that wasn't the case. This guy was random and he wasn't the guy who had sex with her; if that was the case then Marlin knew he would be looking for a different killer altogether.

One day the victim is a homeless man, the day after a priest? The rhymes and gods and sayings were applied, but the people were random and seemingly unimportant. If the Doc was right, this person was justifying an uncontrollable lust for killing. Yet it seemed to have stopped. For every seeming shred of sense there were innumerable contradictions. How do you find such a person? How could they stay hidden? He tried the Doc's mobile one final time, but once again it went to voicemail; checking his watch and seeing that it was after 8pm he chastised himself for thinking that Al would be available or sober. He thought again of the pretty blonde girl he'd seen on two occasions and smiled at the man's luck, even if it was costing him. Placing his files in his bag he headed for his car and home.

Opening a bottle of wine, Marlin sat among the papers and lit a cigarette, drawing deeply and sighing with pleasure. He filled a glass and sipped before picking up his notebook and switching on his computer. Scanning down his list of crimes, copied to accord with the Doc's board, he looked at the gaps in the list of days and connections on his notepad. As he made some amendments he looked for something new to leap out at him and was aware of a certain futility in doing this. Then again, at least it gave him something to do.

In front of a flickering computer screen the man sat staring at the picture of Dr Aldous Andrews. It was from 10 years earlier and Al had always thought it was a pretty good one, so he'd left it. The man looked intently as if expecting some animation or response. He read the introduction and clicked for the bibliography, pausing at 'Inside the Mind of the Serial Killer'. He smiled a wry, joyless smile and glanced across the room at the spine of the self-same book. Scrolling through the pages of the website he paused only occasionally if a quote or photograph caught his eye, but he was really just satisfying himself that he had been through every page. He believed in thoroughness. Eventually he reached the final page and the information he'd been seeking - the contact e-mail address. He clicked the icon and reached for the paper that lay at the side of the computer, the paper that he'd prepared carefully. He began to type.

Dr Aldous Andrews (Dr Al)

I hope I find you in good spirits today Dr Al, after all spirits are your second speciality are they not?

I am glad that the police chose someone I know, although I personally feel that Professor Peters of Cambridge University has a much greater insight into these matters. Perhaps I just prefer the more academically challenging tomes? There is no doubt however that he has nowhere near as much of a high profile as yourself. True, your star has somewhat faded, but I still enjoy your sporadic utterances on TV and radio, even if the books have dried up.

You may wonder why I have rambled on so entertainingly, but I thought I should explain some things, if only to give you some guidance and hopefully move things along.

Firstly, if you haven't thought of it yet go to your computer and do a search on each day of the week. I favoured Wikipedia but you can certainly try other more reliable reference points. This will give you my first group of themes and to be honest I was not so highbrow as to avoid pop culture references or even pop song titles. The theme quickly bored me, but to be honest I had better things to do and it was time to move on.

Secondly, I was thinking about a name. If there is no name then I feel I am probably not getting people's attention sufficiently and, as you struggled with the theme, I thought it unlikely that you would have made any progress in this area. So, once again in the interests of expedition and clarity I will offer my advice. 'The Phantom' is my nomination as a sort of homage to The Phantom of Texarkana (sorry Dr Al, that case is covered in Peters' book but cheer up; you have the celebrity and this message).

Thirdly and finally, for now, you and your police friends are probably wondering why I have stopped? Well to be honest I haven't, I just thought that maybe I would pause for a while - not too long - and take a well-earned rest. Do you know I've been working without even a weekend off? Oh yeah that's right you do - don't you? Well, I think my work probably deserves a bit more quality and a bit less quantity now. I am committed but flexible if you have any ideas?

See you soon

The Phantom?

Without pause for thought he pressed send and closed the machine down. Standing, he moved to the window and stared out into the gloom as if searching for some message, as his body ached with desire and anticipation. Palms stretched wide and flat on the pane of glass before him, he pulled back his shoulders in search of relaxation or some form of ease. Then bringing his face forward he grimaced at his reflection until the image was fogged by his breathing, slow and heavy.

'WHY AM I?'

'I AM WHY?'

His lips met in a cold mirror kiss and, as he touched himself, he felt his soul shifting.

Al sat in front of his laptop blankly for some time, partly sobered by his message and yet unable to obtain clarity or shape. Clumsily he typed and searched and then, with some difficulty, he cut and pasted the now blurry passage before forwarding the message to Marlin.

Marlin

A phantom for fuck's sake! Look at the message below and this.

The Phantom Killer of Texarkana.

On February 22, 1946, the Phantom Killer murder spree began on a quiet road known as Lover's Lane with the homicide of 23 year old Jimmy Hollis, who was parked in a car with his 19 year old girlfriend, Mary Jeanne Larey. Hidden away in the secluded darkness, the victims were attacked at gunpoint and ordered out of the car. Hollis sustained a fatal injury from a blow to the back of his head, while Larey made a run for it down the dark and desolate road. However, the killer caught up with Larey and taunted her with rape until a passing vehicle illuminated the highway, enabling Larey to escape.

This vicious cycle of death would continue until May 4, 1946, claiming 8 victims and 5 descendants in the states of Texas and Arkansas. Although the victims did not share any significant characteristics that would link them together, the method of operation of the Phantom Killer would yield some strange and curious signals as to when he would attack. Many of the crimes were committed under a full moon and became known locally as the "moonlight murders", sending a chilling fear through the region when the lunar cycle was complete. Law enforcement has had their theories on who the Phantom Killer could have been, however, no one was formally charged with the string of midnight murders.

Once sent he drank in whiskey and fear in equal measure. Closing his eyes he was oblivious to the music playing; the frantic beating of his heart and insistent throbbing of blood in his ears was deafening. The study, the theory, the black and white words from history, had taken shape before his eyes; born in flesh and cold blood they now reached out to him. He was shaking now as he drank quickly in panic, his mind racing as over and over his thoughts circled. Death speaks to me, death knows my name. Death knows my fucking name!

Marlin sat awake, sipping wine as he flicked through page after page until he was not sure which file he had open anymore; his eyes were tired, his body heavy. He stretched to turn off his laptop and as his touch brought the screen to life, he raised his eyebrow at the icon in the bottom right hand corner; *I have mail from Dr Al.* Lighting a cigarette he coughed and pressed open. His immediate thought was that the Doc was completely hammered as he saw the first passage.

'Phantoms, Doc? Are you tripping?'

Marlin scrolled down until he saw the message then swallowed heavily as he tried to shake himself awake. He read the message again and again and tried to phone the Doc.

'Voicemail again, Doc. Pick up for fuck's sake, we need to talk about this message.'

What is it with that guy? Pouring a small glass of wine he put his cigarette out and lit another, his eyes fixed to the screen, greedily eating in each word. He stopped at the end when he saw the sign-off 'See You'. He was worried now for the Doc and he rang yet again but still to no avail. Sitting back down he blew smoke rings into the air as he thought of the Phantom of Texarkana and the full moon. He really did take time to pay homage, fucking hell! Marlin glanced at the page again and looked at the e-mail address - deathnow@hotmail.co.uk. He shivered involuntarily as he read and stood up.

'Fucking hell, death now! Fuck's sake.'

He paced around the room as if searching for some unknown exit and then, calming himself, sat again and picked up his phone.

'Hello, is that the desk sergeant? This is DCI Marlin and I've got some important information. You better get hold of DCS Thomas. Oh, and can you see that a car goes to check on this address over the course of the night? 32 Albert Road, Camden, NW5. A Dr Andrews lives there and he may be in danger. Thanks.'

Pulling on his jacket, he headed to his car.

MONSTER STORY

The incessant ringing echoed in Al's head and resolutely refused to go away. Carefully opening one eye he shifted uncomfortably. A pain shooting through his shoulders and neck, along with the numbness in his left leg, informed him that the night had been spent on his not so luxurious sofa. The ringing continued now, accompanied by a rapping of the letterbox

'Dr Andrews? Dr Andrews are you there?'

The voice was unfamiliar but clearly concerned, so Al forced himself to his feet and out towards the door. Attaching the chain securely he eased the door inwards and peered through the slim gap.

'Dr Andrews?'

A young uniformed officer eyed him suspiciously, the dishevelled half-glanced mess clearly not what he'd expected.

'Yes, I'm Dr Andrews. How can I help you?'

The young policeman had leaned in to better hear the dry croak of a voice, but quickly withdrew from the noxious odour that was Dr Al's breath.

'Are you alright sir?'

'Yes, yes. What's this about?'

'DCI Marlin asked us to check if you were alright sir. Oh, and he asked if you could switch on your phone and give him a call?'

'My phone? Oh right. I was going to call him later this morning after I'd woken up properly.'

'Sir, it's half-past four in the afternoon.'

'What?'

'It's four thirty, sir.'

'Oh brilliant. Look, I'll call him. Is there anything else?'

'No sir. Good day to you.'

Hand over his face, the young man pretended to have had an extended attack of itchy nose but, as he stepped away, he couldn't disguise his deep inhalation of fresh air. The door had closed behind him and, lungs now refreshed, he headed back to his car.

'Is he in? Our friend, the Doctor?'

The young officer was slightly taken aback as he had not seen this small bearded man approach him.

'And you are, sir?'

'Jeff Stanley, *the Herald*. Is he in? Have you got any more information? Were you briefing Doctor Al on a new killing?'

'Mr, er, Stanley, whether I was or wasn't giving Dr Andrews any information is none of your business. I suggest you get off his property and leave the man alone.'

'Come on officer, give me something? Please? I've been hanging around here for bloody hours. Apart from our friend Dr Al there rolling in half drunk this morning, there's nothing.'

'You've been watching this place?'

'Well sort of, the editor thought it could be worth a gamble and since I couldn't possibly have anything better to do on a Sunday, here I am. I thought you turning up might have meant something was actually happening?'

'Look Mr Stanley, could I see some id please.'

The reporter stroked his beard as he sized up the policeman, head cocked and eyebrows raised. He looked as though he was going to speak and then, shrugging his shoulders as if he'd thought better of the whole thing, he then reached for his press pass and driving license. It was usually better to be thorough. The policeman took both of the plastic encased cards and again studied the man in front of him as he clicked on his radio and carried out the check. All the while the reporter looked beyond him to the house; his eyes searching as if some clue may be found hidden in the very facade of the building. The policeman received the 'all clear' in a crackled radio message but kept his eyes fixed upon this edgy man, all nervous energy and questions, now talking excitedly into his mobile phone all but oblivious to the policeman.

'You're fucking kidding me, Dan. You must be really fucking kidding? Thanks man.'

Putting the phone away the reporter wagged a finger at the young officer and grinned as he tutted slowly.

'Very, very naughty son. Ha, very sly.'

'What?'

Puzzled and slightly annoyed now the policeman handed the ID cards back to the reporter.

'What? What? The fucking Phantom is what. Jesus Christ man, this is a fucking monster story.'

'Look sir, I don't know what you're talking about so please go now and leave Dr Andrews alone.'

'With this story, no fucking way. This is massive officer, and talking to that guy is my job. Free country and all that.'

The policeman was noticeably angry now, but also unsure where the conversation had gone and he wanted to get away.

'Don't let me hear of any complaints here, ok.'

'Of course officer.'

The mock deference was again a source of irritation and the young officer wished he could arrest the little toad. If truth be told, arrest was the least he wanted to do, but he walked to the car and pulled away with only a brief glance at the man. The reporter, for his part, had all but forgotten the existence of the PC as he was eagerly ringing the bell and beating the door. Now it was out on the radio he'd be joined at any moment by his peers, all hungry for the scoop. Leaning down and pushing the letter-box open with his fingers, he shouted through.

'Come on Doc - give me something about the Phantom? Just a first comment and I'll leave you alone. Come on Doc, please?'

Al had washed his face while attempting to sweeten his breath and tame his hair. His head however thumped and his eyes had retreated in surrender to his lifestyle. He had seen the reporter outside with the PC and ignored the matter, despite the banging on the door, until that word. Phantom. How? He moved to the door and again peered through the secured gap.

'The Phantom? What are you talking about?'

'Doc, Doc, don't treat me like an idiot. The police released the details of his message at a press conference less than an hour ago. Since the message was to you, I'd think you might have a comment. No?'

'The police? Fucking wankers.'

'Can I quote you on that? Ha!'

'Yes you can, the incompetent idiots. And as for the Phantom, there is no Phantom, there is just a fucking psycho playing games with days and rhymes. A fucking sexual inadequate who can only get off through death. Even his name is pathetic. Print that why don't you.'

Slamming the door shut Al could feel his heart pounding in his chest. Then, as he moved uneasily towards the living room, he was aware that his whole body was shaking. At the door the reporter still pounded, shouting indistinct questions, and Al was forced to rise again to close the living-room door. If only shutting out the world was so easy. He felt like crying and searched for a bottle in the mess that was now his room, his darkened, curtain drawn refuge. Among the now realised asylum for empty vessels he found a bottle that was a third full; noting that it was hidden by an old gatefold Made in Japan Deep Purple cover, he almost smiled.

Sitting once more he realised that the hardness pressing into his kidney was an unopened half-bottle, stuffed tightly into his coat pocket; his coat that was half forced down the back of the sofa, the coat that had been his blanket. Glass full he picked up his phone from the table and suddenly thought of the angry comments. What was he thinking? He glanced out of the curtains furtively, careful to ensure that the movement was minimal, and saw the press pack assembling. A flash of a camera took him away from the window. He picked up his phone, turning it on, and sat glumly as he perused the messages and missed calls.

Marlin wanted to talk.

Marlin really wanted to talk and was worried.

Marlin was angry with the drunken so and so.

Marlin was going to check in on him and wished he would just pick-up his fucking phone.

Marlin was sorry but there was nothing he could do since certain people wouldn't answer or turn on their phones.

Lara wanted to know if he was ok and whether he needed cheering up.

Shirley wanted to know if he was ok and thought it might be wise to have a chat about any possible response to the press.

Al sat looking ahead, sipping quietly in his self-imposed house arrest, his mind swimming with thoughts. Shirley was going to kill him, maybe Marlin too, although he might want to get his retaliation in first in that particular case. The thought of Lara walking in through the assembled press pack filled him with absolute terror and he tried to blank the thoughts again. He dialled Shirley for the first apology.

Marlin sat smoking in his car. He'd set off for home, after all his Sunday was ruined as a result of the e-mail. He'd sat in a room with DCS

Thomas and tried to argue his case for restraint in releasing any information; but the total absence of the Doc and any argument with a psychological basis had hamstrung his point of view. Adding information to his reports and standing like some embarrassed mannequin as the DCS briefed the press had made up his day. It was an aspect of the job that had never become any easier for Marlin, his discomfiture more than obvious on each occasion.

Standing in the press room he'd looked out at the gathered paper and news teams, as he'd done many, many times before. The normal feel of the occasion was one of tedious habit; the flavourless police speak, dryly spoken, in a featureless room of recycled warm air. Notes were taken by sleepy reporters grateful for filled column inches, but numbed by the familiarity of both the setting and the crimes. The 'short straw saloon' was not a venue of choice for any of the participants.

Not today, though. Today was a day not unique, but rare and unwelcome for Marlin, who was in a certain minority in finding death and mutilation unpleasant; worthy of respect. Today the story, one story, took shape and rose; a beast formed of headlines and fed by hearsay and gossip. Born of half-lies and unspoken truths, the creature would find refuge in tabloid front pages, paraded for money until the public's attention fell on another creation; then archived beyond fickle human memory.

The Phantom was a story trying to write itself. The journalists and old hacks feasted greedily on every word and phrase, the room electric with excited anticipation. It was not only the press. DCS Thomas was buoyant and glowing; sunning himself in the public gaze of the camera crews, his eyes seemed glassy, drunk on the occasion. Beside Marlin stood Detective Susan Scott. Intelligent, diligent and honest, she was a fine police officer reduced to a statue. A female presence to back-up the DCS's equality initiative. Slim and pretty in an easy, understated manner, Marlin liked her enormously but too often found himself avoiding her clear green eyes. That he even recognised that her dark brown hair framed her face to perfection was only due to furtive looks and stolen glances. He would really have to talk to her. Maybe after the case? He deferred even in thought.

As he tapped the ash out of the window of his car, he stared across the road at the assembled newspaper men, cold and bored outside the Doc's house. He checked his watch - 7.30pm. They can't be far from giving up, surely? He's clearly not coming out. He tried his phone again, and was preparing yet another message, when a hoarse voice spoke bitterly.

'Hello Marlin, my apologies for missing the baptism.'

'The baptism?'

'Our friend 'the Phantom'? You named him, just as he asked you to.'

'Well, you know what incompetent idiots we are. Your friend, Mr Stanley, called to ask if we had a comment to make about your opinions, if you can describe calling us wankers an opinion.'

'Ok Marlin, I'm sorry about that. Really I am. Look, I was somewhat hung-over and he blurted out the whole Phantom thing. It pissed me off.'

'I'll take the apology but Doc, whilst I'm also sorry that the 'name' and the e-mail came out, I couldn't do anything. You see, my main defence for silence was suddenly incognito again. Where did you go Al? Why the fuck did you turn off your phone?'

'After the e-mail, I may have reacted somewhat badly and perhaps drunk a bit too much. I don't really remember intentionally turning off my phone and, as for the rest of the time, I was sleeping. None too comfortably either, my neck's killing me.'

Al was staring ahead at the half-bottle of whiskey, but considered his trip to the off-license a bit of an irrelevance; especially so as he couldn't actually remember making the journey. After all, it wasn't a new situation.

'Can you keep your phone on tonight and stay at least half-sober? I need to talk to you about where we are and where we go from here. I've got to go home first but I'll come back; it should only be a couple of hours until the majority of your fan club have left for the night.'

'Are there still a lot there? They're doing my head in.'

'There are quite a few at the moment, but it's cold and you're keeping pretty well hidden.'

'You're out there now?'

'Yes, but just to check up for the time being, as I say I'll be back along later, ok?'

'Yes ok, but bring a bottle, I can't get out.'

'Jesus Doc, you really should look at changing the record.'

'Why, Marlin? I really like the song.'

'I give up, I'll see you later.'

Ending the call, Marlin dragged on a cigarette while slowly shaking his head. Glancing down, he brushed the ash from the daily reports he'd taken from the duty officer. The Doc may have a point, preferring pro's and drink to cold cars and administration. Shaking his head again, as if to banish the thought, he rolled up the window and eased the car onto the road, heading home. The press men were filing away gradually and he recognised some as they made their inevitable journey towards *the Red Lion* at the end of the road. Further on down a hooded figure stood, quiet and still at the side of the road, invisible to all.

At home Marlin showered and sat with a coffee, trying to relax sufficiently without giving in to sleep. He arched his back and craned his neck before sinking into the settee and yawning widely. Topping up his coffee he picked up the daily bulletins for Friday, Saturday and Sunday (up to the point where he'd left the office anyway). Assaults, muggings and domestics were a welcome sight, much to his chagrin. He glanced through quickly, knowing that the Sergeant would have pointed out anything of note and again he yawned. Three quarters of the way down the 'Sunday' page a line caught his attention.

14.32 Officer Turner responded to a call at 124 Buckingham Rd (Flat 3) in Kentish Town, the body of a woman 28, found beaten and strangled. Alarm raised by returning flat-mate. Murdered woman Alice Short worked as a prostitute.

Marlin felt a wave of tension ease in his body as the last word appeared, prostitute; that particular series of deaths was being handled by Detective Scott and the public interest was absolutely zero. All the same he scribbled down the details and made a mental note to mention it to the Doc; after all, he'd looked at the other two killings. Again he chastised himself, for being so pleased to dismiss a crime, just because it didn't fit his own case. He sat back and wondered when he'd become so hardened to think this way; then he wondered, how long would it be before he didn't chastise himself for such thoughts. Draining the coffee, he picked up his case of papers.

'Ok, Doc, here I come.'

CRUMBLING CERTAINTY

Al had checked through the curtains once or twice and was relieved to find that Marlin was right; the press were bored with him, for now anyway. He checked his watch and noticed the scratches across the glass. They made the expensive timepiece look shabby. It was 9.45pm now and he was expecting Marlin with some anticipation. His half bottle looked sadly alone on the table and he just wished Marlin would arrive with its companion.

He smiled to himself at his exaggerated alcoholic panic, not because it pleased him, but because it was better than worrying about the self-titled psychopath. A killer who not only spoke to him but scared and threatened him; this 'Phantom' had critiqued his skill and not too generously he noted. He was in a bizarre and new position, a serial killer that knew more about him than he did about the killer. His thoughts were interrupted by the sound of a car door. Checking through the window he was only too pleased to see Marlin with his typically weary walk, bringing provisions to the door.

The two men sat drinking, Marlin smoking enthusiastically, as they took some time to appreciate one another's silent company before the work took over.

'I have to say, you look like shit Doc.'

'Thank you, that makes me feel a lot better.'

'I like to do my bit.'

'Well can I say thanks? I really do appreciate you sending the police cars to check on me. However, if they hadn't woken me up I might look a hell of a lot better. But seriously, thanks for checking.'

'You're welcome Doc but, to be fair, the guy only managed to wake you up in the late afternoon. How much beauty sleep do you need?'

'Obviously more than that.' Al framed his face in his hands in his best silent movie actress pose and the two men laughed loudly, aware of the tension easing. 'Don't leave your phone off again, Doc. At least not till this whole thing's over, ok?'

'Look, I'm sorry about the whole silent thing. The message really got to me.'

'The message or the whiskey?'

'One was a result of the other.'

'Come on Doc, you don't need a creepy message to hit the whiskey. You don't need any excuse.'

'Maybe you're right, but I do normally emerge the next day. On this occasion I think I'd every right to drink. Anyway, what did I miss?' Al smiled, trying to evade the truth of the conversation.

'Well, you know that you missed the press conference and about twenty calls. You should also be aware that DCS Thomas is unlikely to be sending you a Christmas card this year.'

'Shame.'

'Oh and I was checking the dailies, you know, the reports? And there seems to have been another prostitute killed, close to Kentish Town.'

'When? Was there a message?'

'Not sure of the time of death, but the body was found this afternoon. It didn't mention a message, but it wasn't a full report.' Marlin reached for his notepad.

'Alice Short, 28 years old, body found by her flatmate.'

'Alice?' Al exclaimed.

'You know her?'

Marlin couldn't hide the concern in his voice, nor the incredulity. Al fell silent, annoyed with himself for reacting aloud. He took a sip of his drink and stared into space.

'Doc? Did you know this girl?'

'What was the name of the girl who reported the death?'

'I don't know yet, why?'

'One of Lara's flatmates is called Alice. She lives in Kentish Town.'

'Buckingham Road?'

Al looked thoughtful for a moment and visibly drifted away, before snapping back and turning to Marlin.

'I don't know Marlin; I've never been to her flat. Even if it was the same girl, I've never met her, only heard the name. Forget I said anything.'

Marlin narrowed his eyes and cocked his head as he concentrated on Al.

'It may not be nothing, Doc. First the Phantom contacts you and now someone connected to you is murdered. As a policeman I don't make a habit of 'forgetting' things, but until we know more we'll leave it for now. Jesus Doc, is there anything simple about you?'

Al smiled uncomfortably and shrugged, looking embarrassed at yet more of his private life being exposed. Marlin felt empathy for Al, but also an annoyance at his child-like attitude to life. Feeling the edginess returning as the silence stretched uncomfortably, he reached for a cigarette and lit it, hands cupped against an imaginary wind. As he drew in strongly he raised his eyes and watched Al filling their glasses with the precision of a man needing something to do. Marlin blew out slowly, watching the blue smoke rise and hang in the air, riding the waves of tension.

'So Doc, the Phantom. What now?'

'Good question, Marlin. Good question.'

Al sat, head bowed, a finger tapping at his nose as if trying to waken his sleeping mind. His eyes were alert, the swollen pupils serving only to intensify his look and he stayed this way for some minutes. Marlin left him to ponder, smoking quietly as if to acknowledge the state of concentration; waiting patiently, yet hoping not to have to wait too long. Al cleared his throat and drank a shot before refilling his glass.

'This 'Phantom', if we have to use this name, is now the dictator of the situation. We handed that control to him when we released details of his e-mail. His name, his agenda. We are literally clueless.'

'So what about the days of the week themes? What about your profile?'

'My profile still holds largely true but, as for the theme, he told us how he worked that out. It was a detail to divert our minds and our concentration, whilst giving us nothing; a test that in his eyes we were too slow in passing, so he stepped in and told us anyway for God's sake! I still maintain though that, for him, it was primarily a rationale; a reason for the incessant blood lust. A true psychopath, this guy is intelligent and therefore needs reason, logic even. A twisted logic can work, but there has to be something behind the outward facade. Marlin, even paedophiles have an inward sense of logic; something that informs their arguments in an effort to excuse their actions. In this case our Phantom is setting himself up as a more intelligent, perhaps even more advanced figure. And, in choosing that name, one that won't be caught. If he feels that all other people are inferior, then why not kill them? He didn't tire of his theme; he tired physically and mentally from the exertions of his gorging. Now we've named him and I've insulted him. He knows about me and has opinions on the subject. I think he's going to try to kill me.'

Al sat back with his drink and looked across at Marlin who was now making notes. Marlin stopped and looked up.

'Doc, I'm no psychologist and I don't understand this fucking freak, but sadly I think you're right. If I had to guess where next it'd be you, after all, it's you he made contact with. You're the TV guy, the one in the public eye.'

Al sat with his eyes screwed tightly shut, a pained expression on his face.

'Fuck it!'

He slammed his glass down on the table as he shouted, making Marlin jump.

'Doc calm down, we've cars passing here all the time and we're going to keep you safe. Now is not the time to lose it.'

'No, no, no it's not that. How can I be so stupid? Always thinking about myself, my big fucking ego. Jesus Al, wake up to yourself.'

Marlin was totally bemused by this outburst and was quick to light up again as he followed the shouting voice and slightly crazed eyes.

'You want to tell me what's going on here Doc?'

'It's not me. Well it is me, will be me eventually, but not now, not first.'

'Slow down and explain.'

Al stopped and breathed deeply, eyes closed.

'I'm a possible trophy kill we agree, but I wasn't the only name and I wasn't considered so prestigious as to be unique. Also he contacted me, warned me almost, to the extent that you're sending cars to check on me. Professor Peters is the man whose text he used for his name and the man he showed respect for ahead of me. Who's guarding Professor Peters?'

Marlin sat frozen, the trickle of smoke from his lips the only indication of life. His mind raced and he felt as though his thoughts were being tied in knots as one seeming certainty crumbled beneath another. Rousing himself, he stood purposefully and looked at his watch - 12.45am. He picked up his phone and dialled.

'Chief Superintendent? I'm sorry to disturb you at this time, but I think we need to contact the Cambridge Constabulary and quickly; they've got to check on Professor Peters.'

*

Cambridge

The M11 was as uncluttered and clear as the man's mind; straight and illuminated it stretched out before him tantalizingly. The city lights were orange in the sky and the streets were dark and quiet. Looking up and breathing in the cold air deeply, the man allowed a brief smile to cross his lips as he focused on the bright full moon. Such poetic justice could be dealt out this night. Hood pulled in close and tight he carried on, occasionally running his hand down his side and feeling the large blade in his pocket. It seemed electric to his touch and, as it pulsed, it was all that he could do to stop himself running. He slowed and calmed himself, almost stopping as he turned into Carlisle Road, the large detached houses glowing with eyes of electric light, some winking, some closing darkly. Only number twelve mattered to the man and the overgrown, dark gated pathway could not have been more inviting.

Bowed in the shadows the man moved through the gate silently and eased towards the house, unseen by all but the moon. Hugging the walls he slid along to the large window adjacent to the front door until crouched, he could peer into the living room. A man sat reading by lamplight; somewhat gaunt of face, his remaining hair white above the ears, delicate half-glasses perched upon his nose. He was still and intent upon the pages before him, seemingly oblivious to the movement in the adjoining room; all footsteps and shadows that the man took to be his wife Helen. 'To Helen for her patience' read the inscription inside his book 'The Psychopathology of Murder: Serial Killers Explained.' Well Helen, to you tonight I offer only my apologies, thought the man. Out of sight and still he remained at the window as twenty minutes became thirty. Finally the grey haired elegant woman came into view, extinguishing her backlighting as she did so. Stopping to kiss the top of her husband's head, the man watched them as they exchanged low spoken pleasantries with genuine warmth and affection in their shared gaze, and then she was gone. Having checked his watch, the old professor returned to his book and, above his head, the man was aware of an upstairs light going on. She was going to bed - it was time to act.

Pressing into the wall, the man felt his way around the far side of the house, until he arrived at the back door which led into the kitchen. Taking from his pocket the glass cutter, the man etched an even square in the pane and gently manipulated it into his gloved palm, then placed it on the grass. Reaching inside he had to twist his hand, but the key was there and turned with no further fuss. As if in slow motion, the door arced open and the man glided forward, holding his breath, drawn to the light. Across the wooden floor and through the open door, silent tiptoe became silent stride, a death march. In an instant the man stood at the chair back, faded green and warmed by the lamp it was but a temporary shield for the unsuspecting Professor. The man enveloped the shape in front of him, left hand clamping strongly and firmly across the startled Professor's mouth, the right arm a fluid movement of blade and skin, bowing an evil tune across the man's throat; one note, two, repeat.

Brutal but quick, the Professor's last moments would be of little comfort to Helen when she rose to chide her husband for staying up too late; no the bloodied head, almost sawn off and hanging, would traumatise permanently. For her, it would have been better that the man had taken them both that night, but his work was over and he was gone. Back to the dark streets, back to his car, back down the M11 into London's anonymous embrace.

*

Sitting waiting for news both Al and Marlin drank on, unable to focus properly. It seemed as though it was pointless continuing, until there was concrete evidence which fork in the road they should take.

'So, Doc?'

'What?'

'What's the deal with you and the... er...,' Marlin paused, struggling to find a tactful description. '...the ladies of...,'

'Ladies of the night? Ha. So in your very Victorian way you're asking why do I pay?'

'Yes.'

'Marlin, you've seen my lifestyle. I wouldn't date me. That doesn't mean I don't like sex.'

'If you were with someone, perhaps the lifestyle would be a little different. Ha, maybe a lot different?'

'Thanks for the advice Marlin. Works for you, does it?'

The flash of anger in Marlin's eyes startled and unnerved Al and he hastened to retrieve the situation.

'Look, sorry Marlin, I'm really not too good at taking advice. I don't know or pretend to know anything about your life so, if I've crossed a line, I apologise.' Al watched as the dark cloud lightened above Marlin, but sensed the chance of a storm was not greatly diminished. 'Ok as we've plenty in the bottle and not too much else to do here, I'll try and explain.'

INTOXICATED AND BEWITCHED

Al settled back in his seat, a far off look in his eye as if trying to make sense of his thoughts, then slowly nodded and turned his focus back to Marlin.

'I was saving this sort of stuff for my autobiography, but what the hell. Are you sitting comfortably? Then I'll begin.' Al smiled briefly and took a sip from his glass.

'I've had to work pretty hard to get where I am, or at least where I was. Put it down to family pressure or whatever, but I've got a fairly single minded ambition; I mean my mother certainly wanted great things for me and I needed to get away from my father.'

'That I can understand.'

'Really? Ok. Well the problem with working hard is that hours spent with your head in a book, are hours missing out on the other pleasures of life.'

'You see hours spent with your head in a book a pleasure?'

'I did. Anyway, from school through college I didn't have too much of a social life.'

'You mean girls?'

'Girls and friends, but yeah, in terms of what I'm telling you tonight, I mean girls. Don't get me wrong I wasn't celibate, but then I wasn't prolific either; let's face it you don't get many dates in a library. So I got my degrees and my doctorate and entered the real world as something of an intellectual giant and an emotional dwarf.'

'Intellectual giant?'

'Ah yes, that's my ego. More of that later.'

'Go on.'

'Twenty-eight years old and I was qualified and writing yet, I dunno, I still felt lost, unsatisfied.'

'Why unsatisfied if you'd just qualified? That's what you'd worked for isn't it'

'It was, and don't get me wrong, I was pleased. But it wasn't me I was thinking of.'

'Then who?'

'Well, about two years before that my father died, the man I could never please, and I suppose I thought it would be some sort of release. It wasn't, the bastard was stuck in my head like some fucking ghost forever being disappointed.'

'You still get that?'

'Not so much now. It tends to be when people call me Aldous that brings him back. It's irrational I know, but it affects me. God, I feel like I'm on the couch.'

'It's ok, talk about whatever you want to.'

'Well, to get back to the point: It was around two years after graduating, in 1990, that I met Anne. I'd written my first book and the publishers were having a launch party in the East End. It was a big deal for me, really big actually, and I was a nervous wreck. Anne was the event organiser; twenty four years old, already the consummate professional and absolutely beautiful, stunning.' Al was animated, glowing as he spoke too quickly. His hands moving in front of him as if to illustrate his story.

'She had this wonderful pale skin and dark, dark, long black hair. And her figure, well. Oh and the eyes, those green eyes.' Al paused as if lost in thought again and sipped on his drink. Marlin did not want to intrude on his musings but felt sure there was more to tell.

'I get the picture, so I take it you fell for her?'

'Sorry, I was lost there for a moment.'

Al continued, but although he spoke more slowly now, he seemed distracted; almost as though surprised by his own disjointed story.

'Yeah, I fell for her. I was intoxicated and bewitched, as I used to tell her. Jesus, I must have been though, because the year after that is something of a blur to be honest. Anyway, she took care of me at the event and afterwards we got together for drinks. I was lucky because she was a sucker for my 'sad, puppy-dog eyes' as she called them.' Al stopped again and looked over to the window, shaking his head slightly.

'Eight months later we were getting married.'

'Whirlwind romance?'

'I guess so, but for two years, maybe three, we were good. Hell, we were great. Then, well you know, it's strange how much a person can change without you noticing it.'

'She changed?'

'No I did.' Again Al shook his head slowly, a look of bemusement on his face. 'I thought she was far too good for me. Too good looking, too bright, just too good. Then once I got onto television, had my books and articles published, nothing seemed too good for me. Nothing and no-one. I wore her on my arm as some sort of badge of celebrity, but otherwise I took her for granted. That fucking ego again you see, always the ego.'

'You had affairs?'

'No, no, I wouldn't call them affairs. I cheated enough, but not affairs; I mean no-one was allowed to get their hooks into me. No-one was going to hold me down. No-one but me.'

'So what happened?'

'America 1995 happened. Or at least it happened in America on a book tour for my second novel; something of a disaster.'

'The tour or the novel?'

'Both if I'm being honest. The writing was tired and no-one knew who the hell I was over there. It was humiliating and draining, but drink helped, so I took to the bottle.'

'Where was Anne?'

'Anne travelled with me and my US agent Steve King, an insufferably patient man, or so I thought. Anyway I kept drinking and I have to admit to being abusive, until I locked myself away in my hotel room in Boston for three days. They tried to get into me, but I saw them off until the third day. Then I emerged, more than a little confused, to find they weren't there. I searched everywhere but no sign.'

'Had she gone back to England?'

'No. I went to the hotel desk and there were two letters for me. The first, from Steve, was a letter of resignation due to my appalling behaviour. The second, was again about my appalling behaviour and also from Steve, except this one explained why he was leaving and taking Anne with him. It said that, given time, she may contact me.'

'It's a familiar story, but go on. Did she contact you?'

Al paused again as he considered that time in his life. He had been as honest as he had ever been so far, but now he felt that he may reveal too much of himself. He sipped his drink to give himself time and collect his thoughts. He was only too aware that the next year or so had been self-deprecation made flesh, made wine, made whiskey. It was a blow to his ego that he had emerged from a self-imposed exile to a world that had not missed him or noticed his absence. Rebuilding his career to its previous level was a long slow process that was still continuing. No, that degradation was private.

'Did she contact me? Yes, eventually, but my focus had shifted to the ladies you asked about. A friend from the television days had a contact in the 'escort' business and I found I had no problem with it. After all, money may not bring you happiness but it can buy short term substitutes. That path led me to Lara, but don't go thinking she's just some escort. Lara is different.'

Again Al stopped himself. How could he explain that having felt degraded in life, he had quickly learned to make it the focal point of the sex 'games' he played? That in thinking about Anne he no longer needed to 'beat himself up'? That, in recent years, it was Lara to whom he entrusted his body and psyche's release? That it was she who would tie, lash and love him; she who would abuse, seduce and rescue him?

'And Anne?' Marlin didn't want to push the point, but he couldn't hold his curiosity.

Al started at the mention of her name as if awoken and spoke slowly.

'She wrote letters. I read the first few and then just burned them.' Al looked away and his cheek twitched as though he were about to cry, he sniffed and sighed heavily.

'I'm sorry Doc, I shouldn't have asked.'

'No, no. It's ok really. I read all about her new life and how she was heartbroken to leave, but would have been even more heartbroken to stay.' Al spoke slowly, long pauses punctuating his recollections. 'She said she loved me and would write again. Said she hoped we could meet up one day as friends. I didn't want to open any more of the letters, feel her pity, picture her face. It's easier to live my life as though she is dead than think of her alive and with someone else.' His voice was still strong but now there were tears sliding down Al's cheeks. He brushed them away roughly.

'Look, I'm ok. Shouldn't there be some news yet?'

Marlin stood, picking up his phone and dialling as he walked, eager to pretend that he hadn't seen the tears; a pretence they both played along with as Marlin strode into the hallway and the Doc wiped his face. Clearing his throat and sniffing loudly, the Doc regained his composure and tried to follow the one-sided dialogue outside the living room door.

Not loud enough to be clear, it was still evident that Marlin was not pleased. Doc waited for what seemed like an age before Marlin appeared again, his face pale and solemn.

'The bastard killed Professor Peters. All but cut his head off for Gods' sake!'

'Jesus, when?'

'A few hours ago I think. His wife was upstairs waiting for him to come to bed.'

'He left her alive?'

'Is that important? I mean does it tell us anything new?'

'Well...,' the Doc stopped and seemed completely lost in thought.

'Doc?'

Al raised his hand as a gesture of patience but his eyes remained fixed on the wall ahead of him. His breathing was regular and deep, but he could feel his heart racing and it was some time before he could bring himself to move. Slowly he picked up his glass and drank, feeling the burn in the back of his throat as he returned to the present.

'He didn't kill her because he wasn't there to kill her. He's showing his control and focus. He's showing us that we don't know him. Not really.' Al went to go on but stopped himself and took a drink. Marlin lit a cigarette.

'We don't know him? What the fuck have we been doing then? Jesus Doc, this isn't what I wanted to hear.'

'Don't worry Marlin; this doesn't rule out the profile, it simply alters it. We thought he wanted me dead and now I think we know that. Also, he's showing that he has a plan; an order for things that must be followed. Forget random, now he really means business.' Al filled his glass, the anxiety turning to fear evident in his voice and etched across his face. 'He almost cut Peters' head off?'

'Yeah, Doc.'

Al nodded slowly and unconsciously brought his hand to his throat, stroking softly. Marlin smoked, eyes fixed on his friend but silent, fully aware that no words of comfort were adequate. He checked his watch.

'Look, Doc, it's late. Why don't you turn in and we'll catch up tomorrow?' Marlin tasted the whiskey on his breath and made a quick mental calculation. 'I'm going to catch some shut-eye down here, you've ensured that I'll be lucky to find my car, never mind drive it.'

Al looked across and smiled for the first time in a while.

'I'm at least reliable for some things. I'll throw you down a blanket but I have to warn you, that thing is not good for your neck.'

Al picked up his drink and made for the door. Thoughtful and serious he walked slowly up the stairs, balancing his glass at the top as he opened the airing cupboard with his foot and dropped a blanket over the banister.

'Sleep well, Marlin.'

Pushing open the door to his bedroom, he paused a few seconds as he gazed into the darkness, waiting for his eyes to adjust. Then, leaning back as if on the edge of a cliff, he felt inside the door for the light switch and as the bulb sparked into life he pulled back sharply, spilling whiskey on his wrist. He could feel his heart pumping and held onto the door jamb as he peered into his now forbidding bedroom.

Damn you, calm down, Al. He poked the door wide open with his toe and stepped forward, quickly scanning around him. Nothing but his furniture and a coat hanging behind the door. He moved towards his bed and, keeping as much distance as possible, looked underneath.

Socks and handcuffs, just the usual then. He managed a quiet laugh and picking up the manacles moved slowly towards his closet. Balling his fist he pulled open the door but there were only clothes to harass. He breathed deeply and moved to place the cuffs inside.

'Doc?'

Al sprang sideways into his bedroom table, scattering the bottles of cologne, a delayed sharpness stabbing his knee as he waved a fist aimlessly in front of him.

'Jesus, calm down Doc, I was only looking for the bathroom.'

'Marlin, don't creep around the fucking place, you're meant to be making me feel safer here, not give me a heart attack,' Al was rubbing his knee frantically, a pained expression on his face.

'Fair enough, Doc. Now why don't you put those cuffs away and get some sleep?' Marlin smiled as the Doc moved to close the closet door, obviously embarrassed. 'Goodnight.'

Marlin pulled the door shut and Al sighed, wondering how the hell he was going to sleep now? Marlin found the bathroom and, as he washed his hands, he looked at himself in the mirror, all too aware of the tiredness in his eyes. He cupped his hands and brought the warm water up to his face, again and again, but the fatigue and concern would not wash away.

Moving back to the living room he picked up his blanket and lay on the settee, hardly able to keep his eyes open. He would be no sentry tonight, no bodyguard. As he curled up, his limbs heavy and tense, he tried to banish his fears. Could he really protect the Doc? This 'Phantom' was brutal and efficient, slipping into houses with ease. Sleep took over anxiety as Marlin slipped into a dreamless darkness, a last thought banished; if I'm looking after the Doc, who will look after me?

*

The return from Cambridge was a blur of numb nothingness, an inevitable anti-climax following the earlier ecstasy. The man had eased his car through quiet London streets with no discernible reason or route, his eyes fixed forward, trance-like. Heading through the centre of town he barely noticed the late drinker's unsteady progress or the prospective lover's eager touches and impatient steps. Passing along the embankment he ignored the dark calm of the Thames and the illuminated beauty of timeless architecture.

Into Camden he steered until his eyes fixed upon Albert Road. Thirty-two Albert Road, his mind screamed and he stopped, allowing himself a brief moment of self-congratulation at his powers of recall. Hours spent staring, studying maps, had ensured that each and every road was committed to memory - London to Cambridge, parking, walking and returning to the City; to Camden, to Albert Road. Here.

Thoroughness was everything and he would not be a tourist in his own world. That which could not be committed to memory was better to be erased completely. This was a land of his mind but solid to the touch, real but soft and vulnerable. Closing his eyes he felt the reality crumbling and ebbing away, like sand through his fingers, and he balled his fist tightly. No, not yet. Eyes open, he stared with a violent intensity at the house before him, noting the lights going out one, two, three. He smiled, curved lips becoming little more than bared teeth, and sucked in the cold air sharply. Welcome to my world, Mr Andrews. I hope you enjoy your stay, but I fear my truth is much stranger than your non-fiction.

Putting the car into gear he pulled away smoothly, eyes once again straight ahead. He must sleep and then start again, as preparation and thoroughness was everything. The man was in a run-down hotel, less than a mile from Doc Andrews in King's Cross. One room was enough and he could come and go as he liked. Paying a month in advance he'd ensured that there was no room service; no interruption and no questions. Inside the spartan accommodation was a 'not quite double but bigger than single' bed; musty and hard, the mattress was only marginally better than the floor. A small table and a worn 1970's wardrobe, doors held together by an elastic band completed the furniture. The closed door to the side of the bed served as a barrier to a stinking room of dripping sinks, barely functional toilet and a pipe which occasionally brought forth warm water; and was generously described as a shower.

The man had no complaints however. The table was adequate for map reading or somewhere to open the newspapers, now that the candlestick and hammers were secure on the shelf within the wardrobe. Alongside his weapons he placed his lock-picks, glass cutter and the knives. On the floor of the wardrobe sat his collection of locks in a brown cardboard box. Quick, quiet entry required practice and this box represented hundreds of hours. Finally, on a small shelf that he'd put up himself, new wood out of place against decrepit yellowed wallpaper, he placed his books. Professor Peters, Doctor Andrews, the Masters book 'Killing for Company'. A Dahmer book that had disappointed lay torn and ragged in the plastic bin by the door. By the bed a lamp sat on a wooden protuberance that barely hung to the wall. Here was balanced his notepad and he held it under the light and studied.

Doctor Andrews - Detective Chief Inspector Marlin - The Girls?

Placing the pad down he reached for the shelf and, selecting the book by Professor Peters, he picked up the black marker pen from the table. Glancing at the front cover for a few seconds he wiped the plastic sleeve with the arm of his hooded top. Balancing the book in one hand, he leaned in close as he carefully printed DECEASED by the author's name. It was now that he noticed the blood along his right arm, and he looked intently as he mimed the bowing motion, nodding his head in acknowledgement and understanding. He undressed and stood naked in the light, examining every stray splatter and drop of blood on the apparel. Picking up the stained clothes, he placed them in a black bin liner from the wardrobe and put the bag by the door. Checking the wardrobe again he noted the three pairs of black jeans and three black hooded tops. Reaching in he picked up the large knife, carefully running his tongue along the blade. He closed his eyes, reliving the moment; his body throbbing and inflamed as he fell back onto the bed with a moan.

BOTTLE SELLS THE DEAL

The alarm on his phone was quiet but insistent, and however unwelcome; Marlin knew he had to get up. Stretching he checked the time - 6am. Wouldn't want to oversleep or anything, he reflected, trying to remember exactly what time it had been when he fell asleep. He moved upstairs quietly and washed before easing the door to the Doc's room open, recoiling slightly at the odour of stale whiskey and fear.

'Doc. DOC!'

'What? Who is it? What time is it?'

'It's Marlin, Doc. Can you wake up for a second?'

Al stirred again and half-sat, blinking into the light from the hallway. Neither fully awake nor sober, he nonetheless was listening.

'Look Doc, I've got to head home now and then get to work. I'll ask for a uniformed officer to be posted here until we know what is going on, ok? Also, I'll see if he can't keep the press off your drive-way; believe me, they'll want to speak to you once the Peters' murder gets out.'

'Ok, can I go to sleep now?'

'Be my guest, Doc. Did you get any of that?'

'Yeah, police uniform and press.'

'I tried. See you later Doc.'

Although he had played it down somewhat, Marlin called immediately for an officer to be posted outside. On this occasion he knew even Thomas wouldn't object. He climbed into his car and lit a cigarette, drawing deeply and rubbing his forehead.

'Whiskey? How do you do it Doc? God, I'm tired. Tired and talking to myself, brilliant.' With that he pulled away and headed home.

The Doc was awake and making coffee at 8.30, despite the lateness of the previous evening. Having been half-woken by Marlin he had dozed restlessly, dreaming of policemen and half severed heads. The picture of Professor Peters from his book floated large and square in his living room, the eyes black and lifeless as he conversed perversely from a gaping wound in his neck. His words slow and indistinct as blood oozed from the framed edges and pooled on the carpet.

'Will you study my case, Andrews? Look at the pictures of my death? Publish them? Will you? You'll have to catch him first, you know that don't you? Find him and catch him. So how do you catch a phantom, Andrews? How do you find a ghost? Who will write up your case, Andrews? What pictures does he have prepared for your chapter?'

Al had found no need to sleep any longer and so, at this ungodly hour, he sipped hot coffee and peered through the curtains at the police car across his drive. I wonder how he ended up with the short straw, thought Al as he moved away to refresh his cup. He had the radio on but, as yet, the news reported nothing of the night before. Maybe Thomas has decided to bury it? The news at nine banished any such hopes. He moved between kitchen and window as his phone vibrated and the gaggle of reporters tried to gain access beyond the not-so-bored-now policeman. He checked the messages and checked in with Shirley, thinking himself fortunate to get her voicemail. Having ignored all pleas for an interview and waited in vain for any news from Marlin, Al was dismayed to discover that it was only 11.30 and he was tired again. Sleeping or, more realistically, dreaming, was not an appealing prospect and Al walked the house peeping out of closed curtains upstairs and down. He was bored. Another coffee? Why not?

He moved to the kitchen and was surprised to see his pedal bin half-open. Despite his organised chaos, he had something of an obsession with areas of cleanliness and tidiness. Chief among these obsessions was closing cupboards, lids, packets or whatever. He believed in being thorough and yet the bin was over-full and ajar. On opening the receptacle he was both angry and pleased. His half-bottle of J&B was half-full and waiting for him. Marlin you bastard, he thought as he grinned to himself and filled a glass.

In the living room his mind wandered again and a half-memory resurfaced. He picked up his phone and dialled.

'Hello, Lara?'

'Is that you Al?'

'Yes. How are things?'

'Did we have anything booked today? It's been a bad week Al; you have no idea how bad.'

'Tell me.'

'Alice was killed on Sunday. Murdered.' Lara spoke slowly as if controlling the pace of speech might lead to control of her emotions. It didn't and she broke-up as she ended the sentence, sobbing loudly.

'I'm so sorry Lara, so sorry. If there's anything I can do?'

'She was killed in the flat, our flat, Al! Christy found her. Jesus Al, the poor girl, I didn't know her well but Jesus. And it could've been me. I know it's wrong to think like that with her dead, but I can't help it. Jesus, Al!' The tears came freely now and she cried loudly into the receiver for some time.

'It's ok, Lara. It's ok.'

'Al, I can't stay here, you know how small it is. There were only two of us then and you thought it was small, but think how it is now, with one bedroom a crime scene and Christy cracking up in another?'

'Look Lara, I've got the press parked outside the place. Even I can't get out.'

'What about later? What time do they go? I'll bring a bottle if you can't get out. And look, I'll be wrapped up and discrete, honestly. What do you think?'

'Ok, they should be bored and away by six if I write something for Shirley to give to them. So come then and don't wrap up too much.'

Lara laughed weakly but he could sense the relief in her voice, 'See you at six, Al. Thanks.'

Al shook his head and smiled to himself as he ended the call. He could picture the short skirt, the panties and stockings. He could almost taste her lips, feeling the excitement, but the bottle had sold the deal. He opened his laptop and began to type a quote to give to Shirley, then stopped himself and called Marlin.

'Hello Doc, you just up?'

'Funnily enough no, your early morning pep talk well and truly put paid to that.'

'Please don't thank me Doc, I can't take it.'

'Ok it's not entirely your fault. Thanks for the car outside.'

'You're welcome. All ok?'

'I've got the press pack hanging around - that I could do without. Look, I want to give a quote via Shirley to get rid of them, but I don't know how much I can give away?'

'What were you thinking of giving away? That you think you're a target? Trust me; they'll camp out for weeks if you do, just in case they get a murder on camera.'

'Thanks Marlin, that would be my murder you're talking about.'

'Sorry Doc, but you know what I mean. I would say trust your instincts and if it's not gratuitous and salacious, you've probably got it about right.'

'Thanks Marlin, I'll try. Oh, and can you tell the policeman outside that Lara will be visiting at about six?'

'For Christ's sake Doc, there's no stopping you is there? I was worried about how scared you might be and there you are worrying about your libido. You just relax and have fun, Doc.'

'Someone sounds jealous?'

'Goodbye.'

Marlin hung up the phone and rubbed his chin, sighing heavily. He was dog tired and frankly yes, he was jealous of whatever it was that Lara did to the Doc; it was surely more attractive than his evening. As he looked up, fixing a point on a strip light, his mind shifted. Lara? What about her friend, or at least her possible friend? Standing, he scanned the office and stretched, trying to focus. Through the bottom doors she emerged, carrying an armful of files and a weary expression, Susan Scott.

'Sue.'

'DCI Marlin.'

'Just Marlin.'

'Ah yes that's right, 'just' Marlin. Well how can I help you, Marlin?'

'The girl, Alice something, killed in Kentish Town. Did you find out anything more?'

Susan Scott looked at him for a few moments, as if his face might tell her more than his words, then she gestured with her head towards her desk, smiling as they walked.

'Let me put these down and check my notes. Ah, here they are. What sort of information or 'more' information were you looking for?'

'Did the girl share a flat?'

'That I can tell you. There were two other girls, although they seem to have rarely been there and not at the same time. Let's just say it was functional.'

'Their names?'

'Christy and Lara, er I have the full names here somewhere.' Susan gestured at the paper mountain in front of her and the files that surrounded her desk.

'Marlin, can I be honest with you?'

'Sure.'

'I'm not going to do you and your new best buddy any favours here, ok? So please don't ask.'

'I'm not asking for anything except information.'

'Really?' Susan was standing hand on hip and eyes wide with incredulity as she slowly shook her head.

'A case you couldn't care less about and suddenly you want information. Next you'll be saying you didn't know your man Andrews was more than familiar with the place?'

'Sue, I'm not pissing about here or looking for favours. I knew there may be a link with Andrews; I just wanted a heads-up if there was. So you're saying he'd been to the flat?'

'A few times; he's something of a regular of the blonde girl, Lara.'

'Thanks, Sue.'

'That it?'

'Yes, that's it.'

'Right then. I'm sorry if I made assumptions.'

Unaware of his potentially starring role in both of the Metropolitan Police's major investigations, Al returned to his laptop and hurriedly typed, thinking of Lara more than phantoms.

Shirley

Updated comment/quote to go to the press immediately - stress the fact that I will make no other comments at this time:

Dr Al is saddened and shocked at the brutal murder of Professor Peters in Cambridge. His thoughts are with his wife Helen and family. Although not definitely confirmed as yet, the Metropolitan Police and he are in agreement that this is the work of the so-called Phantom. Dr Al is continuing to work with the top detectives on this case and would ask that you leave them to get on with this and not look for information outside his house - no comments will be made there.

Thank you

Tapping the 'send' button, Al relaxed and drained his glass, tired and bored by the seemingly endless day. Lying back he rested his eyes and, terrified of his dreams or not, he slept.

*

It was four thirty when Marlin pulled up in his car at Albert Road, waving at the PC to let him through the now sparse group of reporters. Huddled together chatting, obviously cold and bored, they went through the motions of shouting questions and even snapped a few photos as he stepped to the door, but it was clear they expected no reply. The tearful wife in Cambridge, shocked and pleading for the 'monsters' capture, would take centre stage in Tuesday's papers. Andrews was good for the throw-away quote, but he had provided one already and it was bland and all but unusable. As for Marlin, most of these newspapermen were familiar with the press conference mannequin and his taciturn nature. If he was the best chance of a comment it was time to pack up and head down to the pub or perhaps even home.

Al was surprised by the knock at the door, rubbing his eyes and yawning as he checked the time - 4.35pm? He walked to the door and, chain attached, opened enough to see Marlin, cold and serious.

'Open the fucking door Doc, it's me, Marlin.'

Al unhooked the chain and opened the door whilst standing out of view as Marlin strode past him, bag in hand.

'What's it like out there?'

'Don't worry Doc, it'll be nice and quiet by the time your little 'more than a friend' girl gets here.'

'Hey Marlin. There's no need for that. What's your problem?'

'The whores, the deaths, the truth and you, Doc, are my problem.'

Al rubbed his face, as if to convince himself that he was not dreaming and looked back at Marlin. Pale and tired, there was no hiding his irritation. Al moved to fill his glass but the bottle was empty and he couldn't hide his disappointment. Marlin reached into his bag to produce a half-bottle and held it out to Al, his features set hard and still.

'This is an advance payment.'

'Payment for what?' Al screwed his face, puzzled, but took the bottle and poured himself a small drink. He was halted as he picked up a glass for Marlin.

'No, not for me. This is payment for the truth, Doc. Level with me now and we can get on with things, piss me about and I'll get Detective Scott to take you down to the station. Now take a seat.'

Al sat, his face a picture of confusion. 'The station? Fuck's sake Marlin, what've I done?'

'Listen to me for a moment.' Al went to speak but Marlin raised his hand, palm towards Al's face, his arm was shaking. 'Don't interrupt or speak until I've finished, just listen Doc.'

Al was worried now; the anger of his friend was clearly evident, if this was indeed his friend anymore. Silenced, he listened to Marlin the policeman.

'Alice Short.'

'Oh Alice...,'

Marlins eyes shut tightly, his body tense 'Shh. I said just listen.' He composed himself again, breathing deeply, and waited for Al to sit back in his chair.

'Alice Short, 28 years old. Murdered on Sunday morning in Buckingham Road, Kentish Town. You said to me that you may know the name but you know nothing of the flat. That, Doc, is a lie. Didn't you think we'd speak to Lara?' Marlin shook his head and paused as he lit a cigarette. 'You've been there numerous times in fact. So I ask you now, did you know Alice Short?'

'I can speak now?' Marlin nodded and gestured with his hand to go on.

'I knew of Alice Short because of Lara, but I've not met her. I didn't say I'd been there because I was kind of spooked to be honest. I know I didn't kill her, so what did it matter if I'd been there with Lara? I kind of thought that it made me look like a regular visitor and I was embarrassed.'

'You are a regular, Doc.'

'I know, I know.' Al sighed and rubbed his forehead nervously 'I'm not a killer Marlin, I just pay for my company.'

'Where were you on Sunday morning?'

Al's eyes widened, 'You really think I'm a suspect? Jesus Marlin, I was here asleep. Unconscious actually.'

'Doc, the fact that you were a visitor there makes you a suspect; it's not just me making this up. Was Lara here?'

'No I was alone; hell you were here Saturday night. I carried on drinking and passed out.' Al stopped, his eyes narrowed, and he ran his tongue over his teeth. 'I did go out and get a half-bottle, but I don't know what time.'

'Where did you get it?'

'Again, I don't actually know. I woke up with the bottle in my pocket.'

'So really you're drawing a blank for most of the time in question?'

Al shrugged and sighed again, this time deeply and he reached for his drink, 'I'm not a killer, Marlin.'

'I don't think so either Doc, but I do need you to level with me. Sue Scott is a good detective, but she already thinks I may try and do you a few favours; I just want to be sure that no favours are necessary. Ok?'

'Yeah, sorry Marlin.'

'Sorry about the Lara comment Doc, I'm just tired that's all. Also be aware, Sue might want to ask you the same questions, so just tell her what you told me, ok?'

'Yes, thanks again Marlin and I am sorry. Just so you know, Lara doesn't sell sex. I buy her time in the bedroom, but whether there is any sex is up to her. She's no prostitute. No whore. And I really am sincerely sorry Marlin.'

'Water under the bridge, let's just forget it for now, eh? See you later.'

Marlin strode out with some purpose, closing the door firmly behind him as he looked out at the now deserted street. The young PC nodded as he backed his car away and Marlin stopped, winding down his window and leaning towards the uniformed man.

'I know it's quiet here now and you'll probably be relieved soon, but keep a sharp eye on things, ok?'

'Yes sir.'

With that he put his foot down, heading for home and hopefully sleep. For once he would leave it to the uniforms and junior detectives to pore over the details. He reflected on the fact that he had been in contact with the Doc for one week and he'd never been so exhausted.

*

Sitting in his living room, Al was thoughtful and still. A suspect? He was a suspect in a murder inquiry? How the hell did this happen? The detective had to be a woman as well, typical!

96

'So Dr Andrews, how long have you been paying this woman to handcuff and beat you? You seem embarrassed, Dr Andrews.'

Al held his hands to his face then picked up a cushion and, holding it close to his mouth, screamed before flinging it back down. Picking up his glass he looked about the room, his eyes finally settling at the board on the side table, beside which sat two white cards; he reached across and picked them up, scanning his own notes. Two prostitutes, one in Oxford Circus, one in Kentish Town. Close enough I suppose, but hardly on my doorstep. He placed the cards down and started to sit back when he heard voices outside. Peering through the curtains he saw the police car sitting across the driveway, the officer was in conversation with what appeared to be a long dark coat with blonde hair. He smiled as he went to the door.

'Officer? Officer? It's ok, she's expected.' The officer nodded for her to continue and Al could faintly hear her indignant 'I told you'. Lara turned and smiled as she hurried towards him, her heels clicking like castanets. As she hugged him and stepped inside he saw the officer roll his eyes as he wound up his window and shivered against the cold.

'Hello, Lara. Some way to wrap up there, eh? You look like a bear on stilts with those heels.' He laughed and felt truly relaxed for the first time that day.

'You don't like the heels?'

'I love the heels. Now put your bag down and let me get you a ...,'

Lara opened her coat and pulled out the bottle of scotch, 'Drink?' She smiled and held the coat open as Al drank in the sight of her body beneath, his delight obvious as she leaned in and passed the bottle.

'So you're pleased to see me as well as the scotch? Yes, a drink please.'

Al went to his cabinet and filled a crystal glass he produced and then placed it on the table. Stepping forward he took her coat and placed it over the back of the chair. As she bent forward for her drink he stepped in front of her, gently bringing her face up to his. He looked at her for some seconds and then pulled her to him, hugging her tightly.

'God, I'm so glad you're ok Lara. So glad. You can stay here as long as you like.'

Lara stayed silent, but he could feel her breathing quicken as she fought to keep her self-control, her hands pressed firmly into his back. They stood embracing for what seemed like an age until Al loosened his grip and eased her face up from his shoulder. Brushing her hair free he kissed her softly, his hand gently caressing her cheek. Tilting her head back, he smiled warmly at her and she saw that his eyes were moist and glistening.

'Don't you go getting me crying, Al. If I mess up this mascara you've no idea how much trouble you'll be in.'

'We can't have that happening, can we?' They both smiled and he hugged her again.

Marlin, fighting against fatigue, had piled the files on the kitchen table and was sipping a glass of wine, hoping this would inspire him to work rather than speed his inevitable descent into sleep. He watched heavy eyed as the blue smoke curled and spiralled towards the ceiling, almost dropping his cigarette at the sound of his phone.

'Hello, Marlin here.'

'Marlin this is Sue Scott, did I just wake you up?'

'You weren't far from it.'

'You sound exhausted. Look I won't keep you from your bed for long; I just wanted to know if you could help me with some info?'

'Shoot away.'

'Have you spoken to Andrews?'

'Yeah, it would seem he was out of it, completely unconscious when it all happened. Believe me if you've ever seen the man drink, you'll not think that an unlikely possibility. I think I was with him on Saturday evening and he was lucky to be standing when I left.'

'Ok, you've made your point, although if you only think you saw him you might want to look at your own intake of scotch. Marlin, I don't think he is a serious suspect, but the sooner I rule him out the sooner I can narrow down some of the others.'

'You've a lot of other suspects?'

'We've enough. Anyway, all I wanted to know was did Andrews tell you where he was when the other two prostitutes were killed? And again, I stress this is just to rule him out, ok?'

'I understand Sue; I told you I'm not in the business of doing favours for people, ok? I didn't ask him, but I will when I next see him. That should be tomorrow.'

'Thanks Marlin, now get some sleep. Oh, and don't get all harassed if I talk to Andrews myself.'

'Be my guest, Sue.'

Clicking the phone down, it occurred to Marlin that he really should have been putting those questions to the Doc himself if only to end this whole sideshow. Then again, how could he deal with everything in this state? How could he deal with anything? Taking one more sip of wine he stopped himself from lighting up again and shuffled through to the bedroom. Falling onto the bed he made a half-hearted attempt to cover himself before the darkness came; the sleep.

The sleep was deep and he was restless as he dreamed. He saw the Doc in handcuffs, smiling as Lara brought a whip across his back, the room dark and awash with whiskey. Lara brought her arm down with a loud 'swish' again and again, but her eyes were only fixed on Marlin and they burned into him. She maintained her gaze and smiled as she brought a finger to her mouth.

'Shhhhhhhhhhhh. It's your turn next Marlin, but what would you like? I think you're already beaten, aren't you?' Shaking her head she tutted disapprovingly and then with a sweep of her arm she brought the dark wall down. In the dim light on the floor lay a half-dressed girl, ghostly white and unmoving, her eyes ringed black and vacant.

'Meet my friend Alice. She'll do anything for you, Detective Chief Inspector, and I do mean anything.' Lara beckoned him forward with her finger as she spoke. Marlin stepped forward, hand over mouth, aghast.

'But she's...,'

'I know Marlin, she's a brunette. So are you a 'blondes have more fun' kinda guy?'

'Brunette? Jesus Christ Lara, she's dead for fucks sake.'

'Mmmmm, a bit picky for a single fella aren't you? We can't all be blonde and alive. And remember Marlin, she's only a prostitute and dead prostitutes don't really count to you, do they?'

Lara stood aside and there was the Doc, sitting on the floor, cradling the body and kissing the girl. As if in slow motion his eyes rolled up and, breaking his embrace, he fixed Marlin with a cold stare as Lara laughed hysterically.

'Doc, no!'

The last words were shouted and Marlin found himself awake and sweating. He caught his breath and checked the time, surprised that it was only just past midnight. Standing he undressed properly and climbed beneath the sheets. Curled tightly he lay, covered and warm, trusting in sleep to take care of him this time.

FALSE OPTIMISM

Tuesday morning came with a cold wind and uninviting drizzle, but Marlin was up at 6.30am. A forced optimism in mind, he had decided that today he would return to good old fashioned police work. He had to speak to DCS Thomas about events in Cambridge and he wanted to check-in with Sue Scott; so he was determined to make an early start. In the back of his mind, he knew that real police work was actually about clues and witnesses, observation and evidence; not phantoms and cryptic riddles, but he dared not allow these thoughts to surface. Today was fresh and new; things would be achieved one way or another.

The raised eyebrows and surprised good mornings were testimony to Marlin's early arrival, the pile of files and paperwork open on his desk, a show of self-discipline or self-delusion. Dark and bitter canteen coffee kept the mind focused and trips outside for a cigarette were both a welcome nicotine fix and a bracing blast of cold winter air. Hours passed relatively quickly but it was clear that progress was not being made, no matter how many times he went over his notes.

Closing his notepad, his finger and thumb squeezed what relief he could from his eyes and he stretched, grimacing as he heard his neck crack.

'Marlin. Thomas wants to see you.' His eyes opened and he saw PC Oliver walking away from his desk. She looked back smiling at him, then flicked her eyes towards the Chief Superintendent's office and nodded. Marlin drained the last of the luke-warm coffee, tasting the polystyrene of the cup. Adjusting his tie as he made his way to the office, he paused to collect himself before knocking and going in.

'Detective Chief Superintendent Thomas, you wanted to see me?' As he spoke Marlin was surprised to see Detectives Carr and Mitchell seated to the side of the desk, and hoped it didn't show as he nodded an acknowledgement to the two men. Thomas gestured towards a third empty seat.

'Please sit down, Marlin. You know Carr and Mitchell?' Again they exchanged nods and half-smiles. Thomas continued, all earnest looks and shakes of the head. 'This whole Cambridge carry-on is a nasty, nasty business. I think we have to step up the whole 'Phantom' angle here.'

'Step it up, Sir? I've looked at nothing else for the past week.'

'Yes, but with what results? What's that? Exactly Marlin, your silence tells the whole story.' Marlin had attempted to speak but, hand raised, Thomas continued and he knew that when the DCS was in this mood it was best to let him finish.

'I have to be honest Marlin; I thought you and that TV clown Andrews were completely off the mark with the whole serial killer thing. But I let you get on with things because I do actually think you are a good policeman.'

'Thank you, Sir.'

'Don't be bloody sarcastic, Marlin. Right, now because of my somewhat shaky faith in your alcoholic pal, I asked Carr and Mitchell here to look into the murders. I got the files copied and divided them between the two.'

'My case and my files? You didn't think about speaking to me?' Marlin spat angrily.

'A case and Met Police files, Marlin. And I don't need to consult a DCI about any decision. Do you understand?'

'Sir.' His eyes were wide, lips tight pressed, and he could both feel and hear his heart racing as Thomas continued.

'The e-mail and now this Cambridge business has changed my thoughts on the matter, and the Commissioner is getting it in the neck from the press. So Marlin, as the senior officer on this case you will lead, but I want the three of you to sit down and go through the files, pooling your information as you go. Basically, I want a result here Detectives, and a bloody quick one! Now get out of here and get on with it.' The men rose. 'Marlin, wait a moment.' Carr and Mitchell left. 'Close the door, Marlin.' Thomas looked away and pinched the top of his nose in a pronounced and obviously dramatic fashion.

'Marlin, you're a good detective.'

'Detective Chief Inspector.'

'Yes, yes Marlin you are a good Detective Chief Inspector. However, this tendency to go your own way bothers me. You're not a team player, Marlin, and I can let that go when you produce results, but not this time.

Work with Carr and Mitchell or I'll get someone who will; you're already lucky to still be on the case.'

'Yes sir.' Marlin rose to leave.

'And DCI Marlin, I won't have you rolling your eyes and giving sarcastic bloody comments in front of junior officers. Nor will I have you questioning my decisions. Do you understand?'

'Yes, Chief Superintendent.'

'Good, now get out and catch this bastard.'

Marlin emerged from the office shaking his head and feeling in his pocket for his cigarettes and lighter. Seeing Carr and Mitchell waiting near his desk, he signalled to the exit and walked quickly outside, not waiting to see if they followed. Sheltering from the strong breeze, he lit up and sucked in strongly through his teeth; once, twice deeply, before turning to face the two men who had followed his lead.

'So then you two, how long have you been looking at my case files, my case?'

Carr and Mitchell exchanged glances before Carr spoke up.

'Almost a week, sir. The Chief Superintendent gave us the files and said we weren't to tell you. We were to report directly to him if and when we found anything and he'd decide whether to speak to you.'

'And what did you find?'

Again they exchanged glances before Mitchell took his turn.

'Not a lot to be honest, sir. There really don't seem to be many clues to go on.'

Marlin dragged deeply on his cigarette and as he exhaled slowly he couldn't help but smile.

'Look guys, this situation isn't your fault and to be honest I could do with some more direct assistance. Also, don't worry about finding nothing – I'm not sure there's anything to find. Did either of you look into the boy who spent the night with the Mile End victim?'

'We looked sir, but no-one seems to have noticed and there's no CCTV from the clubs,' Carr explained.

Mitchell narrowed his eyes in thought and looked as if he was about to speak as Marlin dropped his cigarette and stubbed it out, shivering against the cold.

'Anything to add Mitchell, I'm freezing here?'

'It may not be anything, but one of Gillian Watson's friends said that she thinks she caught a cab outside the Starz club.'

'Black cab?'

'No, an unlicensed car. Unmarked and touting for business type. It just occurred to me that there had to be some way this nutter picked her out and that was a possibility.'

'Good work, Mitchell, I agree with you. Check the roads and buildings around the club for any CCTV and see if we can get something. Also, one of you check with PC Wilkes, he's interviewing the girl's friends again, and then get back to me, ok? And Carr, can you see if the MI6 boys came up with anything we missed on their admin boy? Thanks, guys.'

Calmer now, Marlin sat at his desk and vowed to avoid optimism in future as he scanned the office. Sue Scott caught his eye with a brief wave of the hand and nodding towards him, started over. Marlin straightened his back unconsciously and met her eyes.

'How can I help you, Sue?'

'My turn to ask for a favour.'

'I didn't ask for one, remember?'

'Yes I do and no you didn't.'

'Sorry, go on Sue. I'm not having the best of days.'

'Would you mind if I talked to Dr Al? I have to get his prints and it would be useful to ask a few questions while I'm at it.'

'Be my guest. Are you bringing him here?'

'No, I thought I'd go out there. More relaxed and all that?'

'Do you like whiskey?'

'What?'

'Whiskey, do you like it?'

'Yes, on occasion, why?'

'You'll see.' Marlin smiled and then more broadly, as he saw the look of bafflement on Sue's face change to a knowing smile.

'Dr Al? Ok, I get it. Quite the comedian, Marlin.'

Marlin watched her smile widen and kept her gaze, appreciating the warmth between them. He felt that he should speak again but words didn't come and the moment, full of expectation, hung in the air and was gone.

'Well Marlin, I've got to get on.'

Watching her walk away Marlin wanted to slap himself for his lack of bravery and his loss of words. The smile, the light in the eyes; he couldn't be sure but he thought that maybe this pretty, bright detective liked him.

'Idiot Marlin, idiot,' he murmured to himself.

*

It had been a long time since Al had woken with someone else in his bed, longer still since he'd had sex in the morning or shared his shower. Having made the most of the window between waking and hung-over sobriety, Al had returned to bed and sleep while Lara dressed and made coffee. Sitting in his living room, she peered out of the eternally closed curtains, glad the press were absent, although there was another police car guarding the entrance.

Walking barefoot around the rooms she examined the contents as if seeing them for the first time which, in many ways, she was. She had looked before, but only in character, and her concentration had been more about the angles of bending; the swaying of the hips, being a subject of gaze and attraction, the seen and not the seer. Having waited an hour or so, and seeing that it was nearly 11.30am, she made a coffee for Al and took it up to the bedroom; chiding him gently for his laziness and waiting until he was sitting awake before leaving. She enjoyed the quiet of the house, the space and, as she sipped her coffee, the world seemed a brighter place. The only dark cloud on the horizon came in the shape of the 'death storyboard' as Al had called it; a stark reminder both of why she was there and why police sat outside the door. Inside the room she was safe and warm though, and she smiled as she heard Al coughing into life.

Al shuffled through the living room dressed and, seemingly at least, half awake, mumbling about more coffee as he turned on his laptop and disappeared into the kitchen. Lara's eyes followed the shambling shape and she sat quietly until there was a loud knock at the door. Al appeared at the kitchen doorway with a glass of whiskey in one hand and his coffee and phone balanced in the other.

'Who the fuck's that?'

'I'll go, Al.'

'Make sure the chain's on.'

Lara, smiling, nodded and walked with a pronounced sashay, knowing that Al was watching each step. All playfulness evaporated at the sight of the female detective she had seen on Sunday, her id in hand.

'You again?'

'Lara? Well, well. Is Dr Andrews in?'

'Al, it's the police to see you,' Lara shouted into the living room. Then, leaving the door ajar and on the chain, she turned and walked upstairs. Al arrived at the door and seeing the id, let the female detective in.

'I'm Detective Sergeant Scott.'

'Ah yes, Marlin's friend.'

'So he mentioned I'd call?'

'He said it was possible.'

'He told you today?'

'No, not today, I can't remember really but I know he said your name.'

'I wanted to see you here at your home because this is really just a matter of tying up some loose ends.'

'Sure. Drink?'

Sue looked at the glass in Al's hand and shook her head with a wry grin.

'On duty and all that?' Al grinned. 'Have a seat.'

'First of all I need to take your fingerprints so I know which are yours in the flat?'

Al nodded and placed his glass down, waiting patiently as the Detective produced a small ink-pad and a fingerprint sheet. As she guided his fingers between the two he looked at her closely. He had to admit that as policewomen went she was really quite pretty. It then occurred to him that he would have to see if Lara had a policewoman outfit.

'Are you finding something funny about this, Dr Andrews?'

'Sorry?'

'The grin on your face.'

'Oh that, no, I was just thinking about something else. Please, no offence intended.'

'The girl, Lara, is staying here?'

'For a short while yes, why?'

'In case we need to get in touch. You're a friend and a client then?'

'That's pretty much true I'd say.'

'How long have you known her?'

'About two years.'

'And you've been to the flat on Buckingham Road?'

'Once or twice, yes.'

'You saw Alice Short?'

'No, she was a flat-mate of Lara's so I've heard the name but I never met her in person.'

'You're sure of that?'

'As sure as I can be.'

Sue produced a picture from her bag; it showed Alice Short half naked and lifeless on her bedroom floor. The bruises around her swollen left eye dark and pronounced against the deathly whiteness of her skin. 'Are you absolutely sure, Doctor?'

Al swallowed hard; his face tense as he looked away from the photo. There was a moment of silence and, when he finally spoke, his voice was soft and quiet.

'Don't you have any other photos of the poor girl? Did you have to show me that one? For fuck's sake, Detective…,' His voice trailed away as he stared ahead into the screen of the laptop.

'Have you seen her?'

'No, no, no. I haven't seen her, ok.' Al's voice was loud and sharp.

'Ok Doctor, I had to ask. Now there are just a few other questions I have for you.'

'Fire away, let's just get this over with.' Al picked up his drink and looked across at the detective.

'Marlin tells me that you were asleep, or should I say unconscious, from the early hours of Sunday morning until well into the afternoon.'

'That's about right.'

'About right?'

Al looked away and grimaced. 'No Detective, that is right.'

'Ok. Right. Finally, now that we have your fingerprints, what are the chances of me finding them at either of the other two prostitute's flats? And what were your whereabouts on the nights in question?' Sue reached into her bag and got out her notepad and searched back for the exact dates. 'The nights of…,'

Al sat back in his chair, a puzzled look on his face. Putting down his drink he leant in and pushed a button on his laptop.

'Dr Andrews I'm terribly sorry if I am boring you, but I'd appreciate it if you could at least try to answer my questions. I've done you the courtesy of coming to your house but I'm more than happy to bring you down to the station if that's what it takes to get a response.'

Al continued to stare ahead, seemingly oblivious to the presence of the Detective and her questions. When he did look up there was wildness in his eyes and he was as pale as the dead girl in the picture.

'We have to get Marlin here. I need to call him.'

'Dr Andrews, what are you talking about?'

'He's back; he's talking to me again.'

'Who's back, Doctor?'

'The Phantom, the fucking Phantom's back. He's sent me another message.' Al drank down his whiskey and hurriedly searched for the bottle, scurrying to the kitchen to get it. Filling his glass his eyes darted nervously. 'Lara, where is Lara? LARA!'

'Calm down, Dr Andrews. Please calm down and let me see the message.'

Lara entered the room, scared by the shouting of her name. 'Are you ok Al?'

Al shook his head and stood. 'My phone, where's my phone?'

Lara bent to the table and handed the phone to Al. 'What's wrong, Al?'

'The Phantom's back. I've got to call Marlin.' Taking his phone and drink, Al moved nervously into the hall.

Lara sat down, bemused by all of the panic, and slightly scared having seen the state of Al.

'What did you do to him?' she asked the detective.

Sue was staring at the laptop, a finger to her mouth, lost in thought. After a while she glanced up at Lara and returned her stare for longer than was comfortable.

'Don't worry about it Lara, he'll have his friend Marlin here soon and he'll deal with it. But while you're here, can you answer a few questions?'

Lara looked slightly surprised and shrugged her shoulders. 'If you're sure he's ok? Go ahead.'

'He'll be fine, I'm sure. Now can I ask you how long have you known Dr Andrews?'

'I already told you.'

'Again please.'

'Ok, about two years or so I suppose.'

'And your arrangement. What is your arrangement? A touch of kink I understand? Are you his exclusive 'Escort' for want of a better word?'

'I'm not an escort and the arrangement is kind of private.'

'Not anymore, Lara. What is it all about? Is there violence involved?'

Lara looked away and shook her head slowly. 'Is this stuff really important or are you just getting off on it? Trying to embarrass Al? I mean you know he's not the killer so why not stop looking for your kicks and go catch the psycho?'

'I don't know anything Lara. Just answer the question, will you?'

'Alright Detective. There's a bit of tying-up, a bit of slapping and stuff, you know? A touch of S&M but nothing heavy.'

'He hits you?'

'Ha, no. I do the slapping when there is any.'

'And you're the only girl he sees?'

'I don't know, I mean I think so but I can't be sure. It's his choice after all.'

'So he could have been a customer of other girls?'

'He could I suppose, but as I say, he's not a killer. Do you think I'd be here if I had even the slightest worry that he could be a killer?'

'And I am not a killer.' Al stood in the doorway, anger written across his face as he spoke slowly and once again calmly. 'If you'd found the time to stop bullying Lara and looked at the message, you might have seen that the job in hand is seeing that I am not killed rather than trying to establish me as a killer. Am I really the best suspect you have in this case? Are you really so short of ideas?'

'I have to investigate this properly Dr Andrews.'

'And knowing who slaps who is an integral part of your investigation?'

'If you're paying prostitutes to slap you, then yes, maybe it is part of my investigation? I'll be the judge of that, though.'

'Lara is not a prostitute, Detective.'

'Really?'

The tension in the room was palpable and the silence that engulfed it was painful to endure. It was then that the doorbell rang out loudly, breaking the intensity of the moment. Sue and Al spoke in unison.

'Marlin.'

Having taken off his coat and sat down, Marlin was aware of the atmosphere in the room, taut and crackling, as he looked around the faces and lit a cigarette.

'You don't mind, Doc?'

'No, smoke away. Second hand smoke is the least of my worries.' Al smiled weakly at his joke as he passed an ashtray to Marlin. Marlin returned the smile and glanced over at Sue Scott. Looking forward she remained impassive and unconcerned as Lara's spiteful stare bore imaginary holes into her. Marlin was not sure what had passed between these two, but he could feel the animosity. Al paced the room drinking and waiting as Marlin flicked at the laptop screen and scanned the message.

Dr Al

How does it feel to be the preeminent scholar in your field? I would like to think that I played no little part in your promotion to this lofty position, but I am not expecting thanks or credits in the front of your books. In fact there will be no more books from you Aldous, although I would hope that I may be able to earn you a chapter when this tale is put into print. I was worried about your health when I noticed how much time you were spending inside that fine house of yours, curtains drawn all day and not even a visit to the off license? But I needn't have worried as you were back to your whoring and drinking in no time at all. Out all night and ordering in during the day, you really are a dirty, drunken dog. Enjoy it while you can Doctor Andrews, as time is short, so short for you.

Get your affairs in order sir. I am your disease, doctor, and I am terminal.

The Phantom

Marlin took a moment or two to collect his thoughts, but he couldn't help glancing at the Doc, only to be met with a crazed stare from his friend, even though his face was stoic and his voice calm and even.

'It couldn't be too much clearer this time Marlin.'

'Doc we can't be too surprised by this, or pretend that it wasn't on the cards. What we may have to do now is consider moving you somewhere safer. I mean he's obviously watching this place.'

'We know he's watching and we know who he wants, so why not leave the bait and wait to spring the trap?' Sue spoke in a matter of fact way as she addressed the conversation to Marlin as though they were alone.

Marlin stayed quiet, but he had to admit that it made a lot of sense to keep the Doc where he was and lure the killer in. He could feel the Doc's angry stare burning and intense, but it was Lara who spoke.

'Maybe you'll get lucky and he'll kill me as well?'

'It would certainly wrap up your investigation Detective Scott and, whilst it may increase your workload Marlin, I get the feeling that DCS Thomas might actually be quite pleased.' Al's words were intended to be angry and sarcastic but came across as tired and not a little scared. Sue softened her tone.

'I'm sorry if my use of the term bait seemed insensitive. Whilst we're never going to be buddies, I don't want to see any harm come to you Lara, or Dr Andrews. I'd want a full protection detail here. Protection for both of you, but hey it's not my call, this is Marlin's case. I'm just suggesting.'

'Can I make a suggestion Detective?' Lara was anything but placated. 'Why don't you just…,'

'Lara! Enough.' Al was well aware where the conversation was going. 'Why don't you run yourself a hot bath and try to relax a little bit?'

'If that's ok with my great protector here? Am I free to have a bath, Miss Detective?'

Sue rolled her eyes 'Do what you want Lara,' she sighed and picked up her bag. 'I'm going to leave you to it Marlin. See you in the office.'

Marlin stood and smiled at Sue. 'Yeah, I'll see you and I do appreciate the input.' He noted her weak smile in response and walked her to the door. Closing the door she turned and held it ajar, leaning in to Marlin and taking him by surprise.

'Good luck with that Marlin, but let me tell you, I don't trust the Doctor and that girl.' With that she turned and left, waving to the PC to make a space for her car.

Marlin returned to the living room wishing he had left with Sue but feeling that he should say something to the Doc. Al was in the middle of the room looking at him solemnly, a protective arm around Lara.

'We don't like her Marlin, no matter how much you do.'

'What?'

'It's pretty obvious Marlin, even Lara noticed.' Lara nodded and then added in a babyish voice, 'Even little Lara noticed.' She smiled but Marlin was uncomfortable, as it seemed more mocking than playful.

'She's just a colleague.'

'Take it easy Marlin; she's a very good looking woman. I'd give you my wholehearted approval to go for it if she wasn't trying to pin three murders on me,' Al shrugged, a wry grin on his lips, and Lara playfully smacked his bottom. 'Don't you be calling *her* good looking Al!'

Al laughed. 'Ok, ok Lara, I promise.' Seeing that Marlin was embarrassed and irritated Al stopped smiling. 'Sorry Marlin, I'm just joking.' Then he turned to Lara. 'See what you've done, he won't do you that favour now.'

'What favour?' Marlin was only too happy to join in with a change of subject. Lara put on her best demure look and fluttered her eyelashes at Marlin.

'I need to get some supplies and I wondered if you could drop me to the shop and back?'

'Do you realise I left the office on the basis that I was attending an emergency call? It was not expected that I'd be rushing to Tesco. Oh what the hell, come on let's go.' Marlin picked up his jacket and gestured towards the door whilst glowering at Al, his mood not improved as Al simply shrugged, his hands outstretched.

The car journey was a fairly short one and Marlin and Lara didn't talk on the way there. She was in the shop for little more than ten minutes, but she emerged with three full carriers. Sitting back in the car the clinking gave a good clue as to the majority of the contents. Marlin sighed heavily.

'I should have known.'

'You should cut Al some slack, Mr Marlin. After all, he's just received a death threat and that bloody woman was doing everything she could to humiliate him.'

'And that's your job, no?'

'What's your problem? For one thing it's none of your business and secondly no. Jesus, I thought you were his friend.'

'I'm sorry.'

'You fucking should be. He's a good man and he's really fucking scared.'

'It's been a bad day, Lara and really, I'm sorry.'

The journey continued in silence and Marlin felt somewhat sheepish as he came back into the house.

Al sat alone, staring at the screen in front of him, sipping gently and trying to remain as calm as possible; ignoring the deafening silence that served to amplify his anxiety. Slowing his breathing deliberately he waited for his heart to slow. He tried to will the tension from his body and focus his mind on anything but the frightening dark shadows of his house. I don't believe in ghosts but I'm afraid of phantoms? He smiled to himself as he reflected that the comment would fit well into his book - if only he lived to write it. He scanned the words again.

'Come on, Al, you're a professional, look beyond the message and into the words; what are they telling you? Why so keen to kill you? How long has he been watching you? Think Al, think.'

The rattle of key in lock took Al by surprise and he instinctively felt around the chair for something to use as a weapon. The chain! He realised that he'd not attached it when they left. He stood quickly, almost falling forward as the door swung open and the hall was illuminated. Lara strode into the living room, sombre and intense. She was followed by Marlin who looked ill at ease and uncertain as he went to speak; then shrugging he removed his coat and sat in front of the laptop. Lara had picked up Al's glass and was opening the new bottle in the kitchen, wordless and concentrated.

Having kicked off her heels Lara returned with two glasses and Al was both pleased and surprised at the more than generous measure she had poured them both. She kissed Al gently as she handed him the scotch and then stepped towards the door.

'I'm going for my bath now.'

'Ok, Lara. Are you ok?' Al's words were wasted as Lara was already half way up the stairs, glass in hand. He looked at Marlin staring at the screen.

'What the hell happened with you two?'

'She thinks that maybe I'm giving you a hard time?'

'Really? And what did you say to give her that impression?'

'I may have commented on the liquid nature of your grocery shopping. Do you ever eat, Al? Solids I mean?'

'It's been known to happen. Look, don't worry Marlin she'll come round, but you have to remember that this has been a fucking dreadful week for her as well. The Alice girl might not have been a close friend, but she knew her and she was killed in her flat.'

'Yeah, ok Al. Are you ok?'

'Honestly? No, I don't think I am really. This Phantom fucking psycho has got me really scared; I mean I almost had a heart attack when you put the key in the door and I'm now literally terrified of the dark. I can't get inside his head to the extent I should be able to.'

'Should you always be able to?'

'I think so. It's my job to do so, but this guy is a chameleon. I get some sort of idea about him and he changes.' Al then laughed gently. 'If I do stay alive, I must admit he'll make a hell of a book.'

'Don't worry, you'll write that book Doc, and if the Phantom doesn't want to be credited in the front cover, you can put my name.' Marlin smiled and checked his watch. 'I'll have to get back to the office Doc, but one thought.'

'Go ahead, any insight would help.'

'This Phantom reads all of your books? And those of Prof. Peters and God knows who else?'

'Yes… and?'

'Well if he's as bright as you say he might be, then he'll know what you are looking for, or what you would normally look for. He's basically getting inside your head, studying you. No?'

'Jesus, Marlin!'

'Sorry Doc, it was just something that I'd thought, I'm no psychologist or anything.'

'No, no, Marlin I wasn't criticising, I think it is fucking genius. You're totally right. That's what I was missing. He reads me, he's certainly watched me, and he's even critiqued me. He's not a chameleon by nature but by design. I wrote about distinct types and he's saying that he can be all of them and none of them. There I was, desperately trying to see what made him unique and he's nothing more than a student of the genre.' Al lurched forwards and awkwardly hugged Marlin.

'Brilliant, Marlin, brilliant and thanks.'

'You're welcome Doc, now can you let go, you are squeezing the life out of me. I really need to go.'

'Marlin, one last question before you go?'

'Shoot…,'

'Did you try to trace where the e-mail came from?'

'Would it comfort you to know that it was in the London area?'

'Nothing more specific?'

'Not yet, Doc. Forward the e-mail to me and I'll see what the tech guys can do.'

'Thanks.'

Marlin pulled on his jacket and wished he could go home and sleep, but he was aware of work beckoning and knew Thomas would have to be told of the new message. Wearily he left.

Al did his best to relax as he contemplated the nature of the beast that threatened him. It hurt his professional pride that Marlin had uncovered the truth of the Phantom's nature, but at least it was revealed now and progress had been made. He wasn't safer as a result, but neither was he entirely clueless; or alone he thought as Lara walked into the room.

Swallowed almost whole by the oversized white towel robe, she had folded back the sleeves enough to carry her glass but the belt was twice wrapped and bowed tightly to hold the folds in place. Sombre and serious as she tried to be, Al had to smile at her, looking like a little girl playing dress-up. Lara saw his grin and the sulk was now emphasised by her pout as she sat across from him.

'I don't see what you've got to be so happy about?'

'Your impression of a 7 year-old drowning in towelling maybe?'

'Very funny. It's nothing to be proud of, fitting into all this snugly.'

'Are you saying I'm fat?'

'Well, you're not Slimmer of the Year are you?'

'Thanks, Lara, and what've I done to irk you so much?'

'It's not you, it's that bloody woman.'

'Detective Scott?'

'Who else? She thinks she's so much better than everyone else, the stuck-up bitch.'

'What did she say to you?'

'You heard most of it.'

'Yes, but not all of it.'

'How long have I known you? Did you see other girls like me? Did you hit me?'

'In short am I a killer? You're right, she is a fucking bitch.'

'Al?' Lara hesitated, uncertain how to go on or even why she was asking.

'What?'

'Do you see other girls?'

'Would it bother you if I did?'

Lara tilted her head and smiled across at Al. 'Just tell me Al, do you pay other girls?'

'Lara, I am 51 years old, overweight and I drink about my weight in whiskey every day. It is a miracle that you don't give me a heart attack every time you cross your legs, never mind looking elsewhere. So no Lara, there aren't other girls, there is you. Just Lara.'

Lara smiled and snuggled deeper in to her towelling retreat. 'I'm glad, Al.'

'Oh, and Lara?'

'Yes?'

'Cut Marlin some slack, he means well you know.'

'Yeah I suppose so, but he's always going on about your drinking and he's always looking at me.'

'Check the mirror Lara, you're more than worthy of a second glance.' Al smiled broadly and filled their glasses; then raising his aloft he announced grandly: 'To the lovely Lara. To you, my dear.'

Lara took her drink and nodded her appreciation as she sipped lightly. Al's measure was dispatched and he filled it anew as the troubles of his day floated away on a tide of scotch.

Returning to the office Marlin was aware of eyes following him to his desk. As he placed his jacket over the back of his chair he saw Mitchell and Carr moving quickly towards him. Impatient as they both were, Carr spoke first.

'We found the man that spent the night with Gillian Watson, or rather he found us. He saw the newspaper stories and was terrified that we'd think he was the Phantom. He has alibis for most of the other murders, although he's quite keen that we don't check too closely, as his alibi is often his wife.'

'Ha, good work. This sort of good news I didn't expect at all.'

'There's more, sir.' Mitchell took his chance to speak. 'I did as you said and checked the CCTV on the streets. There's a guy in a black-hooded top with a black VW. He only picks up one couple and I would swear it is Gillian and our man.'

'Right I want to see the film and I want an address for the man...er...,'

'John Sutton.' Carr spoke eagerly.

'Great work, guys. How did we miss the CCTV the first time?'

Mitchell smiled. 'The guys checked all of the street cameras and they were right to say that he wasn't on them. He'd picked his spot well, but missed the camera on the warehouse over the road. It does them little or no good as it's come loose, but helpfully it now points out onto the road at the junction. You said to look for any CCTV and it got me thinking. I got lucky.'

'Again, good work guys and to be honest we needed some luck.' Marlin checked his watch. 'It's getting on a bit so give me Mr Sutton's address.'

'Here's his work address, he asked if we could see him there if possible.' Carr held out the page from his note-pad, a wry smile on his lips.

'I bet he did. Ok I'll start with this.' Grabbing his jacket he headed for his car.

Pulling up in the car Marlin looked across at the bright, red-framed window of Bearlake Properties, a typically characterless estate agent that was perfectly in keeping with the others in the area. As he entered the office he was aware of the eyes assessing him, his suit and tie, his worth, and he smiled as he saw their disappointment; they would be making no jackpot commissions today. The three women returned to their computers and Marlin was about to make enquiries when he appeared from the back room coffee in hand. Smart and confident, bordering on arrogant, about forty three or four years old; it had to be.

'John Sutton?'

The man looked at Marlin with a fake smile and judgemental eyes.

'I'm John Sutton, how can I help you?'

'DCI Marlin.' He held up his id, looking with interest as Sutton's smile froze and his eyes signalled panic. Marlin could almost hear the cogs and wheels whirring in his brain as he placed the coffee down and grabbed for his jacket.

'Ah yes, Mr Marlin, I have just what you are looking for. Please come with me.' Scared and suspicious, he ushered Marlin out of the office and into the street.

'You don't mind chatting as we walk out here Mr Marlin?'

'DCI. And no, walking is fine. I guess having police in the office is not good for your reputation?'

There was a brief flash of anger in Sutton's eyes as he looked across, but it quickly vanished. 'No, I don't think it's good for anybody. Police are rarely welcome, are they?'

'I suppose not. Would you prefer me to call in at your home later?'

Again the panic returned. 'No! God, no. Look I'm sorry DCI, how can I help you?'

'Gillian Watson, you went home with her after a night in the Starz club?'

'I only knew her as Jill, but yes.'

'Why didn't you tell us sooner?'

'At first I didn't think Gillian was Jill. Then I was scared that you would think I was some sort of psycho. It's scary, all of this, you know.'

'Even scarier if your wife found out?'

'Ok, yes, I was worried about that as well.'

'Right, well tell me about the night.'

'I told the other officer.'

'That's good. Now tell me.'

Sutton sighed deeply. 'We met up in Starz. We were both a bit pissed and had a few shots and a dance. She snogged me and asked about getting out of there and, once I knew she had a place of her own, we got going.'

'You caught a cab?'

'Yeah, you know they're always touting down the road there. You usually don't have to wait too long.'

'What do you remember about the guy who picked you up?'

'It's strange, but until the other cop asked me I'd almost forgotten about the driver. He was odd. If it wasn't for the fact that I was well into the girl, I wouldn't have gotten into the car.'

'Odd how?'

'Well, apart from the fact he was in a black hoodie and mumbling, it was the eyes. They were almost black and they seemed to look straight through you. I couldn't wait to get out of there.'

'Do you remember what sort of car it was?'

'Be serious, I was hammered and otherwise engaged.'

'Go on.'

'Well, he got us to her flat in Mile End and one thing led to another, you know? Afterwards she fell asleep, but I knew I had to get home, so I left. I managed to get a black cab near the station and that was that really.'

'Ok thanks, just one more thing. Do you think you would recognise the man again if you saw him?'

'His face was all but covered, but those eyes I'd recognise.'

'Ok, that should do. Don't go disappearing; I may need to talk to you again.'

'The office, come to the office. And maybe phone? Yeah?'

'Yeah, maybe.'

A PROBLEM

Marlin could only wish for an end to a very long day. He sat at his desk staring forward into his screen with no focus or attention other than on keeping his eyes open.

'Marlin?'

Pulled suddenly back to reality, Marlin looked around, clearly startled to see Sue Scott.

'Sorry, I didn't mean to give you a heart attack.'

'Sue, oh er, it's ok I was just miles away.'

'So I saw. Could I have a quick word or two?'

'Yeah sure, I was thinking about calling it a day anyway. I'm getting nothing done here.'

Sue checked her watch and then, eyebrows pulled low, she moved her head from side to side, weighing up her thoughts.

'If you're finishing here do you fancy popping into the Crown for a drink? We could discuss things there if you want?'

Marlin had prepared himself for the journey home and the question took him by complete surprise.

'The Crown? Now?'

'It was just a thought Marlin, it doesn't matter.'

'No Sue, I'd love to grab a drink with you.' As soon as he said it Marlin wanted to dig a hole for himself and disappear. 'I mean a drink would be good.' He was now blushing, his cheeks hot. Good work Marlin, you idiot. Sue noticed his embarrassment and smiled but didn't dwell on his discomfort.

'Ok, I'll get my coat while you finish off here.'

'Yeah, give me five minutes Sue.' As she turned and moved away he breathed heavily as he cursed himself and yet he felt good that he was going for a drink with her. Quickly saving the document he had avoided working on for quite some time, Marlin closed down his computer and reached for his jacket and cigarettes. He walked towards the exit and, at the door, signalled over to Sue that he would wait outside; she was on the phone but acknowledged his gesture.

Outside he lit up and inhaled deeply, hoping that he was drawing in some sense of calm as he leaned into the breeze to wake himself up fully. Sue appeared through the main doors and pulled up her collar against the cold as she searched for Marlin, finally seeing him loitering by the corner wall, pacing as he smoked. Catching sight of her, Marlin smiled and came forwards throwing away the remains of the cigarette.

'You don't have to finish that quickly on my account.'

'It was all but finished.'

'Ok, shall we leave the cars here and walk? It's only five minutes down the road.'

'Yeah sure, come on, you look freezing.'

'I am, Marlin.'

They walked quickly and in silence along the familiar route to *the Crown*, appreciating the warmth as they stepped inside. Sue went up to the bar and ordered the drinks. Sitting in the corner, Marlin tried to remember the last time he had been in the 'coppers' pub. The cleanliness of the red carpet and relative whiteness of the walls certainly showed at least one redecoration in the intervening years.

'A pint and a shot, very old fashioned Marlin.'

'You got the same.'

'I'm easily influenced and it sounded good. I feel like a traditional TV cop now. Apart from the female bit of course.'

Marlin smiled, surprised by how relaxed Sue was, although his nerves were far from gone. He drank two generous gulps from his pint and, wiping his mouth, chased it with the scotch.

'Quite the conversationalists aren't you Marlin?'

'Sorry, it's been a while since I came here or did this.'

'What? Had a drink?'

'No, not that. I mean it's been a while since…er…well socially at least… ,'

'Don't worry Marlin, I'm teasing you.'

Again he smiled as his cheeks reddened and he wondered if he should raise the white flag and leave. He resolved to pull himself together.

'I've not been out socially for a while and not in this pub for a long time now. I was just taking it all in really. But thanks for the invite; I'm really glad you asked.' With that Marlin raised his shot and they touched glasses.

'So you know I didn't ask you here just to talk about the case?'

'I hoped it was more than that.'

'I do need a word but it seemed a good way to get you out. I was pretty sure you weren't going to get round to asking me.' Sue smiled broadly as she brought her drink to her lips and again Marlin blushed, although this time it was accompanied by a shrug of the shoulders and a smile of his own.

'I've thought about it enough times, but I was working the long game.'

'Some long game, Marlin. As I'm not getting any younger, I thought it was probably a good idea to shorten it.'

Marlin held up his hands as he raised his eyebrows. 'Fair enough, Sue. Fair enough.' He caught her eye as he spoke and they maintained the look for the extra second, smiling as they returned to their drinks. Marlin rose and moved towards the bar. 'Same again, Dixon of Dock Green?'

'That's the TV cop you see me as? Thanks Marlin, yes I need a drink now.' She was laughing freely and, relaxed like this, she was transformed and even more attractive to him. He got the drinks and sat down, a more serious look on his face.

'Shall we get the shop talk out of the way?'

'Yes, lets.'

'So what was it you wanted to say?'

Sue cleared her throat and a serious look came over her again, thoughtful and business-like.

'I'm sorry if I allowed my irritation to show when I talked to Andrews and the girl, but as I said, there's something not right there.'

'Why so irritated?'

A brief laugh escaped from her lips. 'Why so irritated? Well this case comes my way and, although there are a million fingerprints at every scene, it would seem that it's three murders by the same person.'

'Why?'

'All prostitutes, all in two weeks, and all with a message left for starters. But anyway, I know you're working with this hot-shot psychologist, so it seems logical for me to pick his brain about who the killer might be. Then he turns out to be a major suspect.'

'Ok now, first of all you said 'for starters' and then you said he is a 'major suspect'. How can he be a major suspect when his prints are easily explained?'

Sue took her shot and drained the glass, savouring the warm burn as she composed her thoughts.

'Ok, I'll explain. I said 'for starters' because they're all prostitutes, all killed in the last two weeks and all with a message written. But also, they were all either specialists of, or participating in, various degrees of S&M play. As for the 'major suspect' part ...well, here is where I have a problem.'

'Go on.'

'The phone call I had before we left confirmed the details from the other two girls' flats. Dr Andrews's fingerprints are all over them both.'

Marlin swallowed hard but stayed silent as he tried to process this information. He picked up his drink and drained the glass as his other hand searched automatically for his cigarettes. He pulled them from his pocket and placed them on the table, sighing heavily. Sue looked across, watching his face for clues.

'You're going for a smoke? Can I have one of those?'

Marlin was woken again. 'Yeah, of course Sue. Will the drinks be alright?'

'In this place?' she laughed, shaking her head. 'Come on Marlin.'

Standing close outside they shivered as they smoked, but Marlin stayed silent, obviously in deep thought.

'A penny, Marlin?'

'I'm sorry Sue; I'm just trying to take it all in. You're saying that he definitely has his prints at the other two crime scenes?'

'As I say, the lab confirmed it today. Look, I'm not going after Andrews for any personal reasons, although I have to tell you that I don't really like him or his lifestyle. I'm going with this because the evidence demands it.'

'Sue, I've never thought this was personal, even though I suspected that you were less than enamoured with Dr Andrews. I also understand how bad this looks, but I just can't see him as a killer.'

'I find it hard to believe he is a doctor of something.' Sue smiled and did her best to catch Marlin's eye. The hard part of talking about Andrews had gone surprisingly well, even if Marlin looked disturbed by it all, and now she felt it was time to go back to more personal matters. Putting out her cigarette she rubbed her hands together quickly and then took hold of his arm.

'Come on Marlin, shop talk's over, let's get a drink.'

Marlin smiled as he allowed Sue to lead him back into the pub, but his mind was racing. Should he act as a policeman or a friend? Was he really Al's friend? After what Lara had said to him, did he owe Al something? He sat back at the table and drank deeply. Sue checked the diminishing alcohol and reached for her purse.

'I'm going to pop to the loo, but I'll get another couple of drinks on the way back ok? Same again?'

'Yes please, thanks Sue.' Marlin watched Sue as she made her way across the bar with no little interest, but his hand was already reaching for his phone.

POKER FACES

Al was all smiles as Lara led him up the stairs, her voice full of pantomime threats and giggled stern promises, a hand reaching back and roaming so that she felt the vibration of his phone.

'I've never had that effect on you before,' she laughed. 'You'd better not answer it Al.'

'Sorry Lara, I have to check the message, but then I'm all yours. Honestly.'

Lara tutted slowly and loudly. 'You know not to upset Lara don't you? I don't know.'

'I'll be quick, I promise.' Al followed Lara into the bedroom and took out his phone as she tapped her foot dramatically; hand on hip, her face a picture of concentrated seriousness.

'Oh come on, Lara, I feel like I'm being menaced by a bath-towel.' Al smiled as she struggled to maintain her poker-faced 'role' and he quickly glanced at his phone message.

Al can't talk now but need to see you tomorrow. They have your prints at the other two crime scenes. Marlin.

Lara looked as all humour drained from Al's face. 'Who is it? Is it bad news? Are you ok, Al?'

Al clicked his phone shut and looked up, a smile returning to his face. 'It was nothing, just Marlin checking that everything's ok. Should I tell him I'm at the mercy of Mistress Terrycloth?' He smiled broadly now as Lara laughed and surrendered himself into her hands; keeping his thoughts to himself.

*

Marlin woke feeling warm and dehydrated, the thickness of the duvet an extra confusing factor that his brain could not yet compute. He opened his eyes and, in the half-light of the morning, contemplated the white patterned ceiling that was decorative but certainly not his. Inching his hand slowly to his left he felt naked warm flesh. The tingle of sweet memory returned as Sue murmured a quiet word from her dreams and shifted slightly. Reaching over to his right he found his watch and checked the time - 6.45am. Not too bad he thought as he felt his erection pressing hard, his bladder as good as any alarm clock. Slowly and gently he slipped from the bed and found the door, managing to stifle a groan as he stood on the clasp from her bra.

Having found the bathroom and eased his discomfiture, Marlin washed his hands and then looked into the mirror; all tousled hair and tired puffy eyes, as he traced his hand across his jaw-line. Stopping, he smiled a broad smile that originated in his eyes and spoke volumes about genuine pleasure, a pleasure he had all but forgotten. He returned to the room, watching his step, and slipped beneath the warm sheets gently. Sue turned, half-asleep, and draped her arm across his chest as her earnest dream conversation continued. Marlin replayed the joys of the previous evening as he sheltered under her touch and, smiling gently, he fell asleep again.

*

It was a cold morning and a light mist hung over the damp street like a veil, the early morning silence broken only by birdsong and distant traffic. Outside the old Victorian house on Albert Road, a young PC was dozing, unable to keep his eyes open as the car heater and the unremitting boredom combined as a powerful sedative. The man sat in his car at a distance from the house, a canopy of trees for cover and as far from street light as he could manage. The foliage created a darkness that gave the impression of an empty car, whilst the stillness of the man within gave no reason to question this assumption.

He gazed from the car to the house and back again, as if measuring each inch. Peering out from within his tightly drawn hood, his eyes alive in contrast to his sombre still face. He had seen the cars come and go, noting every move. Policeman; Policewoman; girl; drink for the Doctor, always drink. The time for watching was drawing to a close; it was time for a message to be sent, time for his presence to be felt. The endgame was approaching and he had to sow the seeds of fear anew.

Opening the car door slowly, deliberately, he slid out into the shadows; a black on black figure invisible to the eye, save for a small white card attached to the black box he carried. Crossing the road into the streetlight glow, he kept close to the wall as he moved fluidly across the pavement until he reached number 32. In one leap he cleared the four foot wall and passed quickly across the front of the drive, past the policeman's sleeping gaze, until he reached the door. Unable to help himself he placed his ear to the door, closing his eyes at the feeling of the cold wood against his cheek. So close, so tempting, he could taste blood on his tongue. You will be mine; mine when the hour is right, and your sleep will be eternal.

Placing the box on the ground, he balanced the card deliberately. Standing briefly, he quickly checked the lock of the door - standard Yale he noted - before crouching again as he moved quickly to the wall and over. Back to the car, back to the shadows. Still again, he sat impassively, his mind drawing maps and plotting plans of action. The lock would be easy, but he had observed the chain was often on and it was in full view of the police car; he couldn't depend on the policeman being asleep. He would have to check the back of the house again. He had tried to look properly some days ago, getting into the back garden, but he was not alone in looking for alternative paths. Disturbed by a news reporter, trying and failing to get in via the neighbours garden wall, he had fled.

Weighing up the options the back route seemed best but he needed to be sure. He reached into the back seat and picked up a small pair of black binoculars. Looking across, the policeman was asleep, his head touching the window so that his breath fogged the glass. The man put the binoculars back on the seat and picked up a small cylindrical torch as he once again squeezed out of the car door. As it clicked gently shut, he moved at pace towards the house to the right of Dr Andrews.

In seconds he was over the wall and gliding down the side of the house, a narrow alleyway all enveloping in its blackness. Once in the rear of the building he slowed his pace and once again hugged the shape of the house. Carefully he passed across the walls and in front of the large bay windows, until he was at the dividing wall. Reaching on tiptoe, he balanced on a stone in the flowerbed, careful not to leave a footprint and used his strength to pull himself up and over onto the other side. It may only have been some sort of reconnaissance, a dress rehearsal, but the man's pulse was racing. Why could the time not be now? Why would there not be blood tonight? Again he forced himself to focus and accept that his destiny would be written another day.

Crouching in the darkness, he looked at the imprint in the flowerbed and, stepping forwards onto the grass, he smoothed it away carefully. Suddenly he was bathed in light as the automatic sensor caught his movement and he froze instinctively. Calmly taking in the illuminated surroundings, he was careful to note the Chubb lock. Looking up to the windows above there was no movement or light, but he was not prepared to take any chances; he'd set off the lights and was angry at having done so. He hadn't been thorough enough in his planning, but post-mortems were for later and the instinct of self-preservation was pumping potent adrenaline through his system. He leapt like some dark feral beast, up and over the wall, sprinting as he landed and moving rapidly along the house and through the alleyway. The smaller front wall was vaulted easily and the man landed in a half crouch as he sped across the road. Once beneath the dark canopy calmness reigned once more. Breathing slowly, he was careful and silent as he slid back into the car.

The policeman had grunted himself awake against the now warm window, and had to shake his head to be fully awake, annoyed at his lapse. As he stretched his neck a shadow traced across his peripheral vision and he felt sure he had seen a fox run across the road. Better a fox than a man or the DCI, he thought, as he cracked open the window just enough to let some of the cold air in. First light was in the sky above the mist and he hoped it would chase away the cold.

The man turned on the engine of his car, ensuring the lights were turned off and slowly reversed down the road under the tree cover. When he was a few hundred yards down he stopped and turned the car using a driveway opposite. Now flicking the lights into life he moved away angry but exhilarated. He calmed his mind as he travelled, trying to take the positives from the day and night. His gift was safely delivered and he had the knowledge he needed for the locks on both doors. The wall was easily scaled and access to it was not too difficult. The downside was the light and he again chided himself for not noticing or looking more closely. He would need to be prepared and quick once at the door; so practise would begin tomorrow until his fingers were as quick as his mind; plans made until his mind was as sharp as his knife. The blood-lust was strong but he had let himself down. He had wished that tomorrow was today, tried to skip pages to get to the end. He had to concentrate and trust in his story, each and every word. He pressed down hard on the accelerator as he felt his frustration surface and, face screwed tight and ugly, he screamed fiercely into the night.

*

Al woke in the night, startled by the violence of his own snoring, and glanced across at Lara sleeping soundly beside him. He could taste the sour whiskey on his breath and his head was gently throbbing, but there was no hangover yet. Stretching, he half-smiled as he felt the lines of the evening's play still tender and warm on his skin. He reached to the bedside table; taking a sip of whiskey from his nightstand glass, enjoying the comforting familiarity of the glow it gave him.

Lying back in a half-drunken repose his mind went back to the message from Marlin. He felt an anxiety about the situation again as he looked over at Lara, a silent silhouette beside him. He would have to make sure he spoke to Marlin when Lara was not around, the whole 'only you Lara' speech would look pretty stupid otherwise. The reality of his travels in the world of sexual commerce was that he had few barriers or loyalties, even if he was somewhat less prolific than in his younger years. He wondered how many places they would find his fingerprints if they scoured London? That however was not the problem, nor was Lara's ire except to him, no the problem was that his prints were found at scenes of murders. Three murders in fact. He had the feeling that Detective Scott was highly unlikely to think that this was coincidental.

Leaning up on one arm, Al squinted in the dark at his glass, pleased to see that there was still some remaining as he brought it to his lips again. What to do then? What to say? He was a bloody psychologist so come on Al, get that addled brain working.

Sipping in the dark he ran through some elements for consideration, as if playing to the gallery in a courtroom, although the nature of this analogy scared him more than a little. Ok, firstly he was clearly not alone in seeing these girls, so what were the chances of there being at least one other person who could be placed at all three scenes? Secondly, and he supposed most simply, was to verify that he was not there at the appointed times. Here he struggled as he could not clearly remember the times or even the days of the killings. His mind had been elsewhere and, even if he could remember, the chances were that he could only say that he was home alone; unconscious and alone. Thirdly would therefore be to reverse matters. So could he remember when he saw the other girls and explain how his prints got there? Here he was stumped because he hadn't asked for names, or if he did he couldn't remember. The fourth pointer was the messages, and the question would be what the hell did they have to do with him? As an eminent psychologist surely he'd have come up with something better than the inanities served up by the killer so far? With that in mind, it occurred to him that he'd not been told what the third message was? He would have to make sure he asked.

Finishing the glass Al lay back, far from comforted by his defence, and thanked heavens he could not be on his own jury. It was then that a thought hit him and it made him sit upright, half waking Lara.

'Are you alright, Al?' she croaked, half turned towards him.

'Go back to sleep Lara, I just need to get a glass of water.'

Al stood as Lara turned away again, breathing deeply as she descended back into sleep. He felt around for the dressing gown and, as he pulled it on and tied the cord, he was pleased that it smelled of Lara's perfume. Walking into the hallway rubbing his eyes, Al thought that he saw the outside light click off and he moved slowly to the window, peering beyond the white lace curtain. As his eyes adjusted in the dark, Al saw nothing and thought of nothing more than hungry cats and desperate foxes. He went into the bathroom and then padded slowly downstairs into the living room. Here he put on a small table lamp and poured himself a drink; grimacing slightly as sore skin rubbed on weary bones, he sat and breathed deeply as he flicked on the laptop.

Scanning his e-mail he found the Phantom's message and read it over twice and then a third time. Taking a piece of paper from the table he picked up a pen and wrote an excerpt,

'noticed how much time you were spending inside that fine house of yours, curtains drawn all day and not even a visit to the off license? But I needn't have worried as you were back to your whoring and drinking in no time at all. Out all night and ordering in during the day you really are a dirty drunken dog'

If he was a long term target of this Phantom, then what if he had been watching everywhere he went? Going everywhere he went for some time. What if he had brought the Phantom to the girls? Was it such a stretch of the imagination to think that he would then kill them? Al relaxed back into his seat and then reached across to the board, picking up the cards for the two prostitutes killed before the unfortunate Alice. For his own peace of mind he wanted to show where he was.

*

DAY: Wednesday

NAME: u/ kn
PLACE: Oxford Circus
FEATURES: Prostitute, strangled - a message (so seems a different killer) 'Are you satisfied now?'

*

DAY: Wednesday
NAME: u/ kn
PLACE: Old Street
FEATURES: Prostitute, strangled - a message 'Now you are fucked'

*

Al studied the cards carefully, but this time there was no revelatory moment. Yawning, he knew that inspiration was unlikely a second time, as once again he felt that fatigue and alcohol were upon him. Draining his glass he pulled himself up and made his way to bed.

SLEEPLESS NIGHTS

Marlin sat at his desk looking from his trays of paper to his screen and back again, seeing nothing and mind a million miles away, as naked snapshots filled his head and warmed his soul. He felt like he was a teenager exchanging smiles and glances as he went for yet another cigarette; and whilst Sue was reacting in a completely professional manner, he still read the arched eyebrows and lip curls that were his response. He had been surprised at the tenderness of their waking, the lack of awkwardness in the situation. Sharing a taxi she had held his hand and kissed him with passion when he was dropped off some way from the office. 'I'm certainly not ashamed, but no need to advertise,' she'd said.

Marlin agreed, but he couldn't wait to see her again, though he really should get some work done in the meantime. He checked his watch and as it was approaching lunchtime he decided to grab a bite, then have the talk with the Doc he had been putting off. Picking up his jacket, he loitered by the door pretending to look for his keys, until he caught her eye, smiling as she looked. Sue glanced for a moment, impassively, and then returned to her paperwork, a small smile playing on her lips; Marlin walked out on air.

Thirty two Albert Road had occasional traffic, but it was generally quiet and the lack of noise always made Marlin feel that he was in the country. As he stepped from his car, he gestured a thank you to the PC for making space and breathed in the cold air deeply as he stretched, appreciating the sharpness. Stepping to the door he saw the long black box and white card at his feet. Bending down to look closer the door opened and Al emerged, peering down at him.

'Marlin? What are you doing down there?'

'Checking this out.' Marlin carefully moved the box in his hands, studying it closely.

'What is it?' Al squinted to focus. 'Oh, a bottle of J&B. You really shouldn't have.'

'I didn't.' Marlin was looking at the card, holding it by the corner. Then glancing over to the policeman in the car he gestured for him to come.

Al was getting irritated now. 'What is it, Marlin?'

Marlin read: *Dr Al, Have a drink on me. No tricks just a gift. See you soon. The Phantom.*

'Oh fuck. Where was that?'

Marlin was distracted by the PC. 'Sir?'

'Get some evidence bags and put this card and box in them, ok? Then call in and get someone here to pick it up for prints. This is urgent! Did you see anything?'

'No sir, I took over at 8.30am and there's been nothing.'

'Who was here last night?'

'Edwards, sir.'

'Ok, when you radio in tell them to get hold of Edwards and give me a call. And yes, I know he'll probably be sleeping.'

Marlin sighed and looked at the wide eyed and irritated Doc. 'Ok Doc, let's go inside.'

'He left that here? At my door? With a policeman supposedly on guard? Jesus Marlin, you said I'd be safe.'

'I'm sorry Doc, we'll look into what's happened and I'll see if we can't get another PC allocated here.'

'Brilliant, let's hope he is as good as the clown last night. My fucking doorstep Marlin. Jesus.' Al's voice was raised and more scared than truly angry. He went to speak again but thought better of it and reached for a glass. It was only now that Marlin saw Lara sitting quietly in the corner chair.

'Lara.'

'Marlin'

'Doc, I'm really pissed off about this situation myself, but I promise I'll get onto it. You have my word, ok? Look, I thought about getting you and Lara to a safe house, but on balance I thought you'd be happier here. I also thought you'd be safe, so long as the security was good enough. I'll make bloody sure it is from now on.'

'Ok, thanks Marlin. I do, or should I say I did, feel really safe here. Bait I may be but I don't intend to get eaten.'

'I understand Doc, really. Look can we talk?'

'Sit down. Drink?'

'No thanks Doc, some of us have to work.'

'I'll have yours then.' With that Al topped up his glass and offered the bottle to Lara, placing it back on the table as she shook her head. 'Lara, could you give us some time to talk over some business here?'

'Business? So you think it'll all be too complicated for little Lara? Don't let her worry her little head eh? Is that it?' Her anger was unchecked.

'No, no, Lara, it's not that at all. It's just that not all of this information is public knowledge; it's also none too pleasant.' Al knew at least the last part was true.

'Ok, I'll be upstairs if you have any parental guidance conversation.' Lara seemed less angry now but not particularly pleased, either, as she left.

'So Marlin, I get the feeling that I know where this conversation is headed?'

'You got my message?'

'Yup.'

'The prints Doc, the prints.' Marlin sounded wearied by the whole subject.

'Has Sue, I mean Detective Scott, spoken to you yet?'

'Sue, eh? No, Sue hasn't spoken to me yet.'

'She will do, but to satisfy my curiosity, what can you tell me?'

Al topped up his glass and sat back breathing heavily, his face solemn and slightly anxious.

'Look, I kind of told Lara that I only saw her these days, but in truth, there have been a few lapses on my part and I've looked elsewhere. Now before you ask, this is a handful of times recently but a lot over the years, so I don't know when the prints might have turned up. Do you have the names of the girls?'

'Not on me, no, but I can find out, although I doubt it would be the same as the names you were given.'

'You're probably right.'

'The second point is, where were you on the days and nights in question?'

'That I've looked at, and I'm afraid you won't like the answers.'

'Dead drunk, alone?'

'That's the truth of the matter.'

'I thought as much. That's brilliant, prints and no alibi.'

'I've thought about this though. Can you tell me what the third message was?'

'Again, I can find out. Jesus Doc, I can't believe I didn't ask about that myself.' Marlin spoke with a genuine surprise in his voice.

'It's not your case and you are not a major suspect, so I think you can cut yourself a little slack there.'

'Thanks Doc, I feel so much better now.' Marlin sarcastically tried to lighten the conversation, although in truth he was surprised how well the Doc was dealing with the new revelations - how calmly.

'Marlin, as I said I've given this some thought, especially because I've got no alibi as such.'

'Go ahead.'

'Firstly, the messages we have from the first two killings; I don't think that any psychologist would argue that they sound like me or something I would say. Secondly, and I think this is the angle to look at, we know that there's someone going where I go and it's someone with an interest in doing me harm.'

'The Phantom?'

'Come on Marlin, it makes sense.'

'Does it?' Marlin sat back and rubbed his eyes as he thought through the logic according to Doc Andrews, then took out his cigarettes and lit one as the Doc slid an ashtray in his direction.

'Alright Doc, let me talk this through. The Phantom has followed you and killed girls that you've seen?'

'Yes.'

'If I remember rightly, the first girl was killed almost a week before I spoke to you for the first time.'

'Yes.'

'So you're saying this whole thing, all the murders, is to do with you?'

'I think it's possible.'

'The days of the week and everything were to make sure the police went to you?'

'I know it sounds a bit OTT, but I've got to consider that may be the case now.'

'You do?'

'Now that I have prints at three crime scenes and no alibis I do.'

Again Marlin paused, smoking slowly to give himself time to pick his words carefully. It was a genuine relief when his phone rang.

'Marlin.'

'PC Edwards sir, you wanted to speak to me?'

'Ah, yes Edwards. Last night did you see anything outside the house?'

'Not really sir, but there was quite a mist last night, visibility wasn't good.'

'A mist? A mist so bad you couldn't see the front door?'

'No sir, but...,'

'But nothing, did you see anyone leaving a box and card at the front door?'

'No sir, I thought I saw a fox run across the road at one point, but that's all.'

'A fucking fox Edwards?'

'Yes sir, running across into the trees.'

'Nothing else?'

'No sir.'

Marlin was angry now as he paced the room.

'Did you fall asleep Edwards?'

There was a silence on the other end of the phone for some seconds. 'I don't think so sir.'

'I'll take that as a yes then.' Shaking his head Marlin moved across to the window and, parting the curtains, craned his neck to look off down the road towards the trees. 'Was there much traffic or any cars parked along the road?'

'I think there was a black VW under the trees.'

'A black VW, are you sure?'

'Yes sir, I'm pretty sure it was a black VW.'

'Was someone in it?'

'It was dark and empty.'

'Really Edwards? So was it dark and empty definitely or was it dark and looked empty? Oh, and was there a registration plate perhaps?' Marlin was almost shouting now.

'I don't know sir...I'm not sure... and I didn't check the plate.'

'Was it still there when you were relieved?'

'Oh...I don't know...I don't think so.'

'You don't know? Surely you know if you saw it leave or not?'

'I'm really sorry sir.'

'Fuck's sake Edwards, you are truly useless.' With that Marlin hung up, angry and frustrated. No wonder he preferred to work alone.

'Doc, I've got to go back to the office to sort this out, but I promise to make sure it's secure out there from now on. Oh and Doc, as far as your theory goes, I don't really buy it, and if I'm honest I don't think you do either.'

Al went to speak but fell silent, a look of dejection on his face. Marlin checked he had everything with him and went to the door, nodding at Al as he went.

'See you Marlin.'

Sitting with his drink, Al considered the conversation for some minutes. Eventually he reached forward, picking up his pen from the table and some paper. As he did so he saw the half-quote he had written the night before. His logic seemed less inspired and assured now, so he turned to the blank side and picked up the cards in front of him whilst checking the calendar on his laptop.

First prostitute 2nd February Wednesday - what did I do that day/ night??????????????

Second Prostitute 9th February Wednesday - what did I do that day/ night??????????

Third Prostitute 13th February Sunday - what did I do that day/ night??????????????

Putting things in black and white was an old psychological trick, but it wasn't easing Al's increasing feeling of angst in any way. He searched through e-mails and phone messages trying to piece together the hours and days of the recent past that could have such a resounding effect on his immediate future. Back to the black and white and he could feel the colour draining out of his world as he wrote;

First prostitute 2nd February Wednesday - what did I do that day/ night??????????????

Lost day - Blank

Second Prostitute 9th February Wednesday - what did I do that day/ night??????????

Lost day - Blank

Third Prostitute 13th February Sunday - what did I do that day/ night??????????????

Asleep but left house at some point to buy whiskey.

He thought back to his conversations with Marlin and looked again at the messages, making brief notes as he went until he slumped back, almost dizzy with fear.

'Marlin wasn't with me last Saturday night, he was here Friday night. FUCK!'

'What's the matter Al?'

Lara stood in the doorway looking concerned and Al tried to smile at her, in an effort to regain his composure. Dressed in a white blouse and black trousers, she was as casual as Al had ever seen her. With no make-up and her hair pulled back she looked so pretty, and yet so young and vulnerable.

'It's nothing Lara, I spilt my drink.'

'I should have known it would be whiskey related.'

'That and the latest message.'

'Message?'

'Oh, when Marlin got here there was a bottle of whiskey in a box and a message from the Phantom to me.'

'Jesus Al, what message?' Lara came over and sat next to Al, putting her arms around his neck. 'Please tell me, don't shut me out completely.'

'Marlin took it as evidence, but the gist of it was see you soon Dr Al, and I don't think he was thinking of sharing the bottle.'

'So where was this message and bottle?'

'Outside the front door.'

'For fuck's sake Al! What was that fucking cop doing? Al, this isn't good. It's not good at all. I thought we were going to be safe here?'

'Calm down, Marlin's sorting it.'

'He'd better do.'

'I trust him. Anyway, I'd rather be here in my own home than some anonymous hotel room they might find for us. Here… and with you.'

Lara leaned into Al and he could feel the dynamic change as he tried to comfort her, but it helped that he could think about her and not himself; it calmed him and the fact that it turned him on was a more than welcome distraction.

'What were you writing on the paper?' Lara's question startled Al.

'What do you mean?'

'The paper you put down when I came in. What was on it?'

'Oh, just some notes for Marlin.'

'Notes about what?'

'Just stuff.'

'Tell me what stuff, Al? I told you I don't want to be left out. We're in this together Al. Just think about it. If this Phantom did get in here do you think he'd let me go? A girl was just murdered in my flat so it's a bit late to protect me from the realities of life.'

'Don't think like that, ok?'

'It's true, so tell me what you were writing.'

Al wearily leaned over and picked up the paper he had placed at the side of the settee and handed it to Lara.

'I'm trying to get that policewoman off my back, but not doing too well as you can see. It's so fucking draining Lara, I'm the victim here. I'm the target.'

Lara looked at the notes and reached forward to the two cards on the table, reading each one carefully as she bit her lip, lost in thought. She spent time shuffling between the paper and cards for some time, occasionally glancing furtively up at Al. Eventually she spoke.

'Lost days? Blanks? What do you mean, exactly?'

Al was silent and he breathed deeply as he looked off into space.

'How do I put this? Let me think.'

'Don't think how to put things, just say it.'

'Ok, take last Wednesday there. What it means is that I had a good time on Tuesday night and had a few drinks. Then a few more. Suffice to say that I didn't wake up until Thursday and I don't have a clue what happened.'

'But you were here?'

'I think so.'

'Do you have these lost days a lot?'

'More than I'd like.'

'Have you ever gone out at these times?'

Al was feeling pressured by the constant questions now and his voice became steely, his mouth tight. 'Look I don't know. How is this helping? How?'

'Don't shout at me Al, I'm trying to help here.' She put her arm on his shoulder then leaned in and kissed him. 'Shhh, let me help you.'

'I'm sorry, go on.'

'Could you check your bank statements to see if you've spent money on any of these occasions?'

'I could.' Al could not hide his surprise at this idea. 'I will. Although,' Al opened his wallet to show the bulging billfolds. 'I like to have cash on me.'

'God's sake Al, there's banks that carry less.'

'Wait, I know. I went out on Sunday, see I wrote it down.'

'I thought you were unsure of the time, not that you went at all?'

'And...,'Al got excited and pulled the laptop closer. 'Friday!'

'Yes, Friday, what?'

'You came here.'

'I do remember that Al. It's not me that is suffering from blackouts.'

'No Lara, don't you remember? You told me I'd phoned on Wednesday?'

'Yes, well you did.'

'That was during a blank.'

'Really? You were dead drunk then?'

'Well obviously.'

'You sound drunker now.'

Al stopped and leaned back his head as he let this information sink in.

'I sounded sober?'

'As sober as you ever are. A bit louder and more serious is all.'

'Interesting.'

'Forget that Al, and listen to me.'

'Ok.'

'Where did you say you were that Wednesday night?'

'I told Marlin the truth. I was dead drunk.'

'What if you were dead drunk in my flat?'

'What do you mean?'

'You didn't ring to book with me; you were with me that night. Later I got you back in a taxi and then you passed out.'

'But...,'

'No but's Al, it's an alibi. I know you're not the killer and we both want rid of that fucking cop, no?'

'Well yes but...,'

'I told you no buts. Put that date in your head and no more blackouts. We get some proper protection here, Marlin catches the Phantom, and we get on with our lives free of the constant questions. Sound good?'

Al smiled a nervous smile 'Once again, I'm in your hands Lara.'

*

Detective Scott's visit was not long in coming, which almost suited Al as he didn't have too much time to think through Lara's plan of action; although he had made it clear that he wanted to do the talking. If at all possible, alone. Lara was happy enough at the prospect of avoiding the policewoman.

Sue Scott was tired and her day had been somewhat disorganised. In addition she was annoyed with herself that she hadn't made this visit first thing. She'd spoken to the policeman sitting on guard, her irritation only heightened as he confirmed that Marlin had called nearly an hour earlier. He'd every right to see Dr Andrews, but she knew that he'd have told him about the prints, so any attempt at springing a surprise was now gone. Still, as she sat in the living room watching Al pour a drink, she was determined to get some questions answered.

'Is Lara out?'

'No, she's upstairs.'

'Good, I may have a few questions for her.'

'I'm sure she'll be thrilled.'

Sue looked at Dr Andrews, her eyebrows raised, and it occurred to her that she might as well be talking to a child.

'Of course she will, almost as much as you.'

'I'm happy enough, really.' He drank a generous mouthful and smiled. 'How can I help you?'

'I take it that Marlin told you about the prints?'

'He did.'

Sue looked at her small notepad flicking back a couple of pages and coming back to a blank page. 'The matter of the fingerprints answers one of the questions you failed to answer last time due to the e-mail distraction. I wonder how you would've answered it then?'

'Without knowing anything about the girls it would've been difficult. I'm not proud of the fact, but I've done this sort of thing a hell of a lot.'

'You're a successful man; surely you can do better than prostitutes and mistresses?'

141

'Mistresses?'

'You don't go looking for some upmarket slap and tickle?'

'Oh, I see.'

'So surely you can engage in a relationship that's not paid for by the hour?'

'You'd think so, wouldn't you?'

Sue looked over at Al and her contempt was very thinly veiled, if at all. 'You're very glib about all of this Dr Andrews but, despite your assertion that you're not proud of this, I think you are far from ashamed.'

'Maybe I hide my feelings well?'

'Maybe. So explain to me what it's all about? Paying women to sleep with you. No, paying women to slap you about.'

'It's not so strange really; I bet you'd enjoy slapping me about right now if that look on your face is anything to go by.'

Sue looked at Dr Andrews, a taut mask hiding a real anger. Yes, she would like to slap him - she would like to beat him to a pulp.

'Wednesday 2nd February, Alison Davidson aka Mistress Scarlett, was strangled in the Oxford Circus area, sometime between 8 and 10 in the evening. Where were you at that time?'

Al, for the first time in the conversation, looked troubled and he took a drink and paused without answering.

'Dr Andrews?'

'Oh sorry Detective. I knew Mistress Scarlett. Alison. She was a really nice woman.'

'Where were you, Dr Andrews?'

'Here. Drunk, asleep, unconscious; some part of all three?'

'Alone?'

'Yes.'

'Wednesday 9th February, Sarah Locke aka Mistress Sarah, was strangled in the Old Street area around 11 at night; so again, where were you?'

'Jesus, Sarah as well? I thought she was getting out of the whole thing?'

'She's out of it now. Where were you?'

'That is cruel and needless, Detective Scott.'

'It wasn't my fingerprints found there. Where were you?'

'He was with me.' As Lara sauntered into the room, fully made up and dressed to kill, Al recognised that she was in character. From her heels to her eyelashes, she oozed the confidence and authority of her role.

'Lara, what timing. So he was with you? All night?'

'Most of it. He turned up drunk about 8.00pm. We played around into the early hours, and then I sent him home in a cab.'

'Did anyone see the two of you?'

'I tend to be discrete.'

'The cab? Which company?'

'I usually use City Cabs, so probably them.'

'I can check.'

'Go ahead.' Lara walked over to her bag and, taking out a pack of cigarettes, she lit up. It was now that Al realised that there were actual nerves behind the bluster.

'It was definitely that night?'

'I remember because we arranged to meet up again on the Friday.'

'Marlin didn't mention any of this, Dr Andrews.'

Al scratched his chin nervously, but Lara interceded.

'He didn't know.'

'What Lara?'

'Look he drinks too much, way too much, and then jumps in a cab to my place and drinks even more. I pour him into a cab late on and he wakes up on Thursday with the previous night a blank or blackout.'

'You said you played around.'

'Yes, as far as he could.'

'Four hours or so?'

'Hey, I was paid for my time, so if he wants to drink and touch and sleep, so what?'

Sue was making notes but she stopped and looked at the two of them, shaking her head slightly as she stood.

'Dr Andrews, how fortunate you are to have an alibi you didn't even know about yourself. Lara, I'll be checking out those cabs. I'll see myself out.'

Sue picked up her jacket and left without looking back, but the slam of the door gave away her feelings. In the living room it was a sound that allowed Al to breathe out deeply and fill his glass with a shaking hand.

'Lara?' She dragged on the end of her cigarette and nodded enthusiastically as she put it out.

'Yes, yes I need one, Christ.' As soon as the glass was poured she grabbed it and drank most of it in one gulp. Breathing in and out heavily, she waited for the alcohol to burn and then finished the glass, holding it out for a refill. She sipped this time and regained her composure, cocking her hip she smiled.

'God I was good, wasn't I Al?'

'You should be on the stage.'

'Maybe, but the bedroom pays better.'

'Jesus, Lara.'

'What Al?'

'Did we just do that?'

'Yes, we did.' She was grinning now and shaking her hips to an imaginary song. 'Yes we did.' She sang.

'But what about the cab?'

'I get cabs for people all the time, including that Wednesday.'

'But not for me.'

'Like the cabby will remember last week? I doubt it.' Lara danced on, a broad smile on her face.

Marlin had felt no affinity with Carr and Mitchell, no real connection but, as they sat in a small meeting room, he was glad of their involvement.

'So Carr, I saw the CCTV footage and I don't think there's any doubt that it's Gillian and Sutton with our man in black. What was it that you had to update?'

'Well sir, I took the plates and checked them against our records. It's no surprise really, but it was reported stolen two weeks ago, from a car park in Hammersmith. The owner checks out. But…,'

'But what?'

'We found the car near King's Cross, or at least a local bobby did.'

'We have it?'

'Blood stains and all, yes.'

'Prints?'

'Not so lucky there, sir.' Mitchell chipped in. 'But the blood is Professor Peters.'

'I take it you are doing a house to house in the area?'

'There are officers out there now.'

'Good, good.' Marlin was pleased but concerned about what this might mean. 'If he's left the car it's probably because of the blood. But that's a careless move for him. Too careless.'

'And why leave the car in the street?' Carr questioned.

'I don't think it matters to him. Whatever he's planning it can't be far away in time or distance. The car's unimportant to him, whether we found it or not.' Marlin looked away again as he spoke, trying to collect his thoughts. 'The box and card, did you get anything there?'

'No prints. He's not that careless unfortunately,' Mitchell smiled 'Also the e-mail trace hasn't yielded anything as yet, the guys think that he's moving around, but we'll keep going.'

'I thought as much. Did you speak to Thomas, sorry Chief Superintendent Thomas, about an extra guard on Dr Andrews's house?'

'Yes sir, he has given us permission for the short term.'

'Good, good. Ok, have a talk between the pair of you and choose a good man. Not bloody Edwards that's for sure.'

Carr again spoke. 'We have talked sir and we think Oliver would be ideal, along with McCarthy. We've spoken to them and they'll see out the nights with regular patrols out of the car. We think the days are less of a worry, but Ellis and Hill are keen officers and we think they'll do a good job. With your approval of course, sir.'

'That's really good work men, you certainly have my approval. Anything else?'

The two men fell silent and having silently checked with each other they shook their heads and gathered up their papers.

'Great. Let's leave it there then and keep in contact, ok? Even if you're just telling me there is nothing to tell me. Oh, and put out a picture of the Phantom; a photo-fit or blown up CCTV with a description. Someone must know this freak and where he is.'

The men stood and Marlin held the door open for them to exit, pleased with the progress. Leaving the door open, he returned to the table to gather the papers and notes as he tried to stifle a yawn. Behind him there was a knock at the door.

'Excuse me Marlin, do you have a minute?'

Marlin turned to see Sue Scott, her face serious and hard, but he couldn't help but smile.

'Sue.'

'Don't grin at me Marlin, I'm angry.'

'With me?'

'No, not you.'

'Well then, let me be pleased to see you.' He leaned closer and gently kissed her, feeling the buzz as she responded in the brief, stolen moment, until she eased away from him.

'Enough of that Marlin…for now anyway.' She was smiling now but he could sense the tension behind her eyes. 'I need to talk to you.'

'Let me close this door and I'm all yours.' He sat and composed himself as Sue checked her notebook and then sat across from him.

'I've just been to see Andrews.'

'I was there myself not long ago.'

'I know Marlin, you didn't go unnoticed.'

'Look, I did mention the prints, but I had to be there for other reasons.'

'It's ok Marlin; you're working with the man after all. I'm not criticising. I am however disturbed by the direction our conversation took.'

'In what way?'

'As a policewoman, I'm more than concerned. As a person, I just feel insulted.'

'He insulted you?'

'Not as such, but the pair of them insulted my intelligence.'

'Please explain,' Marlin suppressed his impatience at the drip-drip nature of the revelation because it was Sue. For her part, she was being slow and deliberate in an attempt to rein in her anger.

'You've talked to Andrews about his whereabouts in relation to the prostitute murders?'

'Yes, you know I have.'

'He was dead drunk at home?'

'Dead drunk unconscious.'

'Well, last Wednesday he spent the hours from 8.00pm until the early morning with Lara.'

'Really? Well that's news to me; he certainly didn't mention that before.'

'Oh he wouldn't, because he didn't know. During one of his drunken 'blank' moments, he went to her flat and she's just told him this.'

'He has mentioned having blackouts when he drinks.'

'Oh come on Marlin, his fingerprints are everywhere and suddenly he has an alibi. It's too convenient, far too bloody convenient.'

'So you really think he's a viable suspect?'

'The more I talk to him, the more I feel I should. There's something I can't put my finger on, something about his attitude, his contempt. If you hadn't become friends with him, I'm pretty sure you'd look at this differently as well.'

'I can't deny that things don't look great, or that he does himself few favours at times. However, a flawed personality is one thing, a murderer quite another.'

'It's more than just flawed, there's something fundamentally wrong with his attitude towards women.'

'Maybe, but I think he's still getting over his marriage. It didn't end well.'

'Oh come on, don't tell me he had his heart broken? Please. And even if he did, it's no excuse for the bitterness he carries around with him; it's little more than misogyny.'

'Misogyny? Oh come on Sue, isn't that a bit extreme?'

'Just keep your eyes open, Marlin. We can agree to disagree on this but at least keep your policeman head on. If I'm totally wrong about this guy I'll apologise openly, but as yet I'm far from convinced.'

As the two stood to leave Marlin stepped across the door blocking the way, and Sue shook her head smiling. 'Not at work.'

'There's no-one here to see.'

Sue kissed him with a loud smack. 'Now, back to work ok? I'll see you later?'

'Oh yeah. Just you try to keep me away,' Marlin beamed as he held open the door.

Back at his desk Marlin considered the facts as far as he could. He tried to look at things from the point of view of someone who didn't know or like the Doc. He thought the alibi was extremely convenient, but only if one thought he was guilty, which he didn't. He couldn't deny that he would be concerned if he was fabricating facts. However, hadn't he spoken of blackouts? Was it really so far-fetched a story? He couldn't concentrate on this with so much new in his own case. Pulling on his jacket, he walked over to Mitchell's desk.

'Have you got the new guard detail in place yet?'

'We gave the go-ahead straight after our meeting, so they should be on their way if not already there.'

'Good, good. You don't mind if I check-in on them do you? There's a couple of things I want to talk over with the Doc, er Doctor Andrews, anyway.'

'No problem, sir.'

'Thanks Mitchell. I need to get out and get some fresh air anyway,' Mitchell nodded and smiled before calling after Marlin as he moved towards the exit.

'You call that fresh air?' Marlin glanced down to see that he was holding his cigarettes and shrugged his shoulders as he went through the door, keenly aware that he hadn't tried to catch Sue's eye. He might have every right to go back to the house, but he felt sure that it was better for all concerned if this visit wasn't advertised.

Arriving at the house the police car rolled aside to let him pass. He smiled at Ellis, the policewoman behind the wheel, and then stopped as Hill came from the side of the house to greet him. He knew of these two by reputation as bright and able officers and, with Oliver and McCarthy to relieve them later; he was at last convinced that the Doc would be ably protected. Shaking hands with Hill he walked with him to the rear of the house, whilst out of the corner of his eye he saw Lara peeking through the curtains, noting the new arrivals with interest.

'I see you've had time to look around the property.'

'Yes, sir.' Hill stopped at the old wooden door that latched loosely against the wall and lead to the back garden via a narrow passage. 'Do you know if this has a lock sir?'

'I don't, but I'll ask Dr Andrews when I go in.' They continued to the rear garden and the PC pointed to the walls either side.

'They're a decent height sir, but not really a great problem if someone really wanted to get in. I'd suggest that both teams patrol round here regularly.'

'Good idea, I was going to suggest the very same thing. Now I'll leave you to it and speak to Dr Andrews.' He moved to the back door and knocked hard. After a faint rattle of key in lock the solid door opened and Lara stood, eyeing him suspiciously.

'We just can't keep you away today can we?'

'May I?'

'Sure, come in.' She stood aside, taller and straight in her heels, her face older, the eyes cold. Marlin walked past and through the kitchen to the living room where Al sat.

'The new protection team are here. Good people and another two for the evening.' It was Lara who spoke as Al looked on.

'So it is two from now on? See I told you Al, I told you Marlin had said he'd try for two.'

'I did indeed, Lara,' Marlin smiled but Lara stayed impassive as she reached for her bag and he was surprised when she picked out a pack of cigarettes and lit one.

'You don't mind if I do?' Al waved to continue and Marlin lit up quickly. 'I didn't know you smoked Lara.'

'Why should you? You know nothing about me. Absolutely nothing.' Lara drew deeply on her cigarette and blew out hard 'There's no law against it is there?'

'Hey, please.' Marlin raised his palms as if in surrender. 'It was just a comment; I'm not trying to wind anyone up here.'

'Makes a change.' Lara spoke sullenly like a moody child. Al leaned forward, glass in hand, and broke his silence.

'So I take it you spoke to your girlfriend?'

'If you mean Detective Scott, then yes I did.'

'That figures.'

Marlin was aware of the combative atmosphere and aware that he was the cause in some way. 'What's the problem here? I'm sensing a certain tension.'

'What a detective.' Lara's contempt was open and raw.

'So what have I done then?'

'It's not really you Marlin, it's the mind shift.'

'Mind shift?'

'I do actually appreciate you getting the protection outside and I'm not really angry with you as a person. As a person I consider you a good man and a friend. I'm angry with the police; with their mind shift away from catching the Phantom to trying to pin three murders on me. How many Phantom suspects have been interviewed? How many times have I? It's beginning to seem as though there's some sort of agenda here'

'I don't think anyone's trying to pin the murders on you, Doc. There's obviously an investigation going on and you feature.'

'Do any other suspects get three visits from the police in one day?' Again Lara's words were spat out rather than spoken. 'We give you a valid alibi and still you come back.'

'Ah yes, the alibi. Well Lara, do forgive me, but you've given an alibi for the Doc that even he can't verify, so it'll have to be checked out properly. It's also true to say that you are less than impartial in this whole thing. Don't forget that I'm arguing on your behalf with all of this.' Marlin paused, waiting for another verbal attack but, as he lit up another cigarette, there was no comment so he continued. 'I came here because I wanted you to know that, until you have the cab details confirmed, there's every chance the investigation will continue. But I can also assure you that there are other suspects and they're also being questioned; it's just that there aren't all that many suspects with their prints at all three murder scenes.'

'All three?' Lara spoke quietly, almost as if she was speaking only to herself.

'Yes, all three.' Al's response was slow and low, a defeated monotone as Lara turned to him with eyes as daggers, her mouth pressed tight and silent. Al's right hand balled into a fist and he remained still, staring at the table. Marlin was aware of the tension rising another notch in the room but it was clear he was no longer the focal point.

'Oh Doc, while I remember, do you have a key for that door to the passageway at the side?'

'No.'

'Is there anything else I should tell the protection detail to help them?'

'Yes, is there anything you should tell THEM Al?' Lara spoke with a controlled anger, each word being slowly enunciated and delivered sharply.

'There's a movement activated light in the back garden.' Al spoke as if the weariness of life had drained him and, as he finished talking, he looked at Marlin with a desperate expression of pleading. Marlin knew it was time to go.

'I have to get back. Call me if you need to know anything.'

As he stood and moved to the door it was as if he had become invisible. 'Make sure that the back door is locked again, ok?' His words disappeared into the intense silence and as he went to the door he glanced back at the frozen scene; Al deflated and unmoving, stared ahead in a trance of despair, while Lara's eyes were burning and fixed upon him as her shoulders rose and fell heavily. Marlin closed the door quietly as if any noise might detonate the incendiary atmosphere.

MALICE AND DEFEAT

Frozen silence was at some point animated but no words were spoken. Thoughts were distilled in alcohol as the room filled with a blue mist that enveloped the atmosphere of malice and defeat. Al sipped and stared ahead, sullen and pale, as if staring into the dark recesses of his own soul. In many ways he was. Lara's heels clicked sharply, as if with evil intent, as she stepped between the living room and kitchen then back again.

Her very being was as taut and stretched as her emotions, her mind a swirling ball of confused disappointment and angry frustration. She wanted more than anything to explode in fury, to unleash a verbal tirade, but somehow the words wouldn't come. Not the words to explain this crushing blow to her person. She couldn't find the words because she didn't know what was happening, to her or her mind. This man, this sad figure before her, was not her husband or her boyfriend; he was her client, he paid. How could he therefore be unfaithful or disloyal? Yet was she not in his house as his friend? His lover?

Two years as his mistress, two years in which he'd become an almost constant in her life; she wasn't paid to sleep with him, she had chosen to. They both played out their roles but she had seen his vulnerability and he hers. Just because they had an arrangement that was mutually beneficial, it didn't mean that it was an act of business. What they had was unspoken, but she could feel it, she could feel it strongly and she felt sure that it was reciprocated. Therefore in this context, in any context, was honesty not a prerequisite? A given?

On she paced, glancing across intermittently as she chain smoked her way through emotional limbo.

Al was careful in his immobility, tactful in his silence, but mindful of his next move. He knew that peace had to be made and order restored. In his very stillness he hoped to allow the gale of emotion to blow itself out, at least in part. He had not bargained for 30 minutes of pacing and silence on Lara's part, or for the intensity within the expressions and stares. He had been confident enough to believe that he could play with her head, but had not thought it relevant to consider her heart. A strategy was required and, as he stared off into the distance, its essence whilst not clear was taking a shape.

'Lara, will you sit down please?'

His voice was calm with a self-assured authority and his low spoken words stopped Lara in her tracks. Nervously lighting a cigarette, she coughed and sat across from Al, her face concentrated and serious.

'I'd like you to let me speak for a moment and, if you can, without interruption?' Lara nodded and in his slow deliberate manner, Al continued. 'We've known each other for almost two years now and it's been a special time for me; a healing time in many ways, but certainly a happy time. I've trusted you with my needs and you've been understanding and kind, even in cruelty. I was broken in so many ways and you've helped to mend me, to bring light back into my world. It's been more therapeutic than you can imagine.'

Al sipped slowly before continuing.

'I'm weak and I know you can't be there for me always, so I've turned to others to help calm me; used them as a way of keeping my sanity when the darkness comes. I couldn't admit this because you are special to me and I wanted you to feel that way.'

Lara sat looking thoughtful for a moment and then spoke. 'So when I'm not around you can't wait? You must see someone, anyone, for this therapy? I'm glad to have helped you Al, I really am, but did you ever hear of using a therapist for therapy?'

'It's complicated Lara, and you've been so good for me. I'm truly sorry I lied to you, sorry that I've hurt you.'

'And why didn't you tell me about the prints?'

'I thought that Detective Scott had mentioned it?'

'She hadn't and you could've tried to tell me.'

'I'm so sorry Lara. I'm sorry about everything.' Al reached for his wallet and threw all of the notes onto the table. 'Take my money or take it out on my body; take whatever retribution you see fit, but please believe me that I'm sorry, Lara.'

Lara leaned forward, picking up the bills, and extended her arm to Al.

'Keep your money Al; it's so not about that so spend it on a shrink or something. I may take it out on you, but not for cash; I'll do it for me. Anything in the future, any future at all, is only on the basis that there are no more lies. Agreed?'

'Agreed.'

'Ok, that's clear now, so pour me a drink for God's sake.' Al leaned over and filled her glass. 'One last point. How long ago did you see the other two girls?'

'It must be a couple of months now. Maybe more.'

'That's the truth?'

'I swear.'

'Ok, that's that for now.' Lara sat back and pulled her feet up under her, kicking off her heels as she did. 'God you're hard work, Doc.'

'So I'm told.

DARK GLOBES

Dressed in customary black, hood pulled tight, the man stood against the wall. A dark figure in cold half-light listening for sounds of life on the other side of the whitewashed brickwork. Looking left and right once again, he breathed deeply and checked that the small backpack was secure, and then leapt upwards, catching the top of the wall. Pulling with all the power his muscled arms could muster, his legs pumped strongly, searching for some purchase. Up he travelled and over, glancing at the tall grass below as he bent his knees to land. To his right he saw his dark image reflected in the large French windows and he paused at the sight. Soon I will need no camouflage against the darkness; I will emerge into the light of recognition and my glory will be seen. No light or sound alerted him as he stared, but time was of the essence and he bent low as he ran to the facing wall and leapt once again.

The second garden was as flat as a bowling green and he had to be careful not to land on the white plastic table and chairs as he flung himself onwards; a barking dog from within only propelling him with even greater pace up and over the next wall. Here he stopped for a second, crouched and still, before moving to the large bay window and peering inside. The sound of a radio playing, somewhere in the house, was faint but audible; the only signs of life in an otherwise dark and seemingly empty house.

Looking to his left he saw that the door was a good solid wood but with two opaque windows running parallel down the top half. He glanced down and, seeing the Chubb lock, reached for his backpack, quickly locating his picks. Half kneeling and yet balanced he manipulated the thin picks with delicacy, listening for the clicks he knew would come and easing the handle down; opening the door. Inside he closed the door and looked about the kitchen, allowing his eyes to adjust to the shadowed gloom of a late winter afternoon. To the left of the door, above the spotless sink and next to the coffee grinder, he saw a key on a hook so locked the back door; almost smiling as he replaced the key. I have my entrance to the mundane world in which they exist, a place of lies where they condemn those they do not understand. There is no need to understand me now; just see me, feel me.

Soft footsteps across the kitchen floor and into the living room, he could now hear that the radio was definitely coming from upstairs. The steady beat and cheerful, if repetitive refrain, bothered the man and, having checked the room around him, he moved more quickly to the stairs. Noting the hallway led to another room, perhaps two, he nonetheless made his way swiftly but softly upwards. On the top landing he paused once more. Looking to his gloved hand gripping the banister, he debated internally the possible advantage of readying his knife. The music played on with ever greater urgency, turning right to face it, he saw light coming from the third door along. He resolved to carry on as he was. At the door, ajar, he looked in and there was the cleaner, just as he had expected.

Standing in oversized blue overalls, the vacuum cleaner at her feet, she had her face pressed tight to the net curtain and window, her neck craned to see into the drive of next door's house. The figures playing out their silent drama came and went, moving with intent. The now familiar police car had been joined by another vehicle; two men, walked in conversation, serious and unsmiling. Briefly they paused before disappearing down the side of the house and out of sight.

The curtain was rough against her cheek, leaving a mark, and the window beyond clouded by her breath. She stepped back, wiping away with her cloth and kicking the vacuum cleaner out of the way. The vacuum barely moved, so turning to look for the obstruction on the floor, she was confused and shocked by the black training shoes; the black jeans a matter of inches away.

'Wha...' The word remained unsaid. The sound was curtailed by the vice like hand encased in leather that gripped her mouth and forced her sideways onto the bed. She felt a fist explode into her stomach, squeezing all of the air from her body; no scream or struggle was possible, as she desperately fought for breath, arms flailing as if air could be caught. The man stepped from her and reached for his back-pack, placing it on the bed and opening it deliberately as he watched her regain colour and oxygen; her mouth open and eyes wide with terror.

'Shhhhhhhh'. A half seen face commanded her silence. 'You are quiet now or forever.'

The woman was still gasping for air, but now tears were falling, a low sobbing amongst the quick breaths as she fought against sound. The man had taken a roll of tape from his bag and, biting off a strip, he placed it roughly across her mouth. Her despairing wail was further muffled as he pushed her onto her front and taped her hands behind her.

Lifting her easily, he threw her face down further up the bed and took her legs, taping them tightly at the ankles. Seeing that her head was now buried in the pillows, he roughly flipped her over onto her back, drinking in the terror in her eyes as her body shook and trembled. Once again he reached into the bag and produced a hammer. With a violent crash he brought it down onto the radio, the room now silent save for the hysterical tears and muffled cries of fright.

Standing, the man approached the window slowly, looking across without getting too close. Leaning to the side to see he was almost crouching lest he give away some sign. The police car sat as always and there was another car parked outside the door. Scanning back across he noted that there were two police in the car. His hand reached back for his bag and removed the small binoculars that allowed a better view, albeit from an angle; it was enough to confirm a man and a woman.

Checking his victim, now paralysed with fear, he left the room and checked the other upstairs rooms. The first was another generous sized bedroom but this time with twin beds and, although spotless, the impression it gave was sterile and unlived in. He moved to the window and had another look; although the angle of view was closer, the thick bushes that divided the properties at the front completely obscured any view. He moved on down the hall and entered the end room, some sort of study; half minimalist furniture and sleek computers, the other half an adolescent boy's fantasy of model aircraft and posters. Once again it was the view that was important and as he looked out he could see the garden and, more importantly, the garden next door. Looking round he saw a chair and pulled it over. Sitting slowly and deliberately he settled, staring out of the window, committing everything to memory.

An hour or so had past and the last of the light had gone as he stared on into the darkness, waiting, until finally the lights in the garden next door came on, shining brightly and illuminating the garden completely. Into view came the policeman, a tall man in his thirties he searched thoroughly as he walked around the garden, the torch he carried unnecessary. He watched as he checked the back door and looked to his watch - 7.30pm. The policeman vanished from view and the man waited for the lights to snap off before resting his chin on his arm again, resuming his vigil.

The wait was not so long this time and, as the lights flared once more, the man saw that it was 8.00pm. This time a young policewoman walked the four corners of the garden, concentrated and studious. He saw that she also checked the door and he noted that there was a risk beyond his usual parameters with this level of security. It was good that he had another plan and it would soon be time to prepare. To be sure and thorough he watched the lights die away once more and settled again, waiting for the next break in the darkness, noting the time and nodding to himself as a half-hour was confirmed.

Leaving the end room he walked along the dark corridor, stopping briefly at the door of the room that had been his second visit. Pushing it open fully he glanced again at the single beds and nodded. Back into the main bedroom, his appearance was a cause of terror once again to the cleaner who had prayed and prayed that the silence was a sign that he'd gone. He stopped by the bed, tilting his head as he looked down at the woman, the blankness of his face in total contrast to the glowering intensity of his eyes. She could not look away from those dark globes which seemed to shine blackly in the dark. She searched for some humanity or mercy, but there was nothing to dilute her horror.

After some time he reached down and with surprising ease, lifted her from the bed. He took her through to the next bedroom, placing her on the furthest of the twin beds precisely and almost gently. He stood staring at her, his head again tilted, as if trying to make sense of this bound figure before him. Now she closed her eyes, hoping that he would somehow disappear, unable to look anymore.

TENUOUS LINKS AND LIES

The City Cabs office was basic and uncomfortable, a functional structure that looked as if it could be dismantled and carried away in minutes. The traditional hatch allowed one a view of Sharif, the controller, who seemed to live there, existing in a constant state of cheerful exasperation. Sue Scott showed her ID and reminded Sharif of their earlier phone conversation regarding his log of calls and drivers. He signalled to her to go back out and along to the rear door which brought her into the driver's area. The selection of torn fabric covered settees and seats were placed at odd angles, as if they had been thrown in randomly. A television struggled to keep its signal in the corner while the drivers that were not on jobs huddled outside smoking. Sharif shook her hand.

'Detective Scott, please sit down.'

'I think I'll just stand, thanks.'

'If you prefer. What can I do for you?'

'The call log? Do you have it?'

Sharif moved across to his ledger and flicked back a few pages. 'Wednesday the 9th and early Thursday? Is this right? And it was Buckingham Road?'

'Yes please.'

He studied for some time and then checked his computer screen, nodding slowly.

'Well Detective Scott, we have a booking for Buckingham Road made at 11.00pm asking for a cab at 12.00pm.'

'Is there a house or flat number?'

'House number 124, one of the girls there; we just beep the horn outside. We are always going there. There was also a booking at 8.00pm for 10.00pm.'

'Who was the driver?' Sue was now taking notes and looking at the ledger. 'The driver for the midnight booking.'

'Let me see. Ahmed took that job. AHMED,' Sharif shouted and a short bearded man entered from the nicotine cloud outside, smiling weakly, his tired eyes telling the true tale.

'Ahmed, my name is Detective Sue Scott and I'd be grateful if you could answer some questions?' Ahmed shrugged and then nodded his head as Sue continued.

'You did a job at Buckingham Road last Wednesday? The 9th? It was at midnight?' Sue was concerned because Ahmed showed no expression whatsoever as she spoke.

'Do you remember?'

'I go there many times, many days.'

'But Wednesday at midnight, do you remember that?'

'I go there at midnight. I go at all hours but if it was Wednesday then I take your word for it.'

Sue took out a photograph of Dr Andrews and showed it to the driver. 'Do you think it was this man you picked up?'

'Ah, the drunken man ha! Yes, I know him.'

'It was him you picked up?' Sue could not hide the incredulous tone in her reply.

'I don't know about Wednesday, but Mr Al we take a lot.' At the mention of his name Sharif looked over at the photo and smiled broadly.

'Oh the television man, why didn't you say? We are always working for Mr Al. He is a drinker alright, but a big tipper. All the drivers want to pick up Mr Al.'

Sue was lost in thought for a moment, but when she did speak it was slow and deliberate.

'So Ahmed, wouldn't you remember if you got a big tip on Wednesday?'

'Last week I have Mr Al in my cab a few times. I have him drunk, I have him sober and I often have him late at night. I don't know if that was the one, I'm sorry.'

'That's ok. Thank you both for your help.' Sue walked out of the cabin, unconvinced of anything in terms of an alibi and angry that the whole area could be so vague. The man was everywhere and yet nowhere. Sitting in her car she slammed the steering wheel as she started it up. 'Damn it!' She checked her mirror and signalled, then stopped, turning off the engine. 'Nearly, stupid girl.' She smiled and stepped out of the car, hurrying back across to the cabin.

'Sharif?' The genial man looked up, surprised.

'I'm sorry Sharif but I forgot to ask. Did you get a booking from er, Mr Al that night?' Sharif checked his book and screen again.

'Is Mr Al in trouble? Ah, here we are. 8.30pm cab for Mr Al, 32 Albert Road, to come immediately.'

'Where was he going?'

'It doesn't say here, but with Mr Al we don't ask. He can afford wherever he is going.'

'The driver?'

'Solly.'

'Can I speak to Sol...?'

'He is not here Detective.'

'When will he be...?'

'No Detective, he has gone to Turkey for a wedding. He won't be back for a week.'

'You're kidding?' Sue tried to hide her exasperation but it was all too clear.

'I'm sorry, but he is away.'

'Do you have a phone number?'

'For Turkey? No. I have his mobile but you won't get anything. When he goes home he is away from everything. But here, you can try?' Sharif jotted the number on a piece of paper and handed it to Sue. She smiled, but disappointment was written all across her face. 'Thank you.' She turned and left again, cursing under her breath as she got back into her car and drove off.

Heading back into town, she could scarcely stop the angry conversation in her head so pulled the car over. Looking at the scrap of paper in her hand she picked up her phone and dialled. The call went directly to voicemail and she spat out 'Shit!' to no-one but herself.

'Hello Solly, this is Detective Sue Scott. I'd be most grateful if you could ring me back as soon as possible on this number...,' Even as she spoke, there was a complete lack of belief or expectation in her voice. Solly was not going to ring the police, if anything the message would mean he might not come back at all; maybe he'd stay put in Turkey.

She finished the message and aggressively moved the car out into the traffic, talking to herself.

'I can't say anything for sure, but I know you weren't with Lara from 8.00pm Dr Andrews. I have one lie confirmed.'

Marlin had no sooner returned and sat down at his desk than Detective Mitchell was there.

'Sir, we have a sighting and a possible address.'

'What?'

'It's from the pictures in the paper. We were called by a guy near King's Cross, two minutes from where the car was found; he runs a small hotel. He thinks our man is staying there.'

'Ok, let's go.'

The journey across North London was no different to any other day, but the need for speed was desperate and every hold-up in the traffic painful. Marlin followed the blue flashing light on the car in front, hopeful more than confident, until they pulled up at the Stanton Hotel. Faded white and dilapidated, the establishment looked as though it had not been painted since the early seventies; it's smell suggested that it might not have been cleaned since then either. The man at reception reeked of BO and cheap aftershave and, in his sweat stained grubbiness, he fitted the place perfectly.

'Mr Osborne? I'm DCI Marlin. You called about one of your guests?'

Reacting in the manner of one for whom time meant nothing, Osborne studied the id and pondered the question. 'The strange guy with the eyes? Yeah, I called.'

'What room?'

'Five.'

'Key?'

'For emergencies I have this...,'

'Just give me the key.' Marlin grabbed the key impatiently, signalling to Carr and Mitchell to follow as he scaled the stairs two at a time. In the corridor he slowed and moved to the yellowing door with an off centre 5. Pausing to listen he could hear nothing, so knocked loudly.

'Police, open up!'

There was no response or sound, but Marlin wasn't waiting for the key as he signalled again to Mitchell. His shoulder forced the flimsy door open and they spilled anxiously into the cramped room.

'Check the bathroom Carr, and be careful.'

Carr was wary as he opened the door, but then recoiled quickly. 'Jesus, the smell.' Looking across he shook his head and Marlin relaxed, taking time to scan the room now.

There were books set along a makeshift shelf and inside the closet he had left his trophies next to what seemed to be a box full of locks. Hanging up was two sets of black clothes. Marlin sighed. 'Get forensics here as soon as possible and speak to our friend downstairs to see what he can give us.'

Mitchell exchanged looks with Carr, surprised by the deflated tone in Marlin's voice.

'What is it sir?'

'Timing Mitchell, timing. I get the feeling we're too late to get anything here.'

'But we've everything here, sir.' Carr was puzzled. 'Murder weapons, clothes, books. Look, even a notepad here. Even if he's left no prints, and I bet he has, we can wait for him coming back here.'

'He's not coming back here, that's the point. He left the car and he's left this place. I don't think he believes that he'll need any of this stuff again. I really don't.' Marlin shook his head slowly, taking one last look around the room as he stood in the doorway. 'Get what you can from here regardless and post a car in case he does come back. I could be wrong.' Marlin's tone suggested otherwise as he headed back to the office.

Checking the clock Marlin considered leaving things for the night and going home, but a sense of unfinished business kept him sitting. He glanced again at the report on the young man Jackson, the unfortunate administrator from MI6, focusing on the post-it note he had attached. 'Spy Wednesday' - the poor fucker was killed for some word-play. Closing the folder he was interrupted as his phone rang.

'Marlin here.'

'Hey Marlin.'

'Sue, well I have to say this is the best interruption of the day.'

'Thanks, I think.'

'What can I do for you?'

'It's gone seven Marlin, so what you can do is pack it in for the night.'

'Where are you?'

'I just dropped my car off and I'm heading to *the Crown*. Want to come?'

'How did you know I was here?'

'Jesus Marlin, you don't need to be a detective to see your car parked down there.'

Marlin was laughing now. 'Just as well then.'

'Don't start on my policing abilities ok? Now get your arse down here and I'll get the first round.'

Marlin flicked off his PC, smiling to himself as he picked up his jacket and left the office. He was pleased to be heading on to Sue, and glad the work day was over.

FASCINATION IS NOT PITY

The man moved into the main bedroom, now only illuminated by streetlights, and picked up his backpack, taking out a small torch and then fastening it securely. He picked up the straight backed chair from in front of the wardrobe and moved back out into the corridor, switching on the torch as he went. Stopping at the top of the stairs, he put down the chair and shone the light along the ceiling, stopping outside the second bedroom as he saw the entry panel for the loft. Standing on the chair he reached up and took hold of the small knob that protruded and pulled firmly; the panel opened downwards and a ladder gently extended to the floor as he did so.

The man smiled at his good fortune and stepped forwards and up the ladder quietly. Torch shining ahead of him, he stood on the wooden flooring between the beams and stood up, his head knocking into something as he did. Bringing the torch beam round he saw the small white plastic at the end of the string cord and smiled again. Checking that there were no windows to signal his presence, the man pulled gently on the cord and the attic was gradually illuminated, as though the bulb were reluctant to shine.

Hardboard floor aside, there were old suitcases and boxes, clothes no-one remembered and pictures that were unhung but kept all the same. The man paused at this forgotten and neglected history, sighing in despair. All of life, all things should be forever or not at all; cherished and written in history or burned and destroyed. What was the use in hiding memories in boxes? Shaking his head, he felt for stability with his foot as he moved across to the far side.

Here the two properties were divided by two thin wooden boards, and the man could see that one of the boards slid back over the other to allow access. Rather than acting as a dividing wall, the boards were leaning almost as boundary pointers for whoever should need them. Looking onto the next section the floor continued onwards except for one section of cut-off carpet, about six feet by three, which lay along to the left.

It was much darker on this side with no bulb and the man had to be careful as he stepped forward. Pulling the board most of the way back behind him he needed his torch again. On tip-toe, his eyes took in everything he illuminated and his ears listened for any creak of board or sounds below. Now the man allowed himself a brief half-smile as he acknowledged his arrival at the point where imagination met reality; breathing heavily, he could feel his very soul shuddering with anticipation as he crossed over the divide. His heart was pounding in his chest and the familiar lust came over him. Patience now, patience.

Testing that solid board lay beneath the carpet, his foot felt around and he moved on until he saw the small round piece of wood the size of a coaster. He gently pushed this to one side and saw the small hole bored below. The man smiled broadly now, his tongue running over his teeth as he lay flat, bringing his eye to the hole; so our model maker has another hobby - peeping tom. His breathing became heavier again but there was only darkness underneath, although he was only too aware that this would not always be the case.

He replaced the disc and stood carefully once again, shining the torch around the floor. At last he found the panel to the corridor below, dusty and unused; he was pleased to see that it too had a small retractable ladder. Making his way back through and replacing the board, the light was clicked off and he returned to the dark corridor by the bedroom. Back in the light he steadied himself and tried to slow his heart; regain control. A dizzying, violent anger, coupled with the proximity of retribution, was proving a volatile cocktail, but it must be harnessed for now. His story arc must be respected.

Helena lay in the dark, all sense of time now gone. She listened for sounds of the hellish figures return, praying for sounds of his exit. Urgently she had tried to loosen her wrists, her legs, but the tape was tight and unyielding. Trying to rock from side to side the realisation hit her that, bound as she was, the fall to the floor would only injure. It was unlikely to be an escape. Again she struggled but the tape was biting into her skin, adding to the pain her arms felt from the angle and pressure.

She sobbed and tried to contain any noise in case it might alert him. She thought of her daughter and her husband; they would be worried now at her absence but would they come looking for her? This was the last house she cleaned, but not the only one, so where would they look? Her car was parked in the pub car park because she didn't have a parking permit, but would the police see that she hadn't gone? She held her breath as a light tapping outside the door signalled the beasts return from the attic above. This was followed by a click as the panel was closed and a light, almost imperceptible, padding of feet as he moved around.

As her heart began to pound again, she was unable to hear anymore because of the blood pumping through her ears. Then he was there. Standing still he bared his teeth and Helena could not be sure if he was pained or smiling. Against her will she was once again drawn to the eyes, the stare.

He stood looking but not seeing, his mind elsewhere as he smiled, thinking ahead and congratulating himself for his successful planning; it was only the movement of the girl that snapped him back to the moment. Yes the girl, what was she, thirty something, forty? It didn't really matter to him as he suddenly strode forwards, making her visibly jump as far as she could within her confines. He moved on past her however and peered from the window at the exchange of cars in front of the adjoining house, reaching for his binoculars to get a better view. Well, well, he thought, again it is one policeman and one policewoman, what symmetry. Putting away the binoculars he looked at the time and noted that it was just past 9.00pm.

He would wait now; sleep if he could, but if he couldn't there were plans to go through, possibilities to consider. But what of the woman? He had walked back to the door but stopped now in the darkness and turned, his nose twitching and sniffing like some feral animal searching for a scent. He fixed his eyes on the woman and approached her, taking out his torch as he did and turning it on. Up and down her trembling body he scanned, stopping to notice the stain of urine now on her trousers; a dark shadow extending across the fabric, as his olfactory suspicions were confirmed. He paused for a moment and brought the light up to shine on her face, now red and swollen with tears, her eyes wide and pleading; the shame and humiliation, the fear that she would bear for more time, for life.

It occurred to him briefly that he had only taken account of the cleaner as a minor consideration, the smallest of obstacles, and yet here she still was. Exhaling deeply the man turned off the torch and for a moment listened to the laboured breathing. He once again felt his heart, inhaling slowly as he felt his calm assurance return. Tomorrow was another day but this chapter was unfinished and needed strong resolve. He understood that all too clearly as he pulled his hood tight and stretched his fingers inside the leather of the gloves.

Reaching forward, he pulled one of the pillows out from underneath the woman's head, hearing the muffled howl as she realised the implications and placed it firmly over her face. It was always a source of great fascination to him that it really did not matter about gender or creed, nor age or size. When he applied the pressure, the fight for life was intense and powerful. This woman was tightly bound but he could feel the power of her struggle, her desire to live as he tried to imagine the maelstrom of her final thoughts. Fascination is not pity or mercy however and the man channelled all of his power as he squeezed the life out of his victim; holding the pillow long after the struggle had subsided, his weight pressing on the lifeless body beneath. He felt the familiar glow of satisfaction for some brief moments, but this was not his aim, his goal; no, this was but a brief aperitif and he would truly feast tomorrow.

POINT MADE

The Crown was busy and warm but Marlin was just happy to see Sue. So happy that he worried that he may be falling too quickly, although on the other hand he recognised his characteristic over-analysis of situations. Sue greeted him smiling broadly and leant to kiss him quickly as her eyes searched the pub for familiar faces. Marlin smiled as his internal dialogue ceased for the time-being and sat at the table.

'Don't be so worried, Sue.'

'What do you mean?'

'I know you don't want to advertise the two of us, but let's not go so far as to make it a state secret.'

'Ok, not a state secret. But you must admit that a bit of a secret helps in this situation?'

'I don't know, I haven't been in 'this' situation before really.'

'You're trying to say that I'm some sort of serial work seductress?'

Marlin laughed. 'I'm saying nothing of the sort Miss Scott, but if there is any truth in the statement I'm more than happy to be seduced.'

'I would say thank you, but I'm not sure that saying thanks is wholly appropriate.'

'No, the thanks are all mine,' Marlin laughed again and was joined by Sue despite her blushing.

'You know Marlin; you are quite the dark horse?'

'You mean compared to my image at work? How I come across to people there?'

'I mean, the way you come across everywhere. Or at least the way you did come across before I found out about the hidden charm and humour.'

Marlin blushed bright red and took a drink.

'And the blushing.' Sue was laughing freely now and, red-faced or not, Marlin was at ease as Sue continued. 'What do you say we have one more then pick up the cars and get a Chinese?'

'Your place?'

'If you're ok with that?'

'Oh, I'm more than ok with that.'

'Great, that's settled anyway.' She drank the last of her glass as Marlin disappeared for a cigarette, calling at the bar on his return. Waiting for him to settle, she took a serious tone.

'I don't want to talk shop tonight, at home that is, but could we have a word here?'

'Of course, go ahead.'

'I checked out Al's alibi today.'

'And?'

'I'm none the wiser. The drivers all know him as some sort of benevolent tipper and he uses the cab firm all the time. The guy who I spoke to went there at midnight and knows he picked him up a couple of times, but can't be sure it was that journey. Plus, they told me they go to that address a lot. I did however find out that he ordered a cab at 8.30pm that night, so he can't have been with Lara from 8.00pm onwards.'

'It's not the longest journey in the world from Al's to Buckingham Road. It only takes 20-30 minutes away from her story.'

'I don't know; I just don't believe the story. But, the cab isn't confirmed as going to Buckingham Road and the driver is in Turkey for a week with no contact.'

'I understand that this is far from clear, as far as you'd like it to be, but look at it this way. He says, well she says really, that he was at hers from 8.00pm until the early hours?'

'Yes.'

'He caught a cab at 8.30pm, that would have taken him to her place quickly, no?'

'Yes.'

'Then we know from your visit, that a cab picked someone up at midnight?'

'Yes.'

'It might've been him?'

'Might have been, yes, but I stress the might.'

'Then as I see it, there are a lot of possibilities to back-up his alibi, but it comes down to what you are trying to prove really.'

'What do you mean?'

'Are you trying to prove he was there? Or that he wasn't there? If you wanted him to be there the comments would be encouraging; if you wanted to prove the opposite they're just frustrating.'

'You think I'm frustrated?'

'I know you think they're lying and the convenience of the alibi has me questioning things, but…,'Marlin paused to consider his words.

'But what.'

'I don't think it's because he's a killer. Look at his life, there are many things he may be covering up, but I don't think murder's one of them. I see him emerge from his whiskey bottle each day and I seriously wonder how he manages to walk, never mind kill someone. And one other thing after which I will shut up.'

'Go on.'

'He's being threatened by a very real, very scary, psycho. I'm not sure my behaviour wouldn't be a little bizarre in the same situation.'

'Point well-made and I take it on board. But I have to say, I think your behaviour is quite bizarre without your serial killer, endearing but definitely bizarre.' They both smiled and Marlin shook his head, hoping that this was the end of the shop talk.

Sue reached across and stroked his hand tenderly but her head was still processing the conversation and she knew that they sat on different sides of the argument; she also knew that she would work to prove that the alibi was bogus. Marlin was also aware that they came from different angles, he was simply not aware that her resolve was so strong in this regard. As her finger traced the back of his hand Marlin put Al aside and enjoyed an intimacy he had believed was relegated to his past.

It was 10.30pm in the evening and Barnet Police Station was quiet and warm, save for the icy blast from the main door as people came and went. Standing at the desk Petr waited anxiously, holding his daughter's hand tightly as much to comfort himself as her. The desk sergeant was sympathetic but realistic in terms of what he could do.

'How long has your wife… Helena, been missing?'

'She is always home 8.30pm. Always.'

'And you can get no reply from her phone?'

'No, nothing.'

'Well Mr Kurczyn, I understand your concern, but we can't say that your wife is missing until after 24 hours.'

'She did not come home, she is missing.'

'She may have gone out with friends and forgotten to tell you.'

'She comes home to her daughter always. Not friends, home. Always!'

'I'm sorry sir, but until 24 hours have elapsed there is really nothing that I can do.'

'Please see the list of work. Then she is home to Paulina.'

The sergeant took the list of properties that Helena cleaned and ran down the list. 'She goes to all of these, every day?'

'No, not all, half one day, half the next.'

'Which ones were today?'

Petr looked at the list blankly and brought his hand up to his face as tears welled in his eyes then ran down his cheeks. He spoke breathlessly, between sobs.

'I don't know, I don't know. It never seemed important. Why don't I know?'

'Please, calm down sir.' The sergeant didn't know what to do as he gazed through the plastic divide between them, noticing that the little girl was now also crying uncontrollably.

'Please sir, please calm down. Don't cry sir, I'm sure everything will be alright. Look, I'll put out the description you gave me to the patrol cars with this list of houses and the car registration. But Mr Kurczyn, you will probably find that she's at home when you get back. These things are normally nothing.' The man nodded, again and again, as the tears subsided and he collected himself.

'Come Paulina, let's go home and wait for your Mother, she is sure to be hungry when she gets in.' His voice convinced neither himself nor the policeman, but it gave the child renewed hope and they began their journey home, the two of them; just the two as it would always be now.

*

Lara had relaxed somewhat, but not completely; the residual anger had lingered as tension in her muscles, behind her eyes. She stood and stretched but this only confirmed the tightness of her body.

'I'm going for a bath Al, and no, I don't need any company ok?'

'Of course Lara. I'll just soak down here.' Al held up his glass and was glad to see his smile returned, even if it was weak and tired. 'I should probably hit the bed soon anyway.'

Lara looked at the delicate silver watch on her wrist and wondered how much therapy she had provided for it, then noted the time.

'Hell, it's gone midnight Al. A bath and sleep I think.'

'Sounds good to me.'

Lara wearily climbed the stairs, doing her best to stifle a yawn. As she entered the bathroom she stopped to look at herself in the mirror. Her eyes were tired and she barely recognised herself, feeling as if she was looking through glass at another girl's life. Thinking of the past few days, how could it be anything but some other girl? Some other life? Whatever it was she wanted hers back. She turned on the water and walked into the bedroom, unbuttoning her blouse. Pulling back her head, she stretched as she unzipped her skirt, stepping out and extending her arms, eyes shut.

Lying flat and still, his eye stared unblinking at the blonde girl below him. Dr Al's young mistress, offering her neck blindly as she undressed slowly; then naked and unaware before vanishing from view. So was she staying with the old drunk? He hadn't been there to see her leave but he hadn't considered her staying. This brought a new dimension to proceedings and although he had not yet integrated her into his plans, he was sure that it would embellish the events to come. He licked his lips and teeth once again, swallowing hard as the possibilities came to life in his mind's eye.

He was about to move when Dr Al appeared, placing a glass of whiskey by the bed and sitting heavily, all groans and breaths as he bent to remove his shoes and socks. Standing, his trousers were dropped and thrown towards a chair in the corner where they hung unceremoniously, spilling coins onto the carpet. His shirt was similarly undone and tossed aside, landing on the chair with one arm dangling as if to get some balance. Sitting with his belly protruding over the top of his white boxer shorts, he pulled over some covers and turned on the radio as he reached for his drink.

The man paused in his prone position for just a moment, watching his prey. He was curious to see the two together, but decided that he could wait until the following day. One last look at the man and he was almost disappointed at how aged he seemed, how soft and flabby; but now there was the girl, so all was not lost - not yet.

As Lara lay in the bath she couldn't help feeling that something was ending and these last few days were merely a limbo or emotional waiting room. She slid down into the hot water to take cover from her cold thoughts of the day. Pleased to be away from the flat, the novelty of Al's place was perhaps wearing off, although looking around the plush surroundings, maybe it wasn't the place?

Was it Al? Maybe, although if he had worn off, why had she been so angry? Perhaps it was her lack of control and an unfamiliarity that caused it. After all, who was used to this lifestyle? A night of entertaining both Al and whiskey had led to sleep, but much too little, until morning coffee was interrupted by Al and the bottle once again. Policeman, policewoman, policeman again and police guards. In the midst of all this a psychopath delivers a bottle of whiskey with a death threat. She laughed quietly to herself. Who wouldn't find the novelty wearing off?

She filled the bath with more hot water and wondered what she would do when all of this ended? Would Al want her to stay around? Could she take him, or at least the drunken him, even if he was to ask? She was aware that she was avoiding a question even within a conversation with herself. So what would bring all of this to an end? How dramatic would events be, and would it also end this nonsense with the policewoman? Fuck, this isn't relaxing me at all.

Lara stood and stepped from the bath, pulling the plug as she did so. Towelling herself dry she was annoyed at herself, at her mind constantly turning over question after question, not letting her settle. Pulling the over-sized bathrobe around her she slipped from the bathroom and crept downstairs, pouring a large glass and taking only two or three swallows to empty it. She half-filled it again and turned, climbing the stairs. Stepping softly she killed the lights as she went, until she came into the bedroom where she placed the drink on the table and threw off the robe, climbing into bed.

'Relaxing bath?'

'A bath, yes.'

'Not relaxing?'

'I think today required more than hot water.'

'Anything I can do?'

'Apart from leaving me alone and letting me sleep, maybe not.'

Al flinched. 'Ok, sorry.'

'No Al, come here for God's sake.' She held Al and kissed him, an exchange of strong scotch. 'I'm not having a go at you, I just want to sleep. A looooooooong deep sleep.'

'Be my guest.'

They both drank and swallowed before Al turned out the light. Then in the dark silence they lay still, side by side, waiting for sleep to arrive; a sleep that suddenly seemed a million miles away.

*

The man stepped down into the corridor and gently closed the hatch above his head, all the while listening for any new sounds. Happy with the silent stillness around him he walked slowly into the second bedroom and trained the thin beam of torchlight on the bed, the woman, the corpse. Holding the torch in his teeth he rolled the duvet over twice, enveloping the body in a padded roll, then stepped back and closed the door.

Moving to the main bedroom, he took a moment to glance down at the police car and waited as he saw the tall man, his own torch bright in the darkness, returning from his patrol. Content that all was as it should be, he lay down on top of the large double bed; still in the blackness, alone with his thoughts. A plan had to be amended, confirmed, absorbed and rehearsed. Two police outside, the girl inside and the regular callers; new factors were new variables and, whilst he would like time to consider his schemes, the cleaner would soon be missed so the clock was ticking. He felt an increase in his heartbeat, but he felt no fear for what was to come, only desire and excitement.

MISGIVINGS

A light tapping on his head and the smell of strong coffee proved to be a slightly confusing introduction to Thursday morning.

'Come on get up Marlin, we've work today you know? The bathroom's all yours.' Sue was half dressed and looking at Marlin via the mirror on her dressing table. 'Sorry about the noise.'

She turned on the hairdryer and concentrated on her reflection once more. Marlin fully woke and reached for the coffee by his side, his eyes fixed on Sue as she got ready, aware of her occasional reflected glances back at him and smiling now.

'Come on, get yourself in the shower. I know you don't think too much of morning working, but my hours are pretty good and I don't intend today to be any different.'

Marlin took another few gulps and walked stiff legged and stretching to the shower.

'That's it old man.'

Separate cars meant that there was less cloak and dagger about the arrival at work. Still, in the interest of subterfuge and his stomach, Marlin delayed his entry with a visit to the local cafe. A hearty breakfast with two more cups of coffee did the trick for him and, as he stepped outside into the fresh morning air lighting a cigarette, he was happy. Marlin was somewhat cynical about happiness, as it often felt uncomfortable and ill-fitting, but today even the news that DCS Thomas wished to see him didn't dilute his mood. Standing tall and relaxed he knocked and entered.

'Detective Chief Superintendent Thomas?'

'Ah Marlin, please take a seat.' Marlin avoided rolling his eyes as Thomas returned to his paperwork, suddenly engrossed in some administrative dilemma. Having confirmed to himself that he was busy, he looked up.

'Have we made any progress with the Phantom?'

'Yes sir, quite a bit. As you know, we got an image of the suspect and his car from CCTV. I got this put out to officers and into the papers. A PC found the car abandoned and then we were tipped off about the suspect's possible whereabouts in a King's Cross Hotel. Unfortunately, he wasn't there and he hasn't returned. We have however recovered a substantial amount of evidence from his room. This is definitely our man. Also sir, since the last message was left on the doorstep of Dr Andrews, we've doubled the guard outside his house.'

'Do you really think he'll try anything?'

'He's made it quite clear that Dr Andrews is his next target and he appears more than bold. The message showed that sir, and he seems to have abandoned the car and his belongings deliberately. I think he's certain to try something but we've good people posted there.'

'Do you think he'll try something soon?'

'Within days I would expect sir. Why?'

'Why, Marlin?' Thomas spoke slowly, his sour expression a clear indication of his distaste at being questioned. 'I have to present a report on how we are staffing at present, in terms of the budgetary constraints we have to deal with.'

'Yes sir, er, I'm sorry but I don't fully understand your point?'

'Staffing Marlin, people, bodies on the street? To put it simply, I can't have four policemen and women sitting outside one property. I need to have people visible in the community and I need to save on the bloody overtime.'

'Are you removing the extra cover guarding Dr Andrews after one night sir?'

'Look Marlin, we don't know if he is a legitimate target and even if he is, we could be waiting for days or weeks here.'

'With the greatest of respect sir, I think he's more than a legitimate target and, with the carnage this Phantom has wreaked over the last week or so, I think it's some gamble to think he'd suddenly wait weeks to attack. Everything points to something happening imminently. As I told you sir, he's abandoned his car and left his room; he's ready to act now.'

'I've warned you about your tone and attitude before, Marlin. Don't speak to me as if I'm some sort of idiot, I know this case Detective and I know it well. I'm not suggesting leaving the man alone; actually I'm not suggesting anything. I'm telling you that there will be a change of approach.'

'Yes sir and what is...,'

'Don't interrupt, Detective. What will happen today is that the guard detail will cease and you will take Dr Andrews to the safe house in Finsbury Park. Tonight, you will look after him there. Tomorrow and the days after are up to you. I'm sure that you can sort it out between Mitchell and Carr who'll take care of things. After a few days, if all is quiet, he can go home. Now is that clear Marlin?'

Mood shattered, Marlin stood tight-lipped and glowering, desperate to speak but afraid of what might be said. Thomas, relishing the power he held in the situation, held his look, a slight smile playing on his lips.

'Is it clear, Marlin?'

'Yes sir?'

'Good, well get back to work then.'

Marlin turned quickly, emerging back into the office red-faced and staring as he moved past his desk and out of the exit. Sue saw the angry figure march out and everyone heard the door, as it was violently flung open against the metal stop; the wood shuddering long after he had gone. She wanted to rush after him, but didn't wish to make it obvious, and then she saw Mitchell looking anxious as he followed.

When Mitchell stepped outside he couldn't miss Marlin, tight-faced and pacing in a blue cloud as his cigarette was consumed rather than smoked.

'Are you alright sir?'

Marlin raised his head, surprised to find another presence in the world then, reading Mitchell's concern, he tried to calm himself slightly.

'I'm ok I suppose, its bloody Thomas who needs help.'

'What happened?'

'He's taking away Andrews' guard.'

'The two extra officers? They've only been there one day.'

'No, all four.'

'What? That's madness sir.'

'Bodies on the street and budgets. Don't ask me Mitchell, how would I possibly understand?'

'So what do we do now?'

'Oh, don't worry. Our great DCS has decided that he should be moved to the safe house in Finsbury Park for the next few days, where I'll look after him. Well, to be clear, it's me tonight and then you and Carr.'

'You're kidding me, sir?'

'I wish I was.' Marlin stubbed out his cigarette aggressively and immediately lit a new one.

'Do you want me to tell Dr Andrews, sir?'

'Thanks, but I think it should come from me. When does the current shift end for the two officers outside the house?'

'The shifts are barely in place but they're due to change at 3pm. Has Thomas really thought this through?'

Marlin didn't answer, his eyes wide and angry as he shook his head and spat out the blue smoke forcefully. Mitchell realised the conversation was over.

'I'd better go and tell Carr sir.' Without waiting for a response that would never come, Mitchell walked back inside, holding the door for Detective Scott as he did so. Sue walked over, checking the car park for anyone paying attention as she came to Marlin.

'Are you ok?'

'Yeah.'

'I don't think I've ever seen you so angry.' She placed an arm on Marlin's shoulder as concern took control, and forgetting about prying eyes she then gently rubbed his neck. He turned, a weak smile on his lips.

'I'll be ok Sue; you know how I love my little chats with Thomas?'

'Yes, but that was some look on your face.'

'He's decided that we should get rid of the security for Andrews, and move him to the safe house in Finsbury Park. To save money of course.'

'I don't understand. It will still cost money to guard him in Finsbury Park, maybe more if it's for a while. And I thought you had decided against the safe house?'

'I had, but it's a few days only, so I'm told, and I'm the guard.'

'What? Are you serious?'

'Yeah, I was volunteered for first watch, then Carr and Mitchell, so you won't see me tonight.'

'Tonight? He is doing this today?'

'The Doc doesn't know yet, but I'll be talking to him some time before 3pm this afternoon.' Marlin sighed, dreading the conversation to come.

'Let me know when, will you? I need to have a chat and I don't want to be going out to the safe house all the time.'

'Yes ok, I'll tell you when I'm going there, but give me some time to break the good news?'

'Of course. Look, I'll have to get back inside and I think you should consider it too, before you get some sort of nicotine overdose.'

'Go in, I'll be there soon.'

Sue walked off, shivering against the cold and Marlin paced away in a semi-circle, unable to escape his thoughts and misgivings.

*

Al lay in bed, head propped up with pillows but unmoving, apart from allowing his eyes to follow Lara around the bedroom; a ritual in progress he could not help but watch. He was surprised by how erotic he found it, watching the familiar striptease in reverse, as Lara, dressed to kill, applied her mask, surprised by the delicate attention to detail of each brush stroke, each dark line or touch of colour.

'Are you going somewhere?'

Lara remained silent as, open mouthed, she applied her mascara with concentrated precision, finally blinking and checking as she spoke.

'No, I'm being prepared as much as I can be in case of visitors. I won't be caught half-dressed again like yesterday - especially if that woman comes around.'

'Well you look great.'

'Thank you, Dr Andrews. Are you planning to stay in bed all day?'

'Is that an offer?'

'This isn't for you Al, well not right now anyway.'

'Ok then I'll get up, but Jesus Lara, you really do look quite something.'

Lara smiled at Al, then carefully slipped on her heels and glided out of the room and down the stairs. Al, fully awake now but lying back, reached for his phone which was sitting by his whiskey glass. Checking for messages he stopped at Marlin's name.

Doc

Have to speak to you so will pop in this afternoon. Detective Scott may also call in the afternoon.

Marlin

Great news for Lara, but I think I may keep the information to myself for now.

*

The man had watched all of this from his vantage point above, and the blood was pumping now, his arousal almost dizzying as he lay; the naked flesh and the knowledge of blood to come as heady a mix as he could remember. He watched Al as he pulled himself from the bed and padded to the bathroom. When the room below was empty, he slowed his breathing and felt to make sure his back pack was secure as he eased to his feet. Moving carefully to the loft hatch he again lay and placed his ear to the wood. Now he listened acutely, straining until he could just make out the muffled sounds of the shower running.

Moving his knife into the tight gap at the side, he pulled along until he heard the catch click and then, agile and quick, he was on his feet. Pushing the hatch open, he winced slightly at the sound made as the ladder slid to the floor with a creak and a dull thud. Moving down at pace he landed softly on the carpet and pushed the hatch back-up, having to leap slightly to re-engage the catch.

'Al, what the hell are you doing up there?' Lara stood at the bottom of the stairs listening for a reply and as none came she started up the stairs. 'Al? Are you there?'

As she reached the top of the stairs she could see the bathroom door was closed and hear the running water. 'Hurry up Al, we haven't got all day. Well we do, but let's not take it ok?'

The man stood knife in hand by the bedroom door, poised until he heard footsteps as Lara returned downstairs. Breathing once again he looked around properly, noting that the lay-out of the house was a mirror image of next door. Then edging along silently, he took a moment to look into the doors as he went. A second bedroom was spacious and dominated by a king-sized bed, upon which lay a selection of dresses and lingerie which had not made the cut during the course of the previous evening's events. He paused, picking up a blouse and smelling the perfume, eyes closed; his face contorted with the intensity of determination within which he resolved that the girl would not go quickly. Today he would feed all of his desires, and his appetite was whet.

Regaining his composure, he moved to the final room and looked at the walls of books, the table and computer, the two black leather chairs. A study and library combined, what else would a person such as Doctor Andrews have? As he stared, he realised that the water in the bathroom was no longer running so darted back along the corridor into the main bedroom, taking his position behind the door.

*

Sue Scott checked through her notes, over and again, as she searched for the crack in the story, some light to shed on the lie that was Dr Andrews' alibi. Maybe Marlin was right about him; maybe he did have plenty to hide. But he had lied to her, she was sure of that, and one way or another she would find out why. The cabs were inconclusive, so what of the other dates? Why had she not looked closer? As she looked out across the floor she couldn't see Marlin, but Detective Carr was returning with a coffee.

'Phil?'

'Sue.'

'Can you spare a minute?'

'Yes sure.'

'I was going to speak to Marlin, but maybe you can help?'

'Is this to do with the Phantom?'

'Yes and no. It relates to information you may have from that case, but the Phantom stuff is all yours.'

'Ok then, fire away.'

'Last Sunday I was told that Dr Andrews was in the house all day. In fact, in all the time from Saturday night until Sunday and onwards?'

'Give me one minute Sue, I'll get my notes.'

Carr walked to his desk, but was quickly back with his notebook and a file which he handed to Sue.

'You can check a lot of the info from the file here, but basically, from my notes, the main point is that he was asleep, probably drunk, until a uniform woke him in the afternoon.'

'The afternoon is the first sighting?'

'Yes, half past four.'

'You're kidding me?'

'No, but as I say, dead drunk.'

'The last time I was told that he was dead drunk, he turned out to be surprisingly mobile. Which of the officers checked on him?'

'I don't remember off the top of my head, but it should be in the file.'

'Thanks, Phil, you've been a great help. I'll get the file back to you as soon as I can. Do you know where Marlin is?'

'I think he's checking out the Finsbury Park place.'

'Ok, thanks again.'

The file confirmed everything that Marlin had told her about the Phantom case, in that it was a series of notes and statements, times and names, which led you precisely nowhere. She only wanted limited information though. Then there it was:

4. 30pm Sunday 13th February – In response to a request from DCI Marlin, an officer – PC Wright - was despatched to the property of Dr Aldous Andrews in Camden (32 Albert Road). The officer checked on Dr Andrew's well- being and asked him to switch on his phone so that he could return the DCI's calls. The man had been sleeping and smelled strongly of alcohol. Officer Martin Wright noted that a reporter from the Herald, Jeff Stanley, had been staked out at the property for some time and asked him to ensure that he did not harass Dr Andrews.

Sue considered the entry and called the desk sergeant to ask if PC Wright could come and see her. Less than 5 minutes later a PC approached her desk, adjusting his uniform as he did so.

'PC Wright?'

'Yes, Detective Sergeant? You wanted to see me?'

'DCI Marlin asked you to check on Dr Andrews last Sunday?'

'He requested an officer check on him, so I went.'

'4.30 in the afternoon?'

'Yes, but I tried a number of times before that, it's just that there was no answer. Then again, having seen the state of the bloke when he did answer, I'm not surprised. The breath on the guy was lethal.'

'So nothing to suggest that he was anything but drunk and unconscious all night?'

'Well, not necessarily all night.'

'What?'

'That scumbag reporter guy, said he'd seen him arrive in the morning, drunk.'

'When in the morning?'

'I have to be honest; it was a passing comment so I thought nothing of it at the time.'

'Did you tell Marlin?'

'No, as I say, I was just there to see he was ok and he was.'

'Thank you, PC Wright, thank you very much.' Sue sat back as the tall officer left, tapping her pen against the desk as she bit her lip slightly. Then smiling, she picked up her phone.

'Good Afternoon.'

'Hello, is that the Herald news desk?'

'Yes it is. How may I help you?' The young lady speaking had an enthusiasm way beyond the requirements of the query, and it almost made Sue think she had the wrong number.

'Oh, err, could you put me through to a Mr Jeff Stanley?'

'Let me see now............Mr Stanley............here we are, I'm putting you through now. Have a lovely day.'

'Jeff Stanley.' The bored monotone now was much closer to expectation.

'I'm Dt Sgt Scott, I wondered if you had a few moments?'

'That depends on what you have for me?'

'A trip to the station sound good? Let's be clear here, I'm not looking to bargain for information.'

'Fucking hell, what is it with you people?'

'I believe you spoke to one of our PC's on Sunday?'

'Sunday? I can't say that I remember.'

'Come on Mr Stanley, outside Dr Andrews' house? Sunday afternoon?'

'Oh yeah, the tall bad tempered one, Scottish wasn't he? Yes I spoke to him but he told me fuck all just like you. Pretended he'd never heard of the Phantom. Jesus, you fucking people.'

'And what about what you told him?'

'Him? About what? What the fuck would I have to say to him?'

'You saw Dr Andrews come home that morning?'

'Yes, the fucking drunkard fell out of a cab and just about got inside. Ha, the pisshead.'

'What time was this?'

'I dunno really, I reckon about 9.00 maybe 9.30. Why are you asking? What do you have on the fucker?'

'Nothing for you to worry about. I'm just establishing time-lines and the like. It's really nothing.'

'Nothing? I think I'll be the judge of that. Thanks Detective.'

'Goodbye.'

Sue had something now, but she was nonetheless annoyed that the toe rag of a reporter had made her feel as if she was giving him some information.

'Damn it!'

'You ok?'

Sue looked up, surprised to see Marlin.

'Marlin?'

'Hello to you too.'

'I thought you were at the safe house?'

'Who told you that?'

'Phil, er, PC Carr.'

'Why were you speaking to him?'

'I wanted to speak to you, but he said you'd gone to Finsbury Park.'

'No, I sent Mitchell along in the end. I just popped out for some more cigarettes. How can I help?'

'I've got the information now.'

'What was it?'

'The PC sent along to check on Dr Andrews? I wanted to check what times he'd been there. No loose ends you understand?'

'Yes, and?'

'And what?'

'Come on Sue, it's written all over your face that there's something you're not telling me.'

'That obvious is it?'

'Yes,' Marlin laughed, but was slightly curious as to why she was withholding details.

'The officer talked to a newspaper guy and he said that Andrews had been out; coming back drunk early in the morning.'

'Really?' Marlin raised an eyebrow but said nothing more. He remembered the Doc telling him about a 'blackout' trip to the off-license and was more than aware that he should have mentioned this to Sue. Too late now though, he thought, as he kept his counsel. Sue, for her part, was trying to hide her delight at having found something and her feeling that this was big.

'When are you seeing Andrews?'

Marlin checked his watch. 'Just about now.'

'Ok I'll give you a half-hour to break the news and then, if it's ok, I want to have a quick chat. Oh and Marlin, can I ask that you don't tell him about me knowing this? It's important.'

'I'll say nothing, I promise.' Marlin at least felt comfortable that he was telling the truth this time as he turned to go.

Sue watched Marlin leave, his hand already taking out his cigarettes as he went through the exit; she shook her head gently and smiled as she reached for the phone.

'Hello, City Cabs.'

'Sharif? It's Detective Sergeant Scott here.'

'Ah, Detective Sergeant Scott, what a pleasure to speak to you again. How can I help you? A cab?'

'Ha, not on this occasion Sharif, I'm after your records again.'

'I will see what I can do.'

'Saturday night and Sunday morning, that's the 12th and 13th this month, did you send any cars for Dr Andrews? Er, Mr Al.'

'Mr Al again, he is in trouble no?'

'Not necessarily.'

'Let me see. Yes, here we are. A cab sent to Mr Al at 6.00am.'

'Where was he going?'

'I can't say Detective, I tell you before he have money for anywhere, so we don't ask.'

'The driver would know?'

'Probably. It was Jay, he is...,'

'He's not in Turkey surely?'

'No, Jay is from Cyprus and he is not there either. Jay is in Tottenham and he is due back at work at 6.00pm tonight.'

'Do you have his number?'

'I have his mobile, but you will be lucky to get anything now. The men who work shifts as long as Jay, usually spend the most part of the day in bed.'

'Can I have it anyway?'

'Of course.'

*

Marlin pushed his car out into the road and rolled down the window, letting the smoke escape as he puffed away. He knew the safe house was an option and it had been his own first thought, but this was not the way to do things. Why let Al get comfortable, not just Al but Lara as well, why let both of them get comfortable? At home, with guards and promises of safety, now suddenly ask them to 'get up and move'.

'Jesus.' He spat out loudly to himself. 'What a fucking mess.' He could feel the anger returning now and, glancing down, he saw that he was doing over 80mph. Slowing down, Marlin turned off and into a side road he knew led to a row of shops. Pulling up the car he stayed sitting for a while, breathing in the quickly cooling air in the hope it would have a similar effect on his head. There would undoubtedly be heightened emotions and raised tempers when he told Lara and the Doc what was going on, so someone had to keep a cool head.

He breathed in three or four times deeply and stepped out of the car, walking slowly and deliberately across to the shops. The crucial part of his proposed peace pact came in the shape of two bottles of scotch, and he knew this would partly placate at least one of them. As for Lara, well he feared that it would take both his head and Sue's presented on a silver platter to go any way towards pleasing her. It also occurred to him that there was a good chance that she might not be there, taking into account the poisonous atmosphere the last time he saw them both. He purchased the bottles and kept a steady pace back to the car, listening to the staccato clinks of bottle on bottle as he went; it was a familiar enough sound, but one he knew would always remind him of the Doc; the Doc and maybe Lara, too. Back in the car, he breathed deeply once more and steered the car back into the day's traffic.

REVELATIONS

Al opened the bathroom door, letting the steam spill out into the corridor and walked slowly to the bedroom, tying the belt of the bathrobe as he went. He paused at the doorway, seeing the door to his study was open, and made a mental note to remind Lara to keep the door closed; surfaces clean, lids attached and doors shut, was that really so difficult? He stepped forward into the room, half yawning, and approached the bed. A powerful weight collided with his back and sent him sprawling across the bed, winded and surprised; scared by feeling such force.

'Lara?' His voice was breathless and falsely hopeful, fooling no-one, not least himself. He managed to turn, preparing to kick-out, but the figure was upon him; a literal dark force pressing him deep into the mattress, then gripping his throat, holding his face. Unable to find any balance or purchase, Al flailed and it felt as though he was drowning as the figure swarmed over him, stealing his breath and spinning his senses. Aware that he needed to move matters on, the man gripped Al's face, holding it still as he brought the large blade into view before letting it rest on his neck. Leaning in, he pushed his head forward in the tightly drawn hood.

'Hello, Dr Al.'

Quietly spoken with a hint of false good humour, the words produced no cheer in Al's heart, a heart he could feel pounding in his chest. He lay still, finally fixing on his attacker's black eyes as he watched them glisten darkly, at once evocative and unfathomable.

'Don't move and don't make a sound. If you do I will not just kill you, I will shred you, your skin, your eyes. Then I'll take the girl and cut the skin from her body as she watches. Do you understand?'

'Yes.'

The word barely registered as Al's mouth was dry, but the croaked attempt and slow nod was enough.

'Lie the other way around and lift your arms above your head.' The man stepped off Al and was signalling with the large knife to lie lengthways. 'I was so pleased to see that you have done most of the work for me.' The man's voice again was filled with a grotesque parody of good cheer, but Al could see no smile as the face remained hidden. The man had hold of one of the loops of rope that were attached at each corner of the bed, and this reminder of more playful times brought Al's mind back to Lara. He had to warn her, keep her away from this demon. As his mind raced, the man was placing his hands and feet into loops that now felt like nooses, the blade twirling in his gloved hands as he glided from corner to corner.

'Lara...uumpmph.'

The blow to his stomach was unseen, quick and of a power Al had never felt. He instinctively tried to ball his body, but he was bound and the reflex motion brought a shooting pain in his shoulder and ankle joints as tears of pain filled his eyes. Groaning, Al fell back, panting for breath. The man had reached into his back-pack and tape was roughly stuck across Al's mouth.

'I did warn you Dr Al, did I not?'

The man waited for Al's eyes to widen in terror and then stepped back behind the door as they both became aware of footsteps on the stairs. Now, for the first time, Al could see the face; black eyes wide and focused, lips curled back revealing a malign grin, as Lara stepped through the door.

'What the...? How the fuck did you manage this Al?'

It was now that she saw his eyes, wide and terrified, and in the corner of her vision a dark shape came close. She turned her head slowly, her neck stiffening with fear, and was met by a dark unyielding gaze, white teeth bared in a twisted snarl. She took a step back, her arms reaching behind her, feeling for some tangible reality. This could not be happening? The dark hooded figure stepped in again, taking her arms in a strong grip that guided her across the room and pushed her towards the chair by the dressing table; sitting her down before she fell, her knees buckling.

'Shhhhhh.'

He brought the knife up to his mouth. The sight of the blade made her shudder and push back in the chair, her eyes swimming wildly from Al to the figure, to the door and back to the knife. Her mouth was gaping but no sound issued, hardly a breath taken, a life frozen in the moment. The man reached again into his bag and produced a rope with a noose which he quickly placed around her hands as he pulled them together. The rope length was wrapped around her and the frame of the chair then tied at the back. The figure leaned in and stroked her left cheek, further in and he breathed in her hair, groaning before stepping back. He spoke slowly and low of voice, but precisely.

'Lara, is it? So pretty, so fragrant.' He breathed in heavily again, his face pinched and sharp. 'I have some business with your friend Dr Al here. You're helping me with my book, aren't you Dr Al, the difficult last chapter and all that? But don't worry Lara; you can rest assured that once we have ironed out some of the plot lines and such, there will be a paragraph at least for you. Oh and by the way, I haven't tied you so tightly my dear, because I need to get quick access to that lovely body of yours. No, not in that way Lara, tut tut, not yet, anyhow. No, I need you to be my face at the door.'

The man brought the knife up to his face again and gently tugged on the side of the hood, letting some light across his stubbled chin and cheek.

'A better face than this one, I think you'll agree? Also one that visitors - should we have any - will not be so surprised to see. I'm happy enough for your police guard to stay outside but they were not invited to our party; no, this is private, intimate. But Lara, it's important for you to understand that you cannot abuse this privilege. I do NOT want to have you struggling to get away. I do NOT want you running. That will make me angry and I will hurt you. More than that, I will slice this man apart. I will slowly and surely butcher him if you disobey me. Do you understand?'

The two words shouted in the midst of the otherwise low monotone made both Lara and Al jump. She couldn't stop shaking now, a sick feeling flooding her stomach. Stammering, she tried to speak.

'Pppplease dddon't.'

The man stepped forward and stopped her with a finger pressed against her lips.

'Shhhh. Don't speak.' His hand reached into the bag again for the tape and he casually bit off a strip. Smoothing it almost gently across Lara's mouth, he stepped back to the door and then was gone. Lara's eyes, dripping tears now, turned to Al, spread-eagled and gagged on the bed. She wept in quiet, breathless sobs that were all but the signature of hopeless despair and terror. In the next bedroom they could hear his movement and it was not long before he returned with another straight backed chair. Placing it down deliberately, he sat at the head of the bed close to Al, resting the knife on his chest.

'So Dr Al, let's get back to that book, shall we? I like to think of it as 'The Psychopathology of the Serial Killer Writer'. Good title? What's that? You see some inspiration there? Well yes, the title is somewhat inspired by yours.'

He picked up the knife once more and placed it on the floor by his feet, then leaning in he pulled the tape off Al's mouth.

'Let's talk, shall we?'

Al licked his lips, his tongue dry as it ran across the sticky residue from the tape.

'Do you need a drink to get you talking? Water? No, whiskey of course.' The man again disappeared and Al heard his feet on the stairs.

'Lara, if you can get out of that rope then fucking run. Don't worry about me; just get away from this fucking psycho.' He began to cough, with the dryness of his throat and the exertions of his hoarse whisper, but he kept his eyes on Lara; wide-eyed and lost in fear, he hoped she heard him.

The man returned and filled Al's glass with whiskey, then cradling his head he poured too much into his mouth, laughing quietly as he coughed and alcohol poured down his chin.

'I thought you were an experienced drinker? Ha!' Al again coughed, but he actually felt better for the drink.

'I've read your work Dr Al and it is not too bad really, not too bad at all. All of your types are fairly standard, but I did enjoy your particular take on it. I'm talking about the good intelligent stuff, before your TV crap of course. So the question is, which am I?'

'You? You are all and none.'

'Really? Explain.'

'You were making a point by seeming to be all of the types and therefore you were potentially none of them, really. The days of the week ploy was you pretending to be a thrill seeker, although I think you genuinely enjoyed telling us what the theme was? Your pursuit of Professor Peters and I was your adoption of a mission to kill certain people. The methods of your killing showed an enjoyment of your victims suffering. By taking on all three types, it can be argued that none are applicable.'

'Very interesting, Dr Al. Very good really, but what I need to know for the last chapter is, what is your name for my type?'

'My name for you?'

'Yes, I want to quote you, so I was hoping for something unique and memorable.'

'You, Mr Phantom, are what I would call a copycat. And the broadest copycat at that. Not even the pathetic name is original.'

The man brought his fist across Al's left cheek with power and rage, once and then again; spinning his senses and sending a burning pain shooting from eye to ear. His glazed eyes saw a blurry vision of Lara in the chair and then there was just blackness as he passed out.

'Go ahead and sleep Dr Al, sleep for a moment. Maybe it will clear your mind, because that is not the end I want to my book. Not the end I want at all.'

The man stood pulling back the hood, his face red and angry, eyes blazing. He moved to the door and then paused, looking back at Lara.

'Don't you dare move a fucking inch.'

He noted the shaking body as the sobbing began again and walked away into the adjoining bedroom. Hearing voices from outside, he rushed to the window, crouching and listening.

Marlin stood by his car, smoking a cigarette and looking at his watch as he chatted to PC Ellis. A few yards away PC Hill stretched his legs

'Officer Hill, do you want to have a last look round the back before you go?' The officer nodded and set off on a final patrol.

'I wanted to get here earlier and warn them of the change in plan, but got kind of side-tracked, so I might as well wait while they get packed and drive them over to Finsbury Park.'

'Seems like a bit of a mess, sir?'

'Tell me about it. I'm sorry you guys were messed about.'

'To be honest, it wasn't the most exciting job, sir.'

'No, I suppose not.'

'A party planned tonight?'

'Oh, this?' Marlin lifted up the bag of bottles. 'A peace offering for the Doc in there. Anyway, I'd better get in so I'll see you guys back at the station?'

'Goodbye, sir.'

Marlin stubbed out his cigarette and knocked at the door. After a few minutes had passed he knocked again, nodding to PC Hill as he re-emerged from the rear of the house.

'All ok, there? Any signs of life that you can see.'

'It's ok. No-one in the kitchen, but there seldom is.'

The door rattled as it partially opened. Pale and red-eyed, Lara peered across the chain.

'What is it, Marlin?' Soft and breaking up, her voice also betrayed tears and Marlin wondered what the hell had happened.

'Hi Lara, I have to see the Doc.'

'He's in bed, can you come back?'

'Are you ok, Lara?'

'Yes, I'm fine. Can you come back?' She began closing the door and Marlin stopped it with foot and hand.

'No, I'm sorry Lara, I can't come back. I apologise if this is a bad time, but this is police business.'

Lara paused and turned her head slightly, a confused look on her face for a moment, then looking at the floor she spoke, 'Ok, come in.'

The door closed and the chain was rattled off. When it opened again, Lara was standing behind the door out of sight. He stepped in and the door closed quickly and loudly behind him. Marlin turned to ask Lara what the hell she was doing, but was stopped in his tracks. Lara stood, a picture of fear as a black hooded man held her tight, a knife pressed hard at her throat.

'The Phantom?' Marlin spoke almost to himself.

'Well done detective, now put down the bag and get upstairs, or I will take this girl's head clean off.'

Marlin led the way up the stairs, totally stunned and confused. Whatever he had thought was the cause for the look on Lara's face, it wasn't this. How the hell did the psycho get in? He glanced back to try and get a better look at the man but his hood was fastened tight.

'Look ahead, not at me. No, not in the main bedroom, the next one.'

As Marlin passed the main bedroom, he caught sight of Al on the bed. Spread-eagled, his face was red and swollen as he lay unconscious; or was he dead? He started to get a dark foreboding about the situation, which only became bleaker as he remembered Sue. Please God, don't let

Sue call here. The thought was curtailed as a sudden blinding pain exploded across the back of his head and darkness took over even before he hit the ground.

SUE

Having waited almost an hour since Marlin had left, Sue climbed into her car and eased onto the roads, enjoying the cold winter sun as it briefly emerged from the clouds, giving the roads a glassy appearance. She eased through the gears but kept a steady pace and even turned on the radio, smiling as she joined in with the song. Making good time she glanced at her watch and, seeing that it was three, it occurred to her that the cab driver Jay would surely be out of bed by now. A little more urgency crept into her mind now and she put her foot down and guided the car to Albert Road. Reaching number 32, she could see Marlin's car parked outside; the police guard gone. Stopping at the kerb, she reached for the number she had jotted down and picked up her phone.

'Yeah?'

'Is that Jay?'

'Maybe.' The voice on the other end was quiet and guarded.

'Jay from City Cabs?'

'Depends on who wants to know, and how you got my number?'

Sue rolled her eyes, frustrated at having to play this familiar game of show and tell.

'I got your number from Sharif and my name is Dt Sgt Scott. I just want to ask you a few questions about some jobs.'

'Fuck's sake, what am I supposed to have done now?'

'Nothing, Jay. I'm only interested in your passengers, honestly.'

'Ok then, go on.'

'You did a job in the early hours of Sunday morning, for a Dr Andrews?'

'Dr Andrews? Mmm.'

'Mr Al?'

'Oh Mr Al, yeah I picked him up. Is he ok?'

'He's fine; I just want to know where you dropped him?'

'It was a shortish journey and he gave me a lot of money for it, but I don't remember where.'

'Could it have been Buckingham Road?'

'That's it, yes. Sometimes we go there, sometimes we bring him back.'

'And this was at 6am?' Sue had to concentrate to hide the excitement she now felt.

'Yeah, around that time, why?'

'It's not important really, but thank you so much for your help.'

Sue sat back in the car and breathed out deeply as she spoke aloud.

'Explain this one, Dr Andrews, what were you doing there? Your safe house may be a cell tonight.'

Stepping from the car she approached the door slowly, determined to keep her composure. She knocked, surprised by the silence within the house, and waited for some time as there was no response. Did Marlin take them to Finsbury Park already? If he did, why was his car there? He surely wouldn't have used the squad car to drop them off knowing he had to pick up his own again.

She knocked again harder, stepping back to look into the upstairs windows for signs of life.

'Come on, come on.' She took out her phone and was about to ring Marlin when the rattle of the chain and lock announced the doors opening.

'Lara? God's sake, what happened to you?'

'Al and Marlin are talking and don't want to be disturbed, so they asked if you could come back later?'

'No.'

'What?'

'This is official business and I really do have to speak to Dr Andrews. Not later, now! If you don't let me in I'll arrest you for obstruction.'

Lara's eyes flicked to her right twice and her expression seemed anxious, then she slammed the door shut and removed the chain. The door swung open widely, presenting an empty corridor, and as Sue stepped in she glanced suspiciously at the empty living room. Where the hell was Marlin?

'I only wanted an intimate party and now look at all the uninvited guests.'

Hearing the quiet but clear voice, Sue turned and once again the man held the exhausted Lara tightly, the knife pricking the underside of her chin.

'Upstairs, please detective.'

Sue started upstairs, but couldn't help glancing back time and again, finally turning around completely when she reached the top. Walking slowly backwards she tried to see the man's face.

'You look puzzled detective, concerned even. Well you should be, you really should.'

Swinging across as he stepped forwards, the man caught Sue on the temple with the butt of the knife handle, his movement so swift that he was able to strike once more as she crumpled to the carpet. Grabbing Lara, he pulled her back to her chair and retied her whilst noting that Al was stirring.

Striding into the corridor, he grabbed the prone and bleeding Sue by her feet and dragged her to the library-cum-study, the journey marked by a bloody track on the carpet. Closing the door he checked on the second bedroom where Marlin lay, hands and feet taped, unconscious. Back into the main bedroom, he slowed his breathing and sat down once more, staring at Al as he came round, his left eye swollen and closed, an ugly colouring already visible.

'Oh God, my head.' The move to raise his hands brought a reality check, stopped as he was by rope. 'Oh, no.'

'Welcome back Dr Al, and no, you aren't dreaming. A living nightmare perhaps, but it's all real and all now. You missed so much while you slept, didn't he Lara?'

Lara sat seemingly broken, staring at the floor, no tape on her mouth but silent all the same.

'Oh come on Lara, tell Dr Al all about it.'

Lara looked up blankly, her eyes welling with tears.

'Marlin called looking for you. He hit him, he hit him hard and dragged him away. Then that woman came...and.....and...I think he's killed her Al.' The sobbing returned now and the tears fell freely.

'That's the basic facts of the matter Dr Al, but it is a very plain account; dull prose when my artistry deserves rich verse. More importantly it has changed some of my plans. The cleaner necessitated a certain degree of rapidity, but with two police as well, I feel a real sense of urgency about proceedings now. So really, I should get to my point. Dr Al? It would seem that we are not on the same page where my book is concerned; a real shame as my other choice of collaborator is otherwise indisposed, having so carelessly lost his head. So to plan B, where I am sole author and the final chapter is you, your renown and your reputation; stripped to the bone - literally.'

'Kill me then. Finish your pathetic story if you must, but leave the others? Leave Lara?'

'Oh, some nobility from the Doctor. It has to be said that I followed you for some time and I never thought of your actions as noble. Is that why the policewoman came? Did she find out your ignoble secrets? I wonder?'

'Please.'

'Shut-up! The cops are not going to save you Dr Al and begging is pointless; your death is not in the realms of possibility, it is an inevitability. I only have one dilemma and that is young Lara over there.'

Lara looked over, eyes pleading, her head shaking no.

'Is she an aperitif or the dessert? It's your choice, Dr Al. I can take her body now, her life; satisfy myself while you look on, helpless? Or I can gut your fat excuse for a body and take my time with her? I'll let you choose, but you may need a minute or two? Think carefully.'

The man left the room glowing as he considered the day gone, and the day yet to come. He always felt the jubilant eruption of ecstasy at the point of a kill, but today there was a girl to share it with. The pretty blonde could give him her body and her blood. The very thought made him dizzy but he knew he could not lose control. Not now that he was so close. He stepped back to the bathroom and, gloves still on, cupped his hands to wet his face with cold water, stopping to look, to stare, to remember himself.

ROOMS

Marlin came to on an unfamiliar carpet, his head screaming in a quadraphonic symphony of pain with his arms and legs. Registering the tethers, he remembered where he was and who put him here. He felt tired and dizzy, but he knew he could not surrender to sleep again as it would certainly be his last.

Moving his legs as much as possible, he tried to get nearer to the bed and a sharp edge, but progress was slow and awkward. With gritted teeth, he concentrated and pushed his body up and to the side, then rolled when he could see he was close. Trying to sit up was a struggle, more so as his head was swimming and he was almost crying with frustration when he finally sat up with his back to the corner of the bed. Leaning to one side he vomited. Again he was aware that he could not rest or stop. Awake and active, awake and active. Making sure of his balance, he felt behind for the sharp corner and began to rub the tape around his wrists with some urgency, ignoring the pain, evading sleep.

The tape was thick and strong but Marlin stuck to his task, his eyes focused straight ahead, his face a mask of pain. Sweat poured down his face, into his eyes, but it didn't dampen his resolve. The Phantom would be back at any moment, each creaking floorboard spoke of his arrival, every sound whispered murder. His face a silent scream, he tore tape and skin as he rubbed against the edge of the metal, feeling some give, and then a tear. Faster he rubbed as his aching shoulders forced his arms apart, testing the strength of cotton mesh and polythene, feeling the resistance yielding to pressure; it must give.

What was the sound? Footsteps? Yes footsteps and then the bathroom door closing softly. The man was moving again and he would be visiting soon, he would be coming for his blood. Marlin became more frantic and each and every muscle tightened, pressing for escape; he spoke under his breath.

'Come on Marlin, nearly there, nearly there. Come on.'

The bathroom door opened and the footsteps, slow and even, came closer.

Not now, not like this. For God's sake don't let it end like this. Please God, no.

Snap! His hands were apart, bloodied but free, as he listened to the even pacing pass by his door.

'Quickly Marlin, get this off your legs, come on, come on, come on. There!'

Standing he was dizzy, his legs numb and disobedient, but he rubbed and stretched, searching the room for some weapon to lead his invalid assault. The bed was strewn with clothes and costumes, for want of a better word. He sank his hands beyond the leather and lace, grabbing a belt of studs and half-inch spikes.

'Yes, yes that will do nicely.'

He moved to the door and listened for movement, or some hint of the events outside but, whilst he could hear some sounds, it was indistinct. His foot brushed against something and looking down he saw the shoe. No doubt expensively designed, the aesthetics were of no consideration to Marlin now. He bent unsteadily and picked up the shoe, his hand enveloping and crushing the toe as he looked closer. The heel was his interest, the six inch, thin, metal-tipped heel. This was a true stiletto; it was his weapon.

The man passed along the corridor slowly, deliberately, calming his excitement and controlling his desires. He paid no attention to Lara and Al as he walked on, passing the second bedroom with only the slightest of glances. That moment was coming, but not now. Pushing open the study door, he crouched at Sue's body, unmoved since he dragged her in. He hadn't tied or taped her limbs because he didn't expect her to ever wake again, but now, as he traced a finger along her neck, he felt a pulse. He flicked her onto her back and, as his hands ran over her chest, he could confirm that she was indeed breathing. Standing again he shook his head slowly. Was he losing his touch or was her desire for life really this strong?

He bent again and moved her head to the right, examining the ugly wound on the left side. Again shaking his head he stood. The hits were powerful enough, but this was a strong woman. She deserved to be conscious when he took her life; she had earned a fighting chance. The man left the room, closing the door gently as if not wishing to wake her, and walked the few feet to the next door; the next body to be dealt with.

This time there would be no mercy. Breathing deeply, slowly, he pulled up his top and drew the knife from his belt, taking a moment to see his reflection in the blade. It was time.

Al listened for the faintest of creaks outside the door, in the corridor or on the stairs; aware that he knew all the locations, the distances from the bed. Nights spent tied and blindfolded, waiting for heeled shoes to bring Lara to his bedside, had honed his appreciation for the sounds made by his aged house. He listened now, for confirmation that this Phantom was in the library, and only then allowed himself to breathe.

'Lara? Lara?' A shouted whisper, hoarse and pleading, as Lara fixed her eyes on the floor. 'Lara?'

'He can take me first, Al.'

'No, Lara.'

'Will it be quick?'

'Shh. Wait.'

Al was twisted as far as he could on the bed, grimacing as his neck stretched. Lara looked over, confused and scared, as Al seemed to be having a fit.

'Al, are you ok?'

'There!' Al raised his right hand, a livid bracelet of rope burn, but free. 'This set up was for fun, remember?'

Releasing his left hand, he paused for an instant as he listened, but the blood pumping through his ears now deafened him to any nuance of loose boards. He freed his legs and stepped somewhat unsteadily over to Lara, finding it surprisingly easy to unravel her bonds. He brought a finger to his lips as her released arms squeezed him as if she would never let go, her body convulsing with almost ecstatic tears.

'Not yet,' Al whispered.

Helping her to her feet, the pair of them tiptoed to the doorway. Al looked at Lara, his eyebrow raised in question as he trusted in her hearing. Lara half shrugged and then shook her head. Al signalled towards the stairs with his eyes and then pointed to Lara.

'You,' he mouthed, 'Go and get help.'

Lara looked puzzled and shook her head, her finger gesturing to the two of them; Al took her hand and leaned to her ear.

'You go now, and quickly. Get help. I won't be far behind, but I have to try and help Marlin.'

Al watched Lara nodding and then held his breath as he peered out to his right. The study door was open but he couldn't see the man.

'Go Lara, go,' he whispered

Lara moved as quickly as she could, but it felt as though she was running through treacle as every muscle tightened with anxiety. She headed to the stairs without looking back and tried to run on tip-toe as she descended. At the door she almost felt like screaming as her shaking hands struggled with a rudimentary door catch. Her tears fell thick and fast, but there she had it, chain off, turn knob, open. Once out her mouth gasped for air as she ran. She only now glanced back and almost stopped as she saw that she had left the door open, almost stopped but didn't. Nothing would drag her close to that beast again and she ran on, she must get help but she needed some distance first.

At the top of Albert Road the pathway split and Lara stopped at the curved, whitewashed wall and caught her breath. Pushing the green wooden gate inwards she staggered onwards and banged loudly on the door; over and over, until a well-dressed woman in her fifties opened the door angrily.

'Would you please stop that?'

She was about to go on, but this figure in front of her was in no way what she had expected. Her blonde hair, now windswept and unruly, clung to her tear stained face; her red eyes were edged with black mascara which ran on down her cheeks. Standing without shoes, a stocking hung at her knee below the short skirt and black stained blouse.

'Who are…?'

'Police now, police. The Phantom, police, police.'

The woman was shocked and alarmed, but pointed to the phone on the table as she looked past the poor wretch and into the street. Lara pounced on the phone and dialled 999.

The man was composed and ready as he turned the knob and opened the door, knife in hand. He was not ready for the blur of colour that exploded into him, sending him backwards into the wall. He kept his grip on the knife, but could not immediately focus, as Marlin landed spiked punches and drove the heel through his cheek- smashing a tooth on the other side. Instinct took over and he drove his right hand upwards once, twice, feeling the puncturing, the tearing of flesh, as the blows kept falling.

Marlin felt the burning in his side, but didn't know he was stabbed, adrenaline forcing him on and keeping the dizziness at bay for the moment. He had wrapped the belt around his left fist, and with the heel in his right, he rained blows heavily upon the head of this demon until a hand gripped his throat like a vice and he felt himself being pushed backwards. He could see the lips curled back, showing the teeth in a grotesque snarl now as the man's bloodied head pushed forwards into his, and again his side burned. It was now that the glint of the blade informed him of its murderous sharpness and he grabbed the arm, scared by its strength. The squeeze on his neck could be felt down to his knees as the man forced him backwards until his back was pushing into the wall. He held the knife away but was aware he was losing that battle, as his right hand brought the heel down, again and again against hand and head; desperate to loosen his grip before all breath was gone. His legs were unsteady and it was all he could do to stay conscious as he felt the knife nearing his stomach, his left arm locked and shaking. He looked ahead and blinked as the black eyes edged towards him, they seemed to swim in the blood all around them, shining darkly. All of his strength and it was not enough; he gritted his teeth.

'Noooooooooooooooooooo. Noooooooooooooooooooooooo.'

The breath of the beast was upon him, it was over now, he was exhausted and finished.

CRASH!

The noise brought him back and the grip was gone, the knife. Eyes and teeth no longer owned his blurred vision. Holding his side, he felt himself slide down the wall until he sat in a half-reality, fighting to keep his eyes open.

'Stay with me, Marlin.' Al was standing above him, a broken whiskey bottle in his hand. Looking to his right he saw the man struggling to get to his feet. On one knee he was staring up at Al, his teeth bared like a cornered animal. Al held the knife that had been dropped but looked less than confident in terms of finishing the job. Outside he heard the loud sound of sirens and cars and Al stepped back as the man stood, shaking his head as if that was nothing too serious. He looked at the knife and then at Al.

'That is my knife, Dr Andrews. Do you really think you can use it on me?' The man made as if to lunge forward and Al leapt back, the knife held out in front of him as he stepped back towards the stairs.

'I thought not.' The man leapt up and the loft catch was opened, the hatch falling down and releasing the ladder. Keeping his eyes on Al, the man quickly pulled himself up and was gone. Al stood transfixed, staring at the hole in the ceiling, as if he expected the man to return.

'Give that to me, Al.' Marlin was standing, holding his side with one hand as he took the knife in the other. 'Tell the officers outside he's going into the house next door.'

Marlin stepped onto the ladder and pulled himself up.

'Leave it to the other guys, Marlin. Look at yourself.'

Marlin paused at the top of the ladder.

'I want to kill this fucker.' With that he was gone.

Al stepped away from the ladder and turned down the stairs, surprised to see an armed policeman already in the house.

'Stay where you are, hands in the air.' Al raised his hands, embarrassed, as his gown opened.

'He's next door, Marlin's gone after him.'

'Stay where you are, sir.'

There were a number of cars and many police milling around as a second armed policeman entered. He looked up at the half-naked man in a bathrobe through his helmet visor and lowered his gun.

'It's ok, that's Dr Andrews.'

'Marlin's followed him next door. Through the roof partition.'

The policeman reacted now. 'Stay here and watch this door, we have men at the back.' Then the policeman was gone.

'Can I move now? Put some clothes on?'

The first policeman signalled to go ahead and Al retreated back into the bedroom, stopping as the far door caught his eye. Following the trail of blood he walked over and opened the door gently, stepping inside and closing the door behind him.

Sue Scott felt a terrible tightness in her chest, a needle sharp pain in her head, and she could hear a terrible gurgling sound as she came round, struggling to open her eyes. It was soon apparent that the gurgling sound was her; she was drowning in her own blood, choking on her back. One eye was swollen shut, the other open as she tried to summon some energy, but with no air she could not seem to move, her limbs heavy and unresponsive. Then in her vision was Al. Her eye widened as she signalled her distress the only way she could as he crouched down beside her.

'Why did you have to go back to the cab company again? I'm a good customer there, maybe their best, so didn't you think Sharif would call me about all the questions? All you had to do was accept the alibi and leave it.' Al sighed deeply and shook his head. 'I suppose I should thank you for clearing up those guilty black holes in my life? But then my suppression was working so well; it'll be hard to get back to that level again.'

Sue's body was shaking now, convulsed through lack of oxygen, but she just could not move; still her eye remained fixed and pleading. Al could hear the policemen moving around the house, they would look for him again soon.

'I hate to see you this way, Sue.' Al reached down and, closing her eye, he held his hand tightly over her face, covering her nose and mouth. He closed his eyes and held his breath as he pressed strongly, until he could feel no further movement, then standing, he opened the door and shouted down to the policeman.

'I need a doctor here quickly. Hurry, please.' He stood at the top of the stairs and watched as the ambulance crew rushed up the stairs and passed him. 'The far room there, please hurry, I couldn't get a pulse. I didn't know she was here.' As the medics fought their pointless battle, Al walked wearily to the bathroom and closed the door behind him. Turning on the taps, he washed his hands over and over, keeping his head bowed so as to avoid his reflection; then cupping them he brought cold water up and over his face. Only now did he raise his head to look. Swollen and discoloured though they were, the empty blackness in his eyes was entirely self-inflicted.

Marlin stepped through the gloom of the loft, the knife held out ahead of him as he went. He felt sick and he could feel the wetness of his shirt as he continued to bleed, but anger drove him on. Edging forward, he tapped with his toe as though testing the water, unfamiliar with his surroundings and all too aware that there may be a real monster in the dark. As he reached the mid-way point between the houses, he could just about make out the thin wooden divide illuminated by the half-light from the hatch. He moved this slightly and now he could see the light from the open hatch on the other side; he stopped, reluctant to step through into this unknown area, but breathing uncomfortably he continued, half crouched, eyes alert. He reached the hatch and again looked all around until satisfied and then, carefully, looked down through the open hole to the corridor. Because the hatch was still open and the ladder down, Marlin assumed the man had moved on at pace, not waiting for pursuers or wanting to fight them. In some pain he climbed down as quickly as he could and, as he made contact with the ground, he moved so his back was to the wall; his head swivelling left, right, left again.

The police were banging against the door, official demands drowned out by the echo of the impact. Marlin looked down at the small pool of blood at his feet and then across the carpet, seeing a line of red leading to the second door 10 feet away from him. He looked back across to the stairs and there was no similar trail. So he stayed here? He waited for me? Marlin looked at the door uneasily, then he heard the sounds of glass being broken at the back door and he remembered his job. Stepping forward with the care of a tightrope walker, he turned the handle of the door with a definite precision, easing it open wide.

The room was large and well-lit in the late afternoon light. A study in white, it had an almost clinical feel and it seemed fitting that the only stains were blood. Two generous sized twin beds dominated the room, but here all domestic normality ended. On the farther of the two beds from Marlin sat the man, his face punctured and bloody, staring at the floor. His back pack was discarded and open on the carpet, in his hand an axe was securely held but hanging towards the floor. Behind the black figure, Marlin could see a duvet rolled tightly; the angled shape protruding at the end now clearly a human foot. Marlin shook his head trying to understand how this wiry figure from the shadows could possibly be responsible for so much misery and death. What caused such cruelty?

The front door capitulated loudly, spilling armed policemen all over the hallway and, fingers on triggers, they screamed for surrender into the empty rooms, killing all silence. The man looked up at Marlin blankly, his eyes glassy black.

'Why? Why all of this? Who are you? Who the fuck are you?' Marlin spoke desperately with a real desire to know.

'I am a cancer. A heart attack, a terminal disease. I am death. There is no why, don't you see that? There is only how.' The man spoke slowly, wearily, his lack of emotion somehow making the words even more chilling.

'That is not an answer you fucking psychopath. That is not an answer! Not for all of this.' Pained and exasperated, Marlin sounded close to tears.

'No, it is not YOUR answer. Do you really believe that you can even start to comprehend me? That you could come close to penetrating a mind such as mine? How could some lines in a chapter understand a whole book?'

The man sighed deeply. An angry and confused Marlin could say nothing. The man sighed again and stood, causing Marlin to take a step back.

'I am written now. It's time to go.'

Marlin stepped towards the man, clutching the knife tightly but aware that his legs were weak and unsteady. Approaching the second bed, he stiffened his knees and balled his left fist in anticipation of contact. His eyes were fixed on the dark figure standing only feet away now and staring at the ground.

'It is not your role or your destiny, Detective.' The man spoke quietly, raising his head to look at Marlin, then the eyes sparked again and in a black blur he exploded into action. Marlin thrust with the knife instinctively but the dark ball of energy sent the bleeding man to the carpet with a primal force, leaving him gasping and bewildered. Again and again he brought the blade across in front of him, but the Phantom was gone.

'STOP!'

'DROP THE WEAPON!'

'STOP OR WE WILL SHOOT!'

'GET DOWN!'

A thunderous cacophony of gunfire echoed around the house as the man confronted his firing squad; a snarling beast charging through the hail of bullets but refusing to go down. Kneeling at the front door, a senior officer took aim for the head and fired as the figure bounded down the stairs towards his stunned colleagues. The bullet hit home but the officer continued to fire away, again and again, until the black-clad body lay at the foot of the stairs; even then his aim was fully upon the prone figure, as if scared he would rise again.

All around officers looked at each other, the helmets not enough to disguise the shock and horror they shared. How had this thing kept moving through that level of weapon discharge? The eyes, what was it about those eyes? What was it that had burned into their collective memories already? They moved slowly forwards to the body, busying themselves with the routine business of the aftermath, as if this was in any way routine, but they all knew that the extraordinary events would not be forgotten.

Oxygen mask clamped over his mouth Marlin was carried on a stretcher to the waiting ambulance. He saw the Doc, now dressed, talking to an officer, but breaking off his conversation as he saw him and coming over. He was serious and looked concerned.

'Hey Marlin, how are you?'

Marlin raised the oxygen mask from his face.

'How do you think, Doc?' He raised a bloody hand as if to explain, but he was stopped by the paramedic.

'Sorry, we really have to get this man to hospital; he's lost a lot of blood.'

'Of course, of course. Get him well, you hear?' Al waved the stretcher on and then paused and leant in. 'Thanks Marlin, and I'm so sorry.'

Marlin was moved quickly on into the ambulance and he could only look back at the Doc; his sombre face and sad eyes seemed to speak of more than concern for a friend and Marlin felt scared but didn't know why.

SORRY

The first few days or so in the hospital were a sedated haze as Marlin kept the doctors busy and the theatre occupied more than they would have liked. Lucky though he was with the position of the wounds, the very force of the knife and the number of blows, had caused a considerable amount of trauma. Blood loss had not helped in any way. Once out of danger, visitors passed in and out in a half-remembered morphine reverie. Marlin was healing and slowly, he emerged from his dreams, his nightmares. By and by he began to talk, to ask questions.

'Just relax and get better, there's plenty of time for questions later.'

Carr, Mitchell, Oliver, McCarthy, Ellis, Hill and others came and went as his periods of lucidity became longer, but he couldn't place them in time or order. Chief Superintendent Thomas talked of heroism and medals but Marlin was pleased to fall back to sleep. He even thought he saw Lara at one time, standing still and serious as she looked at him from across the room, but of any of this he couldn't be sure. Not till the day of the rain.

The wind was strong and it whipped the water across the window of the hospital room, waking Marlin to his first day of sustained reality and reduced sedation; his first day of searing pain sound-tracked by the lashing of rain against glass. Eyes open, he forced himself to try and focus as the burning in his side refused to go away. With an open mouthed groan, silenced by the dryness of his throat, he scanned the room for help.

'Here, drink some water.' He recognised the Doc's voice as a cup was placed into his hand. 'Go on, drink. Nurse? Nurse? Ah, you'll see that our friend is awake now and in some pain.'

Marlin drank and gradually his vision cleared so that he could see Al seated next to the bed.

'Hang on Marlin, the doctor is on his way and he should give you something for the pain. Oh and try not to speak just yet, just drink.'

Al refilled the cup with water from the jug on the table and then held the cup for Marlin as the nurse returned with the doctor and they began the examinations. Al watched as Marlin was gently moved about, glassy eyed and grimacing with the pain until eventually he was given some pills and sat up more comfortably.

'Mr Marlin, those pills will help the pain but they will make you very drowsy.' Dr Chang then turned to Al. 'Have you spoken to him?'

Al shook his head and Dr Chang looked concerned for a moment before continuing.

'The pills will hit him soon so you have about ten minutes, ok?'

'Yes, thank you doctor.'

'Spoken to me about what?' Marlin eventually spoke, albeit hoarsely. Al gave him some more water as the doctor left and Marlin noted the look of concern on the face of the nurse as she closed the door. He drained the cup of water and handed it back to Al, who placed it on the table carefully.

'So come on Doc, what is it? The fucker is dead isn't he? Gone?'

'Yes, there's no more Phantom. It's Sue.'

'Yes, where is she? I know she wanted to keep things under wraps, but isn't she visiting at all? Or was she here when I was out of it?'

'Marlin, she came to the house after you.' Al had to look away.

'What do you mean, after me? She wasn't there.'

'He put her in the next room to you.'

'No, she wasn't there.' Marlin shook his head in hopeless denial, but the cold, sharp pain in his side spoke of a different truth.

'She was, Marlin. She was in the next room to you. He hit her Marlin, he hit her hard and...well...she didn't make it. I'm so sorry.'

Marlin went to speak, but he didn't know what to say and lay back staring, trying to take it in. He remembered the words as he was on the stretcher 'I'm so sorry.'

'You knew that night? When they put me in the ambulance?'

'Yes.'

'You knew where she was?'

'Yes.'

'You let me go after that bastard, knowing she was injured a few feet away behind a door? You let me leave her?'

'I'm sorry, I wasn't thinking.'

'Sorry? Sorry? You, you weren't thinking? If it'd been Lara would you have thought? She died in that room alone.'

'I tried to help her but…,'

'You tried? You? You...,'

'She was already gone, Marlin. You couldn't have done anything.'

'You...,' Marlin's voice broke off and tears came freely, washing down his cheeks as his shoulders shook.

'I'm sorry Mar...,'

'Please just go.'

'You want....,'

'GO! Please just go now, Doc.'

Inconsolable, Marlin wept as Al left, and he kept on weeping until the drugs took his conscious thought away; his dreams were already destroyed.

IN CONCLUSIONS

The press conference was well attended and crackling with anticipation as DCS Thomas stood to speak. Beside him sat Al, still bearing the discolouration of his beating, a fractured cheekbone the diagnosis. Flanking Thomas, Detective Mitchell and PC Ellis stood in position much as Marlin and Scott had done so many times before, listening solemnly.

'Ladies and Gentlemen, I would like to thank you all for being here today, a day which is a source of so much pride and sadness for the Metropolitan Police.

'Firstly, I would like to pay tribute to the bravery and dedication of Detective Sergeant Susan Scott, an outstanding police officer who I have recommended for a posthumous bravery award; she will be missed by us all. I would add that our thoughts and prayers are with her family at this terrible time.

'Secondly, we would like to wish a speedy recovery to the heroic DCI Peter Marlin, who has also been recommended for a bravery award and who is in hospital as a result of stab wounds at this time.

'Now ladies and gentlemen, I'm sure you are all aware of the circumstances surrounding recent events, but please let me clarify.

'In previous weeks we alerted the press to the activities of a suspected serial killer who went by the name of the Phantom. Having killed indiscriminately for some time, we ascertained that his focus of attention had turned to the psychologist helping us with the case, Dr Aldous Andrews. Although we established a secure boundary as far as we could, the Phantom did manage to gain entry via an adjoining house. But, due to the efforts and bravery of Detectives Scott and Marlin, aided by the armed response unit, he was found and trapped. In the course of this action Detective Scott was brutally assaulted and killed and, when the Phantom refused to surrender or lay down his weapons, there was no alternative but to open fire on him. He was shot and died at the scene. I would also like to say that we have identified the body in the second property as Helena Kurczyn; we would like to offer our sincere condolences to her family at this time.

Finally, I would like to thank Dr Andrews for all of his help in solving this case and another which we had not realised was connected. Any questions?'

Al sat listening to the man who had wanted nothing to do with him, offering thanks and condolences in equal measure, and tried to take his mind elsewhere. As his eyes roamed around the room he saw cameras flash and lights pointing forward, searching for sensation. Amidst it all, he was drawn back to two persistent eyes that ignored the DCS and were fixed wholly upon him. Al thought the bearded man familiar but couldn't place him as he tried to see more clearly against the brightness. Was he smiling at him? How odd. Al looked away and again connected with the speech. 'Any questions?'

'Detective Chief Superintendent Thomas, Jane Hughes, Sky news. Have you identified the Phantom yet? And do you know what his reasons for doing this were?'

Thomas glanced at Al uncomfortably and cleared his throat.

'Well Jane, in terms of his reasons we have better qualified people here to answer that question. But as to the identity of the Phantom, all I can say is that investigations are on-going, but he seems to have worked very hard at hiding his identity. Dr Andrews, could you help with the second part?'

Al stayed seated but pulled his microphone a little closer.

'Jane, the question of why is too complicated a matter for a quick response today, but I do appreciate that everyone is curious for answers here. I am currently putting together a detailed description of this case and an explanation of the Phantom as we speak, and hope to have it ready for publication as soon as possible. I'm sorry but I can't give any more information at present.'

Al sat back and listened as the same question seemed to be asked in eleven different ways; Thomas replied anyway, enjoying the sound of his own voice too much not to. Some mention was made of Marlin, but it pained Thomas too much to dwell on his heroism, and so it seemed the whole event was going to ebb away to nothing. Then the bearded man stood.

'Chief Superintendent Thomas. Could you tell us what the other case was that Dr Andrews helped you with?'

'Excuse me, you are?'

'Oh sorry, Jeff Stanley, The Herald.'

'Right. Well Jeff, we had become aware of the deaths of three prostitutes in the London area in recent weeks and it emerged that the Phantom was also responsible for these.'

'How did you discover this?'

'During his time being held prisoner, the Phantom confessed this to Dr Andrews and one of the other captives.'

'Dr Andrews, may I ask you a question?'

'Go ahead, Jeff.'

'Is it true that you were a major suspect in this second case?'

Al was stunned as he looked with some alarm at Thomas, and then back to this upstart of a reporter, desperately trying to regain some composure as he searched for an answer. For once he was happy when Thomas spoke.

'Ah Jeff, I think you'll find that Dr Andrews was assisting us, so he was not a suspect, no.'

'Mm. Really?' *The Herald* reporter sat while making a few notes and then resumed his previous position, staring at Al who could not return his gaze.

Al survived the press conference, although his composure had been badly disturbed by the reporter; both his question and his look had unsettled him. He was travelling to see Shirley, but the cab ride there was quiet as he searched for a memory of the bearded man with the mocking eyes. As he entered the familiar offices in a Soho backstreet he chose to put it all to the back of his mind. Shirley stepped from her office to meet him and Al could taste her perfume long before she offered her cheek in greeting; well-dressed and elegant as always, she nevertheless always seemed to remain hidden behind a barrier of powder and scent.

'Dr Andrews, how good to see you in person for a change.'

Al smiled; the fact that Shirley called him Dr Andrews was always a sign that she was pleased with him.

'Hello Shirley, you're looking well.' Shirley smiled, her plump cheeks dimpling as she did so and then adjusting her glasses, she sat.

'I'm always well when I know I have a book coming. I do have a book coming, don't I Dr Andrews?'

'It's on its way Shirley, but let's not rush things ok?'

'Let's not lose the moment, either.'

'When do you need it?'

'Yesterday?'

'Come on.'

'It can't come too soon.'

'I can give you a crap version right now and then I think you'll think it's too soon?'

'The frenzy over this? I don't think it matters how good it is. People want to read about the Phantom now!'

'Ok, I get the point, but please allow me some sort of professional pride?'

'Of course, Dr Andrews.'

'No really. This is going to be THE book for me and I'm not going to fuck it up. But the good news is that it's not too far away. If you give me three weeks, I'll finish the book.'

'I can work with three weeks.'

'I'm going to go away for a wee while, relax a bit and finish it there.'

'A holiday? I'm not sure I like the sound of that.'

'Not a holiday as such, more a working journey. Some sunshine, some time to get away from it all.'

'Not a drinking session abroad?'

'Only a few, I promise.' Al smiled and he could see the doubt and mild panic in Shirley's eyes as she tried to smile back at him. 'Shirley, I really do promise, ok?'

'Ok, but even if you are away, keep in touch?'

'As always.'

Al stood before the to and fro could continue anymore.

'I have to see Marlin again and then I intend to get away, ASAP.'

'How is he?'

'The Phantom cut him up pretty badly and the female detective that was killed? Well, that was his girlfriend and he's taking it really hard. I think the body will heal in time, but the mind is something else.'

'Wish him all the best from me.'

'I will - bye Shirley.'

Stepping from the office into the fresh air, Al breathed in deeply and felt good at the thought of getting away from it all as he hailed a cab to the hospital. Sliding into the back of the black cab he noticed the driver looking back in the rear-view mirror and it pleased him to know that he was recognised again, relevant. He did not want to talk though, and quickly pulled out his phone and dialled.

'Lara?'

'Al, where are you?'

'I'm going to the hospital and then home, but listen to me for a second.'

'Yes.'

'Get your passport and pack a bag. Two or three bags in your case, but anyway, we are going away.'

'Away?'

'Yup.'

'What sort of clothes do I pack?'

'Don't worry, it'll be a warm place, although I can't for the life of me think of any clothes you have that are not designed for hot weather.'

'You don't usually ask for me to wear my thermals, you cheeky bastard.'

'That's true, but anyway, get packed. If you want to come, that is?'

'How long?'

'Two weeks, all expenses and that.'

'I could do with a holiday.'

'That's settled then.'

The cab dropped Al at the hospital and he dallied on his way to Marlin's room, not sure of the reception he might get. Opening the door quietly, he saw Marlin hidden behind a newspaper held at an angle, as he could not yet extend his left arm; it gave the impression that the room had been tilted.

'Marlin?'

Marlin lowered the paper and then folded it in half across his lap as he looked at Al. He was pale and his eyes were tired and red.

'Doc. Have a seat.'

'How are you?' Al felt obliged to ask the stupid question as he sat, and was not surprised by the raised eyebrow in response. 'Sorry, it's kind of an automatic hospital question.'

'It's ok, but could you try to stop apologising to me, it kind of reminds me.'

'Sorr...I won't.'

'I heard you on the radio with Thomas.'

'He needed someone with him and, with you in here, I guess I was the next best thing.'

'Two cases?'

'What?'

'You cleared the prostitute murders as well?'

'I didn't, it was just what the Phantom said.'

'He just came out with it.'

'We weren't expected to walk away from this, as you know Marlin, so who was going to tell? He was boasting.'

'He talked about all of the killings? Boasted about them?'

'No, not as such, but then we knew about the others.'

'He said it just to you?'

'No, Lara was there as well.'

'Lara again?'

'Again?'

'One alibi and a verification to back up the alibi.'

'What do you mean by that?'

'I don't know, Doc. I just don't buy the Phantom for the other killings, never did. If you hadn't been a suspect, I doubt you would either. In fact, you were the one who told me to stop linking them in the first place.'

'I also said the days of the week were relevant and that was wrong.'

'There were links though; it just wasn't the reason why.'

'But not right, though?'

'The messages at the crime scenes: 'Now are you satisfied' - 'You're fucked now' and well... ,'

''Was that hard enough?''

'You know the third message?'

'As do you.'

'I didn't actually; I never got a chance to find out.'

'Oh, well.......I talked to Sue...sorry......well she told me.'

'She didn't mention it to me.'

'What can I say?'

'The last girl, Alice, was on Sunday morning.'

'Yes, and?'

'The Phantom killed Prof. Peters late on Sunday night. You think he killed the prostitute, leaving a joke, a bad joke? And then travelled to Cambridge?'

'It seems at odds Marlin, but then, everything he did was to lead us to wrong conclusions.'

Marlin stayed quiet, but kept on looking at Al, making him feel uncomfortable.

'Look Marlin, I'm really sorry but...,'

'I said not to say sorry.'

'I'm s...,' Al stopped and cleared his throat. 'I have to meet Lara; we're going away for a while.'

'A nice break, eh? Are you paying?'

'What?'

'Forget it Doc, forget it. Just know one thing.'

'Yes.'

'I don't buy the Phantom for the killings of the girls. It makes no sense to me at all, but more than that, it was Sue's case. I intend to do right by her, no matter what that means or what it takes. So. Did the Phantom confess?'

Al stood and shook his head slowly, anger and frustration writ large across his face.

'I have to go, Marlin.'

'Did he?'

'Lara's waiting and I have a book to finish. I'll send you a copy because it's all explained in there. In a few weeks or so, when you are better, we can have a drink and catch-up. In time, when you're not hurting so much, it'll make more sense to you. You look after yourself and get well. Bye, Marlin.'

'We'll talk again about this. We will talk, Doc.

Al travelled back in his cab, angry and confused but determined to regain his sense of well-being. As he paid the man in the battered green Ford he made sure the tip was a generous one.

'Thank you Mr Al, thank you very much.'

'That's ok Jay, you're always welcome. Now remember to tell Sharif to get back to me with that phone number, ok? I hope to fly out later today, so the sooner the better. Oh, and this is between us, ok?'

'I will make sure of it, Mr Al.'

'Thanks.'

Stepping into the house Al threw his coat onto the sofa heavily. Moving to the table at the side of the room, he poured a generous glass of scotch, sipping as he ambled out of the room and up the stairs. At the top landing he walked past the main bedroom, past the guest room, and opened the door to the study. At the door entrance he stopped, his eyes drawn to the stained carpet where Sue had breathed her last; staring quietly he sipped his drink as his mind wandered. How had he missed how Marlin had fallen for the woman so quickly? Yet again a woman getting in his way, just like Anne. Shaking his head, he closed the door and moved away to the main bedroom; placing his drink down he pulled a large suitcase from the top of the wardrobe, filling it quickly with a random selection of clothes and shoes. What he forgot he could buy.

Closing the case he felt for its weight, then picked up his glass and took the luggage down to the door. Draining the glass he walked back into the living room and picked up the bottle before sitting. Refill accomplished, he picked up his phone.

'Lara, it's me again.'

'What is it Al, is everything ok at the hospital?'

'Yeah, pretty much. I just wanted to let you know that we are going to Turkey and we are going tonight.'

'Hell Al, you didn't waste any time.'

'I know, I said I would finish the book out there and I also have a bit of business.'

'Business?'

'Sort of. It's just someone I've got to see out there but it won't take long, I promise. Be here for 9.00pm and the cab will pick us both up.'

'Ok, though you know I find that place a bit creepy now?'

'I know but we'll be gone soon enough.'

'Ok, see you later.'

Al put the phone in his pocket and leaned forward, picking up the cap of the bottle and screwing it tightly in place. He had restored order and security once more so, closing his eyes and taking a drink, he relaxed back into his world.

If

Printed in Poland
by Amazon Fulfillment
Poland Sp. z o.o., Wrocław